Happy Da

edges of

me

[signature] x

GAYE POOLE

CRANTHORPE
— MILLNER —
PUBLISHERS

First published by Cranthorpe Millner Publishers (2024)

ISBN 978-1-80378-215-7 (Paperback)

www.cranthorpemillner.com

Cranthorpe Millner Publishers

Printed and bound by CPI Group (UK) Ltd,
Croydon, CR0 4YY

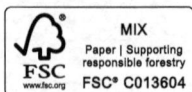

MIX
Paper | Supporting
responsible forestry
FSC® C013604

For the three wonderful men in my life:
Keith, Jack and Barney.

PROLOGUE

2016

I
John

It was Jenny's final winter and her chest gently rose and fell. John, his exhausted head propped in his big hands, waited.

He realised he was holding his own breath as the time between his wife's breaths lengthened. She, and so he too, had been like this for days now. Hooked onto her borrowed hospital bed, the newly-inserted syringe driver whirred its persistent doses, even as the catheter bag drained the last of Jenny's life's juices. The digital clock by her bed clicked to 2:07 a.m.

He held her loose wedding-ringed hand on the new crisp white bedlinen – he had remade it only that morning, a lifetime away. The detail of death. At 2:09 a.m. the air changed; she was really gone.

Nothing else had altered in the room and, yet, everything had. At last, stirred by a brazen chink of light which seared through the straining blousy curtains (Jenny never did master sewing), he mustered himself to tuck her in tenderly. He laid the picture of Evie (gap-toothed at seven) face down on his wife's quiet heart, bringing the sheet up under her chin, not able to cover her face, not yet, and switched off the digital clock at the wall. Wrong that time was still moving on.

Amidst the detritus of final days – the wet wipes, valiant room deodorisers and drug timetables – John found Jenny's lists of things to do and people to ring, now death was an official visitor. Amongst the bottles of morphine and rescue remedies, he found a bottle of sherry. This and vodka jellies had become her new "five a day". He poured himself a large tumbler and went into the garden. He stood shrouded by the long unpruned leylandii – guarding like giant white sentinels – still in his shirtsleeves, oblivious to the chill air.

'Claire?'

'Oh, John... has... oh, god!'

'At 2:09 this morning. She just didn't wake up. Sorry, I didn't know if it was too early to phone you?'

'I couldn't sleep. I had a feeling. Do you want me to come over?'

'No!'

This was said too forcefully. He didn't know why, but he had a gut feeling Jenny wouldn't want Claire there, especially her... or possibly anyone just yet, and neither did he. He had just needed to say the words to someone. He softened his voice.

'Thank you, but Doctor Perry's on his way. I ought to phone the funeral directors. I just don't want to set all that in motion somehow, not yet. I want to sit with her awhile. That's okay, isn't it?'

With the saying of these words, it was all becoming more real and John, a previously unfaltering man, began the "falterings".

'Of course. There's no right or wrong way. Take your time. Does Evie know?'

'No, I should tell her now, I just—'

'I'll call her right away.'

'I should really—'

'No "shoulds". I'm family really too, remember? And I'm here for you.'

'Thank you.'

'I'll come over this afternoon to be with you. No arguments.'

'Oh, no, it's—'

'John! I'm coming.'

When the doctor had left, John bolstered himself with another sherry and coke. It felt wrong to open a red just yet. He filled the plastic washing-up bowl with warm water in their newly replaced country kitchen and carried it carefully up to her bedside. Then, dipping her flannel, he soaped it up with some lavender soap he found at the back of the bathroom cabinet. The cloying smell hit the back of his throat and he knew Jenny would say it smelt of old ladies, so he emptied the bowl and started again with her everyday soap.

'No fuss, Jen, I know, but got to get it right, eh?'

He spoke, wanting to believe she was still listening, still there.

'Face first, eh? There you go, love... Now your arms, please, Jen.'

The washing was easy compared to the hugely difficult dressing of her unhelpful body.

'Sorry, love, never was much good at bras, was I? But this is a first, doing one up!'

Yes, this had to be right, this last act of love. And he had all the time in the world. He was glad of the time – seven, then eight o'clock – so that rush hour was over and the road outside was rightfully quiet. And he hadn't wanted strangers turning her flesh, although he knew soon they would have to handle her. But at least he had done this, prepared her in the chosen dress. A mauve silk that she had selected online, knowing that it would suit this new pallor and would shroud her – gossamer clouds enveloping her (she had joked) "once in a lifetime svelte figure". John had mostly mourned cancer stealing her once fulsome body, her supine splayed belly that used to shake with their Sunday morning lay-in laughter; she had always loved a lie-in.

He arranged the silk folds around her legs – fanning the fabric out – and stood back like a window dresser appraising a mannequin.

He tried a wolf-whistle, but it petered out, and every ounce of John's six-foot-two and sixteen-stone frame folded in on him.

'Oh, Jen.'

Feeling this weight of his fifty-four years corpulent past and empty present, he traipsed downstairs to the notepad of IMPORTANT NUMBERS. He slumped onto their well-worn leather sofa. Their Labrador, Lewis (after the detective), found his lap and weighted him still with his big heavy head. He fondled Lewis's velvety ears, stalling just a little longer. Then, when Lewis finally sunk by his feet, he set the whole funeral fiasco in motion. He made his way through all the unsurprised relatives and friends, calling them, ticking their names off Jenny's list, crossing through her feeble handwriting.

'Hello, Jan, I didn't know what time it was out there, but you'd said to ring whenever...'

'Margery? It's John... Yes, early this morning.'

'Laura... yes, I'm so sorry.'

Stopping after every batch to climb the stairs and check in again on Jenny.

'Daft.'

The saxophone doorbell rang. Jenny had chosen it ironically for their unmusical family and he welcomed the sound as the noiseless funeral directors hushed in. Each item of furniture these men slunk past screamed Jenny at them. John couldn't understand why they didn't see that. Her console table in the hall piled high with hats and scarves nobody wore, but Jenny kept in case visitors needed one. The desk on the landing with drawers stuffed with Evie's playgroup paintings and displaying her wonky clay pots and netball trophies. Their marital bedroom, where she had revelled in her Sunday lie-ins until life was all lie-in. They lifted her, *tenderly*, John thought, and then they hushed out again.

He hoped they had Bob Marley, or Led Zeppelin even, playing at full volume, when safely alone in the hearse with Jenny. From Beethoven to The BackStreet Boys, she'd had an eclectic musical taste, or "tragic" as Evie had described it, but her mother had just liked human family noise around her best.

He was sure they had to keep the hearse free from crumbs too and obviously couldn't be seen to eat when on view at traffic lights say, but maybe on the open road they could go about their normal lives; perhaps stop for a Big Mac. Maybe they had special compartments under the coffin bit where they could store their rubbish. He realised he was thinking just like Jenny, but buried that thought quickly. She would feel more at ease if it wasn't too tidy though. She had always prioritised living rather than tidying the house.

'Lived in, that's what it is, and the cobwebs? They're performance art!'

He went back upstairs, pulled back the curtains just a little and sat on their empty bed. Then he opened the "D-Day note" Jenny had penned for him.

"Now you're reading this, I am presuming the cheery coffin collectors have carried me off and you are left on your tod, or with Evie if she's back. Sooo, first make yourself a milky coffee and a cheese and pickle sandwich to soak up the booze. See, I know you so well! Then, why don't you put the football on, or an episode of Only Fools and Horses, and then face another day. Live your life to the max for me and encourage Evie to never look back... Always yours, loveliest man, Jenny xx"

2
Olivia

The winter sun may have been warming their cat Neville's tabby belly, spread like dough on the cracked paving stones outside Liv's flat, but the temperature had suddenly turned very frosty inside. Conor had broached the subject... again. So, Liv had bristled... again. And leapt up to make a coffee, and to remove whatever non-existent dust she could purport to find on the few items of flatpack furniture. Anything rather than go "there" again, just yet, or ever.

Olivia, or Liv as she was known, was an English teacher, and had met Conor when on her first placement at inner-city Bridewell Senior School. The austere Victorian redbrick exterior belied an interior of peeling, graffitied partitions and bumping swarms of head-phoned students, necessitating shouting as the norm. Conor was already an established and popular PE teacher there and a shoe-in for the 2020 Olympic swimming team (he had just missed out on selection for the 2016 squad). They topped the bill of the staffroom small talk and the student backchatting-banter from term one, and their relationship was thus written.

So, they followed the script and, yet, suddenly, now where the marriage scene should be, set in the quiet haven of her pokey bolthole, Liv was stalling. And affable, uncomplicated Conor couldn't understand why.

'Well, why ever not now? Talk to me, Liv?'

'I don't understand what the rush is. You'll want to concentrate on your swimming for the next few years.'

'Yes, but—'

'And we're already taking a huge step buying a place together. That's commitment enough, isn't it?'

'Is it though?'

Liv clattered cups in the kitchen, but as it was all open plan, she couldn't pretend not to hear.

'Liv?'

'It is for me.'

'I know your parents' marriage didn't work out but—'

'You don't. I don't. So, how can you?'

'Sorry, you know what I mean.'

'Yes, I know what you mean. But you don't know what I mean.'

'Huh, you've lost me?'

'That's just it.'

'Come on, Liv, you're the one with the lexicon, you'll have to spell it out for me.'

Liv sat with her coffee, filled her lungs and stilled her pulse.

'Well, you know I told you my mum left my dad when I was tiny...'

'Yes...'

'Well, there was always this big secret around her. Neither Aunty Jan nor Dad would never talk about her.'

'Yeah, I know that. I don't get what that has to do with us getting married?'

Liv scraped and re-scraped her long brown hair back away from her face into a polished conker of a bun, all the time avoiding Conor's steady gaze, then reluctantly gave him a small bite of conversation to chew on.

'I don't know half of my genes... So, I am only half-known, and I'd want to know if—'

'Lots of people don't know their genetic history; it doesn't matter to me and when we do—'

Liv sprang up once more, saved by the doorbell. She had never been so grateful for a delivery of an all-seasons pizza.

Plates were placed loudly and decisively, drawers forcefully opened – almost spilling their contents – but knives and forks were thankfully laid on the table, rather than wielded.

Once more the conversation was iced out; another reprieve.

THE FIRST ERA

1981

The year the Iran hostages were released and the first space shuttle was launched.

3
Claire

Claire had phoned home for solace and understanding and had found "another" laughing in her place.

'Hello!'

'Who's this?'

For a moment, Claire thought she had mis-dialled, mis-everything.

'Ella. I live here. Who are you?'

'Claire, I live there too.'

'No, you don't, silly!'

Her mum's voice called, 'Who's that on the phone, Ella?'

'She's called Claire.'

A gasp then tickling, giggling footsteps came together.

'Hi, love. Sorry, we're having an Easter egg hunt. You okay?'

'Yes...'

Claire felt her ear burning as the phone pressed into her auricle (as just this week she'd learned it was called), but it didn't bridge the distance with home and, after an expectant silence, her mum prattled on.

'Oh, that's good then... That was our new foster child, Ella; we've bought her a rabbit, so she's a bit over-excited. Her own Easter bunny. Remember you had one for Easter once; Brutus, you called him. Remember?'

'Yes, I do.'

'You eating okay?'

'Yes.'

Ella was obviously finding it hard to contain said excitement.

'What are we gonna eat?'

'Coming, Ella. In a minute, I'm talking.'

Janet ruffled Ella's hair and shooed her away.

'We're taking her to Bodcombe beach for a picnic tea; you loved it there!'

'Oh, I won't keep you now.'

'Don't be silly. It's sooo good to hear from you.'

'No, I'll call another time.'

'No, please, love...'

'No, really, it's no problem, I'm fine.'

'It's just that she's quite needy at the moment but settling in well. You'll love her; she's very like you at eight.'

Claire rang off quickly before tears showed in her voice. She couldn't remember how she had been at eight. She didn't know how she was at nineteen. The laughter continued from next door. Her fellow King's College physio students getting ready for another rowdy night "on the pull".

'Come on, Claire, come out with us, it'll be a laugh. Don't be a stick in the mud.'

That was exactly how she felt, an ugly stick in a huge slick of mud. She had looked it up in her "Origins of Phrases" book. Meaning: "unprogressive person". So be it.

'I've nothing to wear.'

'Borrow something of mine.'

They all offered. All of them size eight but with a variety of supposed body issues. Claire had the monopoly on body issues and screamed inside whenever any of them dared to complain about their lot. The trouble was they were all lovely kind girls – sickeningly lovely. All about to pass their first-year physio exams with ease. Claire should have found uglier, dimmer friends that she could have outshone. But no: Cesca, Katrina and Lottie had invited her to move in with them when they had to leave the halls at the end of the year. How could she refuse to be in this shining group? Her mum always said "comparison is the thief of joy", but these were like a ready scab she just had to pick.

They all barged in, half-cut already, as was Claire, but it didn't make her into a gay, giggly, frothy being, trilling about whether hair should go up or down. She smiled a feigned interest and continued her excuses as to why she wasn't joining them for a night at "The Cat's Whiskers".

Lottie cried, 'But we are the four musketeers!'

'There were actually three of them.'

'Yes, but...'

They all fell about laughing.

When they tottered on their way, Claire sat in her small, dark study bedroom. Alice Cooper and Blondie stared down at her from their glossy un-attainment. She turned to face the Habitat mirror her parents had bought for her new life and spat at her reflection. That wasn't nearly enough. She hurled the empty bottle of Cinzano. Splintering into more and more ugly parts, the mirror threw a shard at her. A shard that said, "Hurt me". She deliberated over the brachial and cephalic vein until it became both a surgical and emotional procedure. She knew enough not to cut too deeply but just enough to see the blood appear and drip down onto the already stained carpet. She slung her handbag over her good arm, locked her door and calmly walked away.

4
Jenny

Never a morning person, especially a morning that cruelly began in pitch black, Jenny grabbed toast and the last smear of peanut butter and sat swearing at her equally reluctant red Fiat Panda's engine. Too many precious minutes later, it coughed awake and stop-started the short journey to the last parking space outside the hospital. Phew! She really needed a new car, or at least a service, but that was for another payslip; it lived to drive another day.

Jenny ran in through the Portland stone columns that surrounded the red brick building, too panicked to be, as she usually was, awe-struck by the history and importance of the place. To Jenny, these columns became the ropes of a boxing ring she stepped into daily, with equal amounts of fear and excitement for the next "bout". And today she was late to her shift, and Jenny didn't do late either.

She pinned her nurse badge to her "civvies" and was brusquely re-assigned to the short-staffed emergency unit, penance for being the last in. Still a newish student psychiatric nurse, this was a scary first experience at this eminent hospital.

The Maudsley Hospital had an earlier existence as a War Office clearing hospital for soldiers diagnosed with shell shock. In 1923, it officially opened with the stated aim of finding effective treatments for neuroses, mild forms of psychosis and dependency disorders; to arrest what were hitherto considered irreversible pathological processes. This was Jenny's heartfelt belief too: that "madness" could be waylaid.

It was the only hospital to run such an emergency unit and madness was said to spill over the threshold in all its most fantastical, florid states, and Jenny felt, thus far, poorly equipped to have any therapeutic impact. She could make beds – well, pretty shoddily – and from the *Hays and Larson Listening Techniques* book that they were studying, say "mmm, go on" fairly encouragingly, she felt. But she was a way off beginning her crusade to save people from, (in her thus far unrefined psychiatric terminology), "tipping over the edge".

Reporting in, she was expecting full-blown psychosis – large in volume, emotion and fantasy – so to say she was both a tad disappointed and relieved was an understatement as large as her overdraft.

'Hello, my name's Jenny, I'll be your nurse today.'

Silence.

'I'm to escort you to Wilson Ward. Can I help you with your things?'

The cowed young woman clutched a sparsely filled, grey plastic hospital bag to her and kept her gaze firmly averted, but compliantly followed Jenny through the twists and turns of grey-green walled corridors (the painters and decorators of hospitals had yet to hear of colours' influence on mood).

Jenny was now at home with the alternate eerie quiet and cacophony of hospital life. By night, apart from the secure unit, which was always a jangling nerve, sound was muted by the closed doors and medicated mollification. By day, other areas came to life and ordinary life outside became a welcome visitor: the everyday clang of canteen cutlery being laid and laughter deep from an easy place, which burbled from staff who took everything in their stride.

Hair nets framed ruddy faces, hot from boiling pans, beaming with pride in feeding hundreds. This comforting rhythm of mealtimes and the solidity of food, literally, in the case of their shepherd's pie.

Jenny moved her patient swiftly past the locked ward and heartrending screams, through the labyrinth she had only just mastered. The young woman started to walk faster, as did Jenny; they reached some stairs and then there was a sign: Wilson Ward. This was an open female ward for patients with "neuroses", but the young woman didn't know that yet.

This was actually Jenny's current placement, so she was on familiar ground again and quickly found the young woman's allocated bed.

'Are you in any pain from your wound?'

A shake of the head as she fingered the new dressing on her forearm.

'Well, here's a nightgown, but you can keep your clothes on during the day here; we're not like a general hospital. And, hopefully, someone can bring your own things in later. Can I call anyone for you?'

Again, a shake of the head.

'I've got to get back to the ED where I'm working today, but I'm on an early here tomorrow so I'll see you then.'

There was no response.

'I'm sorry you feel like this, Claire.'

A large, long face reminiscent of a sad beagle looked up at her with sorrowful, deep brown eyes, connecting with Jenny's cornflower blue, open gaze. They both recognised the moment.

'Take care.'

Although at the beginning of her training, Jenny had already learnt about, and experienced, the transference of powerful emotions. Once again, she felt as if she was harbouring a little piece of someone's heart. A familiar heaviness settled in, and it definitely wasn't the peanut-buttered toast.

Why would a nineteen-year-old physio, her own age, someone at the very same stage of her career, attempt to take her own life? Jenny doubted she had meant it and, not for the first time, also doubted the appropriateness of admitting someone who was perhaps just temporarily sad, not "mad".

A few drunks, then a "real" suicide, to be monitored continuously took her up to her break. All staff and patients ate in the canteen together, which was ideologically brilliant but sometimes appetite challenging. The only differentiations obvious were the badges staff wore, and the occasional reply to non-existent voices, or one regular routine from Tom, a young Tourette's sufferer. He had a teasing disposition, enhanced by his bipolar highs, and perfected a regular mealtime floor show of "almost" dropping his tray of food, accompanied by an explosion of expletives, much to the consternation of the canteen staff, but others' hilarity. Thus, it was never a "break" really unless it was sunny enough to take your food outside for the few minutes left after queueing or if you were on of the organised Tupperware brigade, who sat smugly relaxing for longer. Jenny wasn't one of them.

The rest of the day passed in a blur and relatively unscathed, but she was still in need of a gin and tonic all the same. Jenny had forgotten the young woman by the time her housemate suggested a top-up. The gin kitty and the party kitty had more necessary funds than the housekeeping kitty. Jenny was lucky to have found housemates who all had similar escapist tendencies and were less hung up about topping up the toilet rolls.

Johnny was a charismatic marketing intern and seemed to have very useful clients if you liked instant whip. These freebies became a staple ingredient of house party cocktails, with the dual purpose of intoxication and stomach lining. One such cocktail still splattered the ceiling from one of Jenny's emergency refills when she forgot to put the top on the blender and chocolate instant whip, rum and banana became the far-reaching results, creating a new "Jenny Klutz story" to add to all others.

Maria, the baby of the group at just eighteen, mooned after Johnny when she wasn't moaning about her very boring insurance job. However, she was generous to a fault when Jenny ran out, often, of shampoo, and most other necessities of life. And she never seemed to comment when Jenny had eaten all her chocolate chip cookies and replaced them with a different brand. The fourth housemate, Paul, had drawn the short straw: the "ground-floor bedroom". This was, in fact, a space behind a flimsy curtain in the partitioned-off front room, but it was handy as a bike-store for Paul's pride and joy. And, as he hardly "saw any action", he was happy enough polishing the trims and surfacing for Johnny's infamous chilli and their even more infamous wildly themed parties. It was a great house to come home to.

5
Claire

Claire awoke to screams. That first open-eyed orientation to a new day shocked her. Pinned to her new iron hospital bed by remnants of the heaviest, drug-induced sleep, she tried to make sense of where she was. Her eyes alighted on an elderly woman, sweating profusely, wringing her hands, mumbling distressingly whilst pacing between other sleep-disturbed, but mostly empty beds; their occupiers having already dragged themselves into this day she was avoiding.

Her eyes swept the ward and she was struck by the blankness, both of the surroundings but also the expressions of those few who sat poleaxed on their beds too. The backing track of a woman quietly crying cued her to look away and as she did, she registered her handbag in the side compartment of her bedside locker. A new toothbrush, toothpaste and hospital flannel were laid out on top, next to a plastic jug of water and a plastic cup. As she reached out for some water to prise her tongue from its welded position, she clocked the bandage on her hand; at the same time, the medicine trolley rattled past. What had she done?

'Morning, Claire, I'm Rhona, a staff nurse. How did you sleep?'

How did she sleep? Claire couldn't believe how easily she was accepted into this "world", but she had no idea how to act as a psychiatric patient, as that seemingly was what she was now.

'Fine, I think.'

'Good. I have some medication for you to take. Are you okay taking tablets?

'Er. Yes, but...'

The nurse checked her arm band and handed her two tiny blue pills.

'It's your first anti-depressant. The doctor will have explained that it will take a couple of weeks or so to really kick in and help you, but we will take good care of you until you are feeling better enough to go home, okay?

'Okay.'

Okay? None of this was "okay". She swallowed the tablets, pulled the thin blue blanket over her head, folding in on herself, and went back to sleep.

6
Janet

Ella had been having nightmares and, once again, Janet had lain perilously on the edge of the diminutive child's bed, so Jeff had taken the call. She had heard the phone ring and then the odd few murmurings from Jeff and had presumed it was one of those staccato, perfunctory conversations he had with his mates, arranging golf or a pint. With Ella safely asleep, she carefully extricated herself, stretched her aching back and padded downstairs to make a cuppa.

As she bowled into their cosy sitting room to ask Jeff if he wanted a brew, his slumped posture told a different tale.

'It's Claire.'

Janet's heart stood still, as did she. Jeff nodded she should sit. She fell into her armchair, bracing herself for the worst news – that she was dead from a car accident, bungled burglary, collapsed building or... Never expecting, or if she was honest fully expecting but dreading, knowing deep down that one day these calls would begin. Claire would always surprise and usually never in a happy way. So, this was how it was to be.

Jeff was shocked his wife took the news of Claire's attempted suicide so well. Unlike some of their fellow churchgoers, they were not as archaic in their beliefs to consider suicide a sin. However, they had never thought to have such a close encounter with their feelings towards this ultimate act concerning their own daughter.

'But she seemed okay when she rang... didn't she?'

And so, the recriminations began, with Jeff taking the opinion that Claire's life was Claire's responsibility and Janet assuming more than her fair share of this "responsibility".

'Maybe if we'd insisted she went to church with us more often, she would have had more of a faith to sustain her.'

'We tried, love, remember what she used to say?'

'By rote, she said it so much: "Jesus was the original Barbie doll created"—'

Jeff joined in, '"To play out life's worst scenarios". Exactly.'

'Do you know that the suicide rate amongst Catholics is consistently lower than with Protestants?'

'Where did you get that from?'

'I can't remember, but it makes you think.'

'Just makes me think we're too scared, at least Claire is her own person through and through.'

'Don't say that.'

'We have to accept, Jan, that there's something in her that you can't hug out or make happy with a few hymns, or some ice cream and a trip to the sea.'

Janet being Janet held onto the hope that maybe Claire would let them visit and bring her home, and they could help their daughter out of this dark place. Ella called out again and she ran upstairs confident that hugs worked wonders for her little body in the here and now, whatever the future held.

7
Jenny

They had the house for two years whilst the owners were working in New York; they were the sort of people who took "sabbaticals". Jenny fancied being like that. So, in their absence, as part of the rental agreement, all housemates were tasked with caring for the sizeable garden which, on divvying of household duties, Jenny had plumped for. She had found she enjoyed coaxing the ageing mower into life, perfecting lawn stripes worthy of a Jermyn Street shirt and discovering which were the prettiest of weeds to spare. The others could keep the dusting and hoovering for sure.

After a luxurious lie-in, Jenny remained weighted to the bed, looking out of her boxroom window at the bare bones of "her" apple tree which, at other times of the year, was rewardingly fecund, resulting in much apple crumble and the more popular boozy baked apples. On a branch sat a starling, or was it a chaffinch? She'd look it up later, or more likely not! Anything to stall leaving this hibernation. Jenny needed eight hours and felt if she was short-changed it was imperative to get more hours in her sleep bank whenever she could. Once up, she was a whirling dervish, but the bed hours, well, they were for pondering and planning, and Jenny loved nothing better than to plan, sometimes forgetting others didn't share her optimism for possibilities and PLANS!

Right! She would get up, do a few minutes of yoga (it was amazing how many downward dogs you could fit into both the bathmat-sized bedside rug and a single song on the radio) and then have a boiled egg for breakfast. This was DAY 1 of "the" diet. This one would work, and she would be super slim. Heads would turn again and, when she was nine stone, <u>all</u> of life would be fantastic.

Jenny loved late shifts; after all, there was still time to go out and party afterwards, but this delicious life-stalling lone time was for now. Once showered, a piece of toast was added to the egg and just a handful of Frosties – well, one needed something sweet to finish. Then, jeans zipped in a reminding way, Jenny had a few minutes over to ring home for a quick check-in with her mum.

'Oh... Hello, love!'

'Why are you puffing, Mum?

'S'okay, love, I had just locked the front door when I heard the phone!'

Jenny was always alert to any sign of her mum's angina. She had already lost her beloved dad suddenly when she was just fifteen, so now it was just her mum and her, she didn't take her for granted at all. After doing unremarkably at A-levels and not having uni to aim for, Jenny had opted for a life in retail as she was determined to stay at home. But, after six months in John Lewis, saying, but not meaning "Can I help you?" she found she did actually want to help. So, it was her mum who suggested nursing and encouraged her to go out in that big wide world.

'Where are you off to?'

'Just into Epsom to get a few bits, you?'

'On a late, then to Helen's for supper, so I thought I'd ring now.'

'Okay, love. How was yesterday?'

'Oh, okay, you'd have laughed; this woman came in with bipolar disorder, as high as can be. I was doing her admission forms and she told me that she was an architect and she had designed the Eden Project as well as the Eiffel Tower. I put all this down and it wasn't until I handed over that I realised that she couldn't have possibly designed the Eiffel Tower; she was only about thirty!'

'Or indeed the Eden Project?'

'Oh, Mum, don't take that away from her, or me! I don't know if I'm cut out for this.'

'Come on, love! You're right, you keep on believing in people, but don't forget that pinch of salt sometimes, eh?'

'Will do... Are you sure you're okay?

'I'm sure!'

'Good. Gotta go then, Mum, drive safely, love you!'

With that, she grabbed her keys, a final handful of Frosties, and cajoled "Trident" into gear (she had just joined the East Dulwich branch of CND, mainly for the hope of "talent" and was trying on "irony" as an accompanying new look.)

At handover, amongst her patients for her shift, she was pleased to be allocated Claire, the new admission from yesterday. She sought her out first and found her alone in the day room with a last year's Woman's Own.

8
Claire

As usual, Claire was in comparing mode. To distance herself from the other patients, whom she most certainly was not like, she chose one of the uncomfortable, upright, green again, geriatric, wipeable hospital chairs and pulled it to face the quadrangle of straggly hospital garden beyond the reinforced windows. (This literal interpretation of her current state was not lost on her.) She stared at celebrity faces in the six-month-old magazine; she was not like them either. She was like no one, and that was the trouble.

As far back as she could remember, Claire had been the odd one out. The shy younger sister to a confident sporty brother. Then the "spare" friend. Sally and Christine were in Brownies with her, they got their sewing badges together and then they went to Guides together. But Claire had felt too fat to "fly" over the toadstool (the Guides' initiation) so said she didn't want to go, thus missing out on Guide camp to Badgells Wood: toasted marshmallows, creepy ghost stories and hidden Milky Way bars. Oh, yes, she'd stored every missed memory.

Thus, she became the third wheel as the other two got even closer and sat together in all the classes at Saint Joseph's. The third wheel in all friendships. Never the steering wheel. No, the wheel at the back. Running behind the in-jokes:

'Claire, are you an A-lien? Get it!'

No, she didn't.

And cults:

'Claire, are you a mod or a rocker?'

'Er, a mod.'

'Oh, god, no, we're rockers!'

As Claire seemed to get more and more introverted, her mother signed her up for elocution classes with Miss Turnbull, who'd had a fleeting flirtation with the stage – as she liked to keep reminding people – and this had impressed Claire's mum.

'In we go, love. Chin up, it'll make you more confident.'

Which it didn't. Every Saturday for months her mother would drop her off before going to watch another of her brother Nigel's winning matches, and Claire would dutifully deliver her learned poems but slink from any offers to join the "little shows". However, her mother did persuade her to take the Guildhall Speech and Drama exams:

'They'll be useful in later life, love, you'll see.'

She was the only one of her cohort to get a mere pass rather than a merit or distinction, and the examiner's comments stung at age nine, and this hurt was also stored:

GUILDHALL SPEECH AND DRAMA GRADE 2

For her poem, The Listeners *by Walter de la Mare, said with good pathos:*

"'Is there anybody there?' said the Traveller,
Knocking on the moonlit door...
'Tell them I came, and no one answered,
That I kept my word,' he said."

The final text from The Reawakening *by Walter de la Mare was a strange choice and rather short:*

"Ye say we sleep;
But nay, we wake;
Life was that strange and chequered dream
Only for waking's sake."

Overall a solid knowledge of the poems but could work on both vocal inflection and facial expression to bring the text alive. I suggest Claire concentrates on a more natural delivery to increase her chances of a merit next time. Work hard and good luck'

Nigel was captain of the cricket and football teams and his parents boasted that he was a cert for the rugby captaincy too. Her only other hobby at the time was swimming, again, an idea of her mother's when Claire had moaned about her chubbiness:

'You're lovely as you are... It's only a bit of puppy fat that'll soon turn into muscle... You'll make some nice friends... Give it a go... All those galas and things, it'll be fun!'

Fun it wasn't, but Claire did enjoy the more solitary lane swimming, the tang of chlorine and then the powdery tomato soup and Mars bar she was rewarded with from the vending machine in the foyer, once out of the cold clinging costume and shouty changing rooms.

In the melee of girls' showering bodies, she noticed she was definitely behind in growing breasts too:

'Oooh, look, Claire hasn't even got a bra yet!'

And with fashion: white socks and frumpy pleated skirts, waiting to be taken to Chelsea Girl on Saturdays, to miraculously transform into Lucy Wilkins – but never asked. Waiting in the large camouflage of Claire-ness. Then, at her girl's senior school always in the top set but nearer the bottom, so she never quite measured up. She revised just in time with her parent's encouragement and managed to scrape enough O-levels for sixth form but then amazed herself and her family by passing enough A-levels to get an interview to Kings College to do physio – and, even more amazingly, got in. She was succeeding at last.

And then to be part of a four, an even number, to be in the flat-sharing discussions for the next year with these beautiful, confident, warm, funny individuals who thought she was hilarious – but then the doubts crept in. Fuelled by those same enemy comparisons: she was the fattest, she had the mousiest, thinnest hair, she had the jowls of a sixty-year-old; nature had been cruel.

She supposedly had molten brown eyes, but what good were they? Plums in a pudding face. Even with careful dressing, and who wants to cover up at nineteen? When she did expose her suddenly fast-tracked size thirty-eight double-D bust, well, she looked tarty, not slim and sexy.

And then, with exams looming, her brain always a pretender had to work harder than these blessed friends' cerebella, who mastered every fascia and every metatarsal by easy osmotic absorption. All whilst their seraphic, porcelain, Teflon skin repelled all spots, all calories, all fat globules, all bad experiences, all bad thoughts and still exuded charm and golden glow. Claire felt dim, in dim light, unseen... dim.

And now she hadn't waited, she had taken action. What had she done? Bloody hell!

The nice nurse from yesterday appeared in the dayroom. She noticed she was wearing a baggy bright turquoise jumper, with the obligatory name badge at a wonky angle (probably hastily pinned) and jeans that looked a bit tight. Claire always felt at home with others who struggled with zips.

'Good, I've found you. May I join you?'

Claire shrugged, but was sooo thankful for this kind nurse who looked about her age and hoped she might offer some insight into what the hell would happen next.

'Do you want to tell me how you came to be here?'

'What d'you mean?'

'Well, you were obviously in some...'

She searches for her words and Claire likes her. She instantly really likes her; she is not perfect, she is probably new at this, feeling her way, just like Claire.

The nurse started again.

'You seem to me to be very sad and must have been, to hurt yourself in that way?'

Exactly but Claire couldn't think how to even begin to explain. Out loud it would all seem so petty:

'My friends are all A-star students with sleek blonde hair. My parents love my brother, even their foster children, way more than me and long ago forgot that I still need their love. And it was Saturday night. I couldn't face Cat's Whiskers, my friends all getting the attention, all getting "lucky" and, me, what would I be getting, the very unlucky night bus home on my own, early, defeated again by my own plainness and ordinariness and, now, emptiness? Unseen.'

She said nothing and folded in on herself, her new go-to position. This nurse looked kindly at her and just waited. Claire, unnerved by this patience and focus on solely herself for once, couldn't help herself,

'Why are you still sitting there?'

'I'm here in case you feel like talking.'

'Well, I don't.'

'That's okay. I'm also here to sit and be with you; it can be lonely when feelings have been so strong to cause you to self-harm... and you haven't wanted anyone to visit you.'

Claire turned to scowl at Jenny.

'My parents are busy with their foster kids.'

'Your mum has rung several times since yesterday to ask to visit.'

'That's what she says.'

Claire fingered her bandage again.

'Is that still painful, I mean, your wound?'

Claire shrugged.

'And... Lottie, is it? She rang.'

'I don't want to see anyone.'

'Okay. Well, I'm here for you until you do.'

10
Janet

The next day found Janet even more out of her comfort zone:

'But ECT, Jeff! That's barbaric.'

Janet had just rung the hospital and spoken to a kind nurse who'd explained that they felt Claire's depression could be shifted with a course of ECT. While Jeff bowed to the professionals, Janet couldn't envisage her little girl with those "Dickensian" electrodes stuck to her head and worried about her losing her memory.

'Well, she doesn't ever remember us as it is, Jan!'

'It's no time for jokes.'

'Did they say when we could visit?'

'Well, no, she doesn't want anyone there yet.'

'Well, then. What can we do, eh?'

'Oh, Jeff... I don't know. Maybe we should just turn up and persuade her not to have it?'

'Claire, for once, might be getting the help she needs, let her be, Jan...'

Janet tried her best but that umbilical cord still somehow pulsed out a remonstrative beat. And that night it was Janet having the nightmares: Claire on a merry-go-round going faster and faster, clinging to one of the horses with two legs in the air (the prancers), which came to life, jumped off the carousel and galloped off with her. Janet could only scream for the fair owner to stop the ride, but the music was too loud and she couldn't make herself heard.

II
Jenny

Handover:

'Jenny, you seem to have developed a good relationship with Claire; can you prep her for her ECT and go down with her?'

Never one to make a fuss or have confidence in her convictions – although she had walked over the hospital picket line though, hadn't she? And joined CND. And was writing to a prisoner in El Salvador – well, once or twice. However, although this situation with Claire's treatment really got to her, she found herself holding Claire's hand, walking beside her trolley and trying not to trip up as the porter sped on. So, they were off to the ECT suite, Jenny having left her resistance a beat too long. All those missed beats in Jenny's life already twisting her path: from failing to say no to the oft-proffered chocolate cake to, more importantly, this.

She had really tried to dissuade Claire from signing the consent, had probably not been very professional and had "overshared" some of her own problems – a big taboo as a nurse. However, Jenny felt compelled to show this young woman that others also shared her fears and her self-hatred, and it didn't have to come down to this.

Yes, she had seen the treatment work on an elderly woman only last week. Trudy was admitted with agitated depression and had lost yet another stone in just a few days, from the nervous energy her tortured body was expending. After just three ECT treatments thus

far, Trudy was calmer, able to sit and eat a whole plate of the canteen's finest lasagne – and, her family, hadn't they seemed thrilled?

But Claire wasn't "ill", Jenny was convinced of it, but she was a lowly student nurse and wouldn't dare offer her insights into Claire's "sadness" to an eminent consultant who surely knew best. She had talked a lot to this sad student physio who, one Saturday night, had just walked over the road from the general hospital she was studying at and found herself in the psychiatric system. Jenny felt, in other circumstances, she could have been a friend going through a tough time. She had to remind herself of the hospital wristband on Claire's arm, the newer cuts to that same arm and the section in place enforcing her hospitalisation and treatment when she had tried to abscond last Saturday.

Claire had asked for Jenny to accompany her on the next three ECT treatments and so she monitored her after each one. Claire was a passive recipient and seemed unaffected by the whole process. Apart from a slight headache, there seemed to be no side effects, memory or otherwise, or indeed any improvements.

Jenny had returned from a fortnight's annual leave. It was nothing fancy, just a trip home to be waited on by her mum, overindulge, and then a night out at the theatre to see *Cats* with the girls. Then here she was back on Wilson Ward.

Trudy was a new woman; she greeted her like an old friend, smiling, sharing her good news that her husband was coming in later to take her home. They were going to have a Chinese takeaway for supper and the grandchildren were visiting on Saturday. Just as if she'd had a gallbladder removed.

Handover:

'Tom, can you get Trudy ready for discharge, TTA's, etcetera... Ruby refused her 8 a.m. chlorpromazine and is isolating in her room,

but none of us was welcome in there, so we just monitored her. Liam, if you can try and see what's going on for her and address the medication situation, thank you. New admission: thirty-five-year-old Clancy, sorry, can't pronounce her surname, in bed nine with paranoid schizophrenia, brought in by the police last night, as she was trying to fly by leaping off her neighbour's bins. She'd had a hefty whack of haloperidol in ED so is still sleeping that off. Liam, can you keep an eye on there too? Claire Thomas has had her last ECT treatment and, suddenly, her depression seems to have lifted. Her parents visited this weekend and we are working towards her discharge now, so that's good. Jenny, can you manage her as well as your other patients, as she's been asking after you?'

As soon as the handover finished, Jenny went straight to Claire's bed and quietly pulled up a chair as she was sleeping. Groggily, Claire opened her eyes, as yet unguarded to the day and, when she saw who it was, gave Jenny the most rewarding of smiles.

'Sorry, I didn't mean to wake you; you're probably still sleeping it off.'

'No, I've just been dozing; just thought I'd escape any upbeat chat from the nurses!'

'Right!... No headaches or anything?'

'No, all good.'

'It's so good to hear that you're going home soon.'

Jenny was met with a now familiar arched eyebrow from Claire.

'I'll rephrase that then: it's good news that you are ready for discharge...'

'Glad to see the back of me?'

'Not at all, it's just that I know you still have doubts about home... I'll miss you.'

'Yeah, I bet you say that to all the attempted suicides!'

'No, honestly, I think... under other circumstances, well, I'm sure we'd have been good friends.'

'Yeah, well, I've got to make room for the next poor soul to listen to your positivity!'

At the end of her shift, Jenny went home to her housemates to find out what antics she missed in the last two weeks and update them on her home time. Instead, she found herself telling them all about her patient Claire, who she felt had played the system but couldn't work out to what effect.

THE SECOND ERA

1985

The year red telephone boxes were phased out and the first calls from mobile phones were made.

12
Claire

Claire leant against the door of her tiny flat and surveyed the scene, unchanged since she left for work that morning. Yes, she'd have to do some washing up; she was down to her last cereal bowl and the air was definitely whiffy with takeaways and careless living. Right! But maybe tomorrow, when she had some energy. Tonight, she would sit in the bathtub of planning and make a definitive plan.

Life had to change.

She let her arms float to the surface of her grimy bath and marvelled at her scars – fading meandering slug trails. She'd looked up why slugs leave trails and found it helps the creature glide forward when pressure is lifted or stick to surfaces when pressure is applied. How apt.

It was three and a half years ago since her hospital admission and a year almost to the day that she had thrown her mortarboard in the air with her fellow physio students. Lottie, spotting her standing on her own, had gaily tried to pull her into a group photo:

'For old times' sake.'

But she had slunk away. On that "signature day" she had left her parents standing with their plastic Champagne flutes and soggy vol-au-vents, looking lost and dislocated from the groups of celebrating families and friends. She had excused herself by explaining she needed to clear her room, then and there, or risk a fine.

'Your dad and I will help then, love.'

'No, I don't need your help... thanks. Besides, you'll be wanting to avoid the traffic.'

'It doesn't matter what time we get back; it's lovely to have this bit of time with you.'

'Mum, honestly, I'd rather do it on my own... say my goodbyes, you know.'

'Oh... okay, love. Well, we hope you'll come home soon.'

'Thanks for coming.'

And here she was slinking away yet again without a backward glance. Her department was fine about her leaving. I think they realised she was never "invested" there and she knew they were secretly relieved to get rid of their "weird" colleague with her sudden absences on her "off days". There were no helium balloons, farewell drinks or exchanges of contacts; she just left her pile of uniforms and walked out of the door on her last day. Nobody had really liked her after all.

And, anyway, like any newly qualified physio, she could drone: 'Good leg up to heaven, bad leg down to hell,' to rehabilitating patients anywhere.

Surely anywhere.

She called home.

'Hi, Mum, it's Claire.'

'Oh! Hello, love, what a lovely surprise. How are you?

'Fine. You?'

'Did you get the parcel?'

Claire had indeed got the parcel, had scoffed the Galaxy bar within minutes and thrown the video in the bin.

'I knew you'd want to see Ella's ballet show as you couldn't get here in person, especially the flower dance, just like Mrs Dibbs did with you. Remember?... But we understand how busy you are.'

'Mmm.'

'Well, what's your news?'

'Nothing much... I'm glad Ella's settled in so well with you.'

'She really is quite a character. I wish you could get to know her properly. You'd love her. I know you would.'

Then, as was becoming Claire's habit, she shut her mum down.

'Sorry, Mum, but I'm ringing to say I won't be home anytime soon. I'm off travelling with my new partner. Er, Rob. He's just got an inheritance; his grandad fell out of a high-rise flat in Honiton and so, we just thought, life's too short, "why not" and all that. When in doubt, travel!'

'Oh, Claire! Wow! You're leaving your job?'

'Well, I can't pound patients' chests from afar, Mum, so yes.'

'So soon?'

'Lots of people move on a year post-qualified; it's not so unusual!'

'Oh, right, I mean, your dad and I are so happy to hear you're going to have some deserved fun at last. When though?'

'All a bit of a rush but tomorrow.'

'Tomorrow! Oh, my, that is a rush. Is everything okay? I mean-'

'I'm fine, Mum!

'Jeff! It's Claire, come here quick! Well, where are you going?'

'Just Europe first: Berlin Wall, Coliseum in Rome – you know, the usual – and then Australia. Rob has a sister in Melbourne who we can stay with and I think I'll be able to do physio for a few months there to earn the fare back.'

Claire found she was good at this lying thing; even her dad's grilling and her mum's tears didn't crack her resolve. How easy it was to create the perfect fictional life. Now why on Earth hadn't she done this before?

Miss Turnbull eat your heart out!

She left an envelope containing the due rent and a note propped up on the pile of dirty dishes apologizing for the flat's mess and her abandoned belongings. She'd cited a "family emergency; a bomb blast in Karachi" and bundled up a few clothes, taking great pleasure in slamming the door behind her.

13
Janet

Ella had the saddest start in life of all their foster children thus far and her temporary placement had turned into a permanent one. Although her bedwetting had stopped and her rages had calmed, she remained a handful and Janet was thankful for her noisy energy which drowned out all the worries about her own daughter. Although Claire had never been an easy child, like Nigel, neither Jeff nor Janet had predicted their sleepless nights would continue into Claire's adulthood.

Janet spent many an hour in bed staring at the flickering kaleidoscopic blackness of her eyelids, trying to go inside herself and find reasons for the very Claire-ness of Claire, but her sleep was always driven back by recriminations. From birth she had colic and remained a restless baby, not going through the night until she was almost three. The tantrums of the terrible twos had seemed to segue into teenage angst and, as much as Janet tried to show her love, Claire fought against it. She would hardly ever be hugged or comforted, and as much as Janet had tried to reach her on her "separate continent", she often felt redundant as a mum. Her role with Claire was defined by Claire... and the constantly changing rules always wrongfooted her.

She had been avoiding going back to her catering career, but once Nigel and Claire were adults she had no other excuses to shirk work. The idea of fostering brought in some much-needed income, especially with Jeff's plumbing business taking a downturn. It also fed their Christian duty, but Janet knew for her the main driver was to mother children – children who would receive her love perhaps without quite as many pushbacks.

However many foster children they tried to help, Janet knew when that call from the hospital came to tell them Claire had been admitted having attempted suicide, that it was her daughter who needed help the most but was the one least able to accept it.

But now Claire was to travel abroad AND she had a boyfriend, some of her desperate prayers may have been answered. She wasn't exactly out of sight out of mind, but Janet felt she need not wait for another painful call in the middle of the night; not for a while at least... please...

'Aunty Jan!'

'Coming, Ella.'

Janet pushed her feet into her slippers and padded quietly out of bed, not wanting to disturb Jeff as he had another early start in the morning on a new housing estate project that would keep them in groceries and the odd special beach trip for some months to come.

'What is it, love?'

'That scary dream again.'

Janet climbed in beside Ella, wiping her tears with her thumb and took her bed-warm, shaking body in her rounded arms, ever hinged to hold.

'It's okay now.'

'I was locked in the back of this dark van. It was going really fast round bends, there was nothing to hang onto and I kept getting thrown around, but I knew to be quiet.'

'Oh, poppet! Well, you know you can always tell me anything at all. No need to be quiet here. It was just a dream. Let's go to sleep, eh, and I'll do us pancakes for breakfast.'

Ella heaved a last sob and fell asleep almost immediately, grafted to Janet's side.

Janet was, of course, wide awake now and thinking even more thoughts, from remembering her gut twisting when Ella's social worker told them of her being trafficked, to "God, I hope I've got eggs now I've promised pancakes," to hoping Claire was lying peacefully asleep in this Rob's arms. Or, as there was probably a time difference wherever she was, maybe hand in hand with him in some grand gallery or sitting opposite him at a beachside café, people-watching, sipping expresso and yes, laughing. She hoped so.

14
Jenny

Orlando's was heaving by the time Jenny tried to slide in to join the packed booth hindered by the stickiness of the especially sticky leatherette. Her colleagues and housemates had already got Hawaiian pizzas and the drinks in. She was unusually late; the reluctant centre of attention. It was seconds after the pre-arranged cocktail hour. She cheers-ed her new life with a concoction worthy of the moniker "S-bend" and fielded all enquiries about why she was leaving. Nine pairs of eyes were drilling into her:

'We still don't understand?'

'You've got the best staff nurse position out of all of us, why?'

To her mum, who was most worried about her decision, she had guiltily said she wanted to help on a wider scale but knew this wouldn't wash with her fellow nurses:

'I could say high-mindedly that I no longer believed in the current models of psychiatry.'

'Yeah, right, neither do we, but what's new?'

Jenny decided to balance it out with something they would understand:

'Okay, you got me. I really want to shag a bhagwan.'

That was enough reason for Kristen, the lead party girl, with her almost empty glass held high:

'Why didn't you say that in the first place! Cheers!'

And she was off to the bar for the next round, her enquiry boxes ticked. Thankfully her landlord needed no explanations, just the remaining rent due.

The truth was she had grown more and more scared of doing and saying the wrong thing. Certain patients haunted her. She had the "dream job" on the children's unit, but at twenty-three did she really know enough to help mend the hearts and minds of such troubled children? Such a child as Eddie, a "lost" child of drug addicts, who'd been from placement to placement whilst his parents languished unaware in prison. Whilst she was in charge on Christmas Eve he had stood on the flat roof of the unit threatening to jump off. That was finally it. She couldn't do it anymore. Jenny had wanted to take him home and love him but knew that wouldn't help. She'd be just another in a long line of "do-gooders" who'd repeat the pattern – fall for his angelic looks, his pleading blue eyes and get emotionally close to him, and he'd start lashing out, testing, waiting for the inevitable rejection. So, she walked away then, rather than later, for all the Eddies she couldn't help and the Terrys, the Claires, but hoped others would help. But what to do?

"When in doubt, travel" was to be her new motto. One late-shift-lazy-bed-ponder, she'd decided on this plan and that had buoyed her all the way through that shift: the resignation, ensuing shifts, this leaving do and now its imminent reality!

Thankfully Jenny found it quite easy to hand her life over to someone else, not in an organ donor kind of way but by visiting Trailfinders where she found Trish, who whisked her around the world from an office chair in her Ealing shopfront:

'You can fly El Al again into Delhi. You'll want to see the Taj Mahal, of course, but make sure you see it at dawn, midday and sunset too. You'll regret it otherwise. Once in a lifetime and you have to tick those wonders of the world off properly.'

'And if I were you I'd avoid Goa, but the beaches in Kovalam are beautiful for a break before your onward journey.'

Trish made landing at Delhi airport and getting a tuk-tuk to the main train station sound as easy as boarding the Circle line; she was hooked. Her colleagues remained as assorted in their responses as the talent in Orlando's. Some barely hid their derision at walking away from such a secure job to, well, "nothing", whilst many unexpected adventurers oohed and aahed:

'You're braver than me!'

'I might even join you; what is a kibbutz anyway?'

'What will you do when you come back, or will you come back? Oh, Jenny!'

She would, of course, she wouldn't do that to her lovely mum, who'd given her blessing selflessly, despite Jenny knowing and feeling that another unbidden hole in her life was about to open up. She'd "be back" a better person who would be able to pull the edges of that hole in, but as "what" or "whom"? She was glad that particular plan was on hold.

THE THIRD ERA

1986

The year the Human Genome Project was launched to understand
the human makeup.

15
Claire

After a few cleansing months off mostly spent lying vacuously on various Spanish beaches with factor fifty as her only companion, Claire felt cleansed by more than assiduous skincare. With this clean slate, Claire figured she could shake off those bitter demons and become a loveable, popular Claire. Step one was to make new friends in this shiny new town. Never one to successfully navigate, even with the A-Z without many unnecessary miles, Milton Keynes was the perfect linear choice for her new home. Milton Keynes University Hospital only opened last year so was also the perfect choice for her new job and new life. Luckily, she had an excellent reference from her old boss. Claire had looked again at the skills and, more importantly, traits a good physio "should have":

- Initiative, patience, sensitivity and tact.
- Excellent communication skills.
- The ability to work in a team.
- Problem-solving skills.
- Excellent organisational skills.
- The ability to be encouraging, empathetic and firm.

Her old boss had emphasised her organisational and problem-solving skills, and she was relieved to see although she hadn't exactly waxed lyrical about her communication skills style, she had diplomatically phrased her dealings with patients as "carried out with encouragement and clarity of instruction".

So, she passed her interview; well, they did need a lot of new staff for a whole new team. The very next week she started her first shift with the respiratory team, even before she had unpacked her few belongings in the studio bedsit in Wolverton, which she hoped was the right distance to and certainly away from work.

New everything. Claire had a new jaunty bob which made her swing her head to feel it swish against her face in a very confident way. It seemed to give her face an urchin look and, what with her new svelte figure, she didn't recognise her reflection and often caught herself doing a double take, almost liking what she saw. Life was looking up. She'd phoned her mum with taped sounds of a Moroccan bazaar in the background (the nearest "atmos", she could find) saying she was in Agra about to visit the Taj Mahal and didn't know when she could ring again.

Three months in, there were still no staff parties and no quick drinks after work. Trish, a fellow physio, had asked her to supper and Claire had said she'd check her diary not wanting to be too desperate, but Trish didn't follow it up and that opportunity was lost. All the others had photos of smooching partners, happy holidays or beaming babies on the inside of their locker doors. Claire had put a magazine picture – which she'd varnished with clear nail polish to look like a photograph – of an obscure handsome actor waving at "her" from what looked like a ski lodge.

Determined not to feel as sorry for herself as "that time", Claire took out an ad in the Guardian singles column: "Professional" (well, she was... hard-earned too, all those evenings in swatting while others in her set partied) "twenty-three-year-old, longing for real connection over dinner and walks in the country". She was going to add: "knows a bone or two" as maybe a clue to her work and to add humour, but thought it could sound smutty; oh, the perils of giving yourself away! "Was that her?" The "real connection" definitely, but she didn't care how that came about; she only knew she was just as lonely as she ever was, and this was the time to fix it – *wasn't it?*

Claire had moved to outpatients and so now had every evening and weekend free; perfect for a social life and, hopefully, a steady boyfriend. Sifting through the replies she realised the importance of her choice. Alfie, who was "twenty-eight going on eight, hungry for all types of fun" was the first rejection. Then followed Justin: "serious, sensitive and in need of understanding" *God help me.* Adam: "Self-made businessman with wealth and love to share" got a closer look but let himself down by adding at the end: "not averse to experimenting in every way". All others were discarded bar one, Tony. His handwriting was big, open and loopy; *should she get it analysed?* He could be a psychopath, but then, so could she. The letter said he lived in Bletchley, so not far away, but far enough if things didn't work out.

Having checked and re-checked the address and the time on her watch numerous times, Claire summoned courage and, holding her breath, entered Revolution, a trendy bar in central Milton Keynes.

'Claire? Great! I'm Tony, good to meet you.'

'And you.'

Two rounds later, pints of lager for him and white wine for Claire, they mutually decided it was safe to go for a meal. They agreed Italian was too messy for a "first" date and settled on a Berni Inn. So there would be a second date. Claire was able to breathe again.

Tony, a freelance graphic designer, resided in what was very much a brown bachelor pad. Claire didn't like being in his brown domain, especially as it was above a pub and early nights felt almost communal with the beery sounds coming up through the floorboards. So, Tony's toothbrush, quickly followed by his weights, three of the pub's Stella Artois glasses and a few other bare, brown belongings (which had been well sifted to this handful of accoutrements) soon littered Claire's streamlined studio living.

By nature, Tony was very affable, although many would say lazy, which made Claire feel positively dynamic and, at last, she had a way of being. She soon enjoyed chivvying him into the shape of at least one of the holes in her life and prayed he was her saviour.

16
Tony

Tony was at his very own local, rehydrating after a game of squash with his friend, Clive, who was even more gauche with women than Tony but covered it with macho bravado.

'So what's she like then?'

'Well, she's... well, hard to describe.'

'Does she even exist?'

'I know you find it hard to believe but, yes, she does. And don't take the piss but I think she's the one.'

'Bloody hell. Come on then, is she a looker for starters?'

'Not stand out in a crowd drop-dead-gorgeous but—'

'You wouldn't have stood a chance!'

Tony punches his friend on the arm but nods in agreement.

'She's got this lovely glossy brown hair and she's magnetic, if you know what I mean.'

'Magnetic... as in the "hook a fish" game!'

'As in she's got these enormous sad brown eyes that I want to make smiley.'

'You have got it bad. What does she do? Hair commercials?'

'She's a physio.'

'Very handy for a massage!'

'Well, I'm not letting you meet her, that's for sure!'

For Tony, sometimes the act of saying stuff confirmed his thoughts. He needed those thoughts to leave his brain as words were said to another's face, allowing him to read their expression and then gauge the response. Clive didn't realise he was Tony's very own bolstering sounding board. He just gaped at Tony but then thumped <u>him</u> on the arm this time. So, yes, maybe she was "the one".

Tony surprised himself with the speed with which the relationship progressed. His last girlfriend was probably three years ago now and lasted only a few months, only reaching the once-weekly pub night out, and didn't feel as if it had any forward momentum at all. Tony wasn't actually a forward momentum type of guy – more a static sort – but this propulsion excited him, and he really felt Claire was made for him. He didn't want to admit to himself that her breasts caught his eye first, especially as Claire seemed hell-bent on covering them up, but they were the stuff of adolescent boys' dreams –large enough to nuzzle between should he get so lucky and not at all droopy like his old science teacher's (Miss Watson had a severe bun on top, a monobrow, wore braless poplin blouses buttoned to the neck, and continuously lifted her breasts up with her folded arms whenever she was cross with him. Tony hadn't ever known where to look: the dipping brow or hoisted breasts). When Tony did manage to lift his gaze, he did really love her eyes – Claire's, that is – which could spit and soften in the blink of, well... an eye. He had early on described her eyes as "treacle pudding eyes, with the treacle all melting in the middle" which had made her laugh, but she seemed pleased. When he learned all the tricks to soften those eyes, well, his heart softened along with them.

'So, cheers! It's been seven months now, practically going steady.'

'Steady, are we?'

'Well, this is the steadiest I've ever got, apart from with Edwina Gumm when I gave her a curtain ring as a wedding ring aged seven so I could borrow her scooter regularly.'

'You are shameless!'

'She got a good deal too! We lived on a hill and we used to go on the scooter together most days after school and then my mum would make us a fish finger tea. So you see, I've always known how to show a girl a good time!'

He loved her hard-won laughter; it was even more of a prize. He loved her work ethic, as he had to admit he found it difficult to get going in the mornings without a few games on his console and several coffees. And most of all, he loved that she seemed invested in them as a unit; he'd felt on his own for far too long. By trial and error, he learned this woman could be won, not by flowers and cheap lockets with their picture in them (that response had stung a bit), but with punctuality, kept promises and a blank diary for her to fill. And Tony had always been rubbish at planning. She added colour to his life; thus far life had all been one season. With Claire, it could be a sunny summer followed quickly by a squally dark winter and he was enervated by these constant emotional changes.

He was sad he didn't have anyone close to check her out, as Clive definitely would be looking for all the wrong attributes. His parents had emigrated to some far-flung Antipodean sheep-shagging area when he was eighteen to join his sister and her new family. They had presumed their formerly meek biddable son would join them. However, he surprised everyone including himself, by getting a place at art school, living in a "studio flat" – a room over a pub – and working evenings in that pub throughout his course, never once going into debt. It was a dream life: meals in the pub, company and beer on tap and then even more free beer when he designed the pub's new look and relaunch. He did well with the unimaginatively named The Green Man and from that first design, the commissions flowed in and a career was begun.

Turning twenty-six and not yet having moved from only his second home in life and the same small social circle, he was trepidatiously ready for phase three of life:

Claire.

17
Claire

The relationship was progressing well. They enjoyed weekend breaks together doing the cultural activities that Claire deemed they ought, and Tony was happy traipsing around any Bonnard exhibition as long as there was a pint at the end and someone to mother him. Claire could now run her clinics blindfolded, which some of her patients might have commented explained her detached approach. So, when the list of museums, etcetera, was drying up, she needed a new distraction from the "holes" and, just as importantly, needed to believe Tony would always be there for her.

A big wedding would entail her parents being involved and she didn't want that – and the lack of a bridal party would be embarrassing, to say the least. Tony did persuade her that he should at least meet his in-laws before the wedding, which Claire grudgingly agreed to and oversaw assiduously.

'Lovely to meet you both at last. Claire's told me such a lot about you.'

Poor Tony. He knew some of the right phrases, but Claire's arch look silenced any further inching towards any relationship, but he was most worried they wouldn't open the malt whisky he'd bought them to ease the day.

'So, how did you two meet, was it when you were travelling?'

'No. It was through a work colleague who wanted a website designed, wasn't it, Tony?'

'Er. Yes, that's right.'

Tony realised he hadn't been given the script for this particular role and so was just going to go along with whatever Claire said; she obviously needed to keep their life private.

'Yes, Claire mentioned you were a designer; business going well?'

'Dad! You're not going to do the "what are your intentions speech" too, are you? We're getting married, so get used to it!'

'Your dad was just trying to get to know him, love! Sorry, Tony, Claire never has liked us being too "involved" as she'd say, but we can't help it!'

'I'm still here, Mum!'

Claire's mum tried a gay laugh that really disguised her teary emotions of wanting this moment of her only daughter's betrothal to be a happy normal beginning of a longstanding relationship with Tony, with the both of them. But she knew he was being wheeled in and, as quickly, wheeled out, not allowed to connect in any meaningful way, lest it quake her daughter's extending bridge of separation.

Tony's parents were conveniently (for Claire) in New Zealand. However, he had a best mate, Clive. They played squash together, which always amazed Claire he had the energy for. But, apart from him, Tony said he only needed her which of course was, for now, the right answer.

So, it was an intimate wedding with two witnesses plucked from the same holiday resort in Corfu. Sunburned noses in the photos and rose petals over the swan-sculptured towels on the wedding bed. Mated forever.

18
Janet

Ella had enjoyed helping Janet bake. She was showing a real aptitude in the kitchen, which both Jeff and Janet were encouraging, as little else at school seemed to interest her. They had both become very defensive when summoned numerous times to Mrs Wallace's office to explain her behaviour, when of course her background did this – but they weren't at liberty to offer such explanations. Instead, they tried to find other talents she may have, and one of these "proved" to be baking!

Overflowing on every scrubbed kitchen surface were quiches, scones, banana loaf, an array of homemade jams and Ella's own speciality, orange chocolate cake. Ella was going out with her social worker that day which she was very aggrieved about. She moaned that she was always farmed out when Claire came around and was only placated by realising her social worker was taking her to see *The Black Cauldron* at the local Odeon cinema and they were to have popcorn.

So, Janet was able to sigh at least one sigh of relief before anxiety took hold again and her jabbering self overrode the calm, prospective mother-in-law she had planned to greet Tony with.

Shrill laugh.

'We are so looking forward to getting to know you... Please do sit down. Can I take your coat or do you want to warm up? We can put the heating up. Jeff?'

'Mum!'

Claire, of course, took charge of the situation and ran it her way and at speed, and before the crumbs had hardly settled on the plates, they had both gone. Not long after, Ella whirl-winded back into the kitchen with bonus ice cream around her mouth, hoping to catch a glimpse of Claire, but then life fast-forwarded on.

Whenever she called Claire and got her answer phone once again, she would hug the thought of Tony to her. Janet had liked him immediately and so hoped this would "settle" Claire down. She hadn't known what to expect from a beau of her daughter's, but he could have been anything for all Janet cared – as long as he loved her and he clearly did.

Even though she had been in and out of the kitchen like an Alan Ayckbourn farce that day, as Jeff had said "brandishing banana loaf like a majorette", she had managed to clock him letting his hand rest lightly behind her as protectively as she would allow and registered his gaze following her around the room like a dog whose owner is going out soon and hopes to go too. He had what Janet's own mother said of Jeff "a nice face" which meant open, kind, forgettable – but who wanted memorably dark and dashing when you had your own trustworthy comfortable slipper of a man? That's what both Jeff and Tony were, "comfortable". She prayed nightly that her daughter would take care of this relationship, thus he would take care of her; she could then live without the mother-daughter catchups, just.

19
Jenny

Thus far, Jenny's travel diary recorded eight months of adventure, unrequited loves, waist inches lost and waist inches gained, and poetic descriptions of the changing landscapes and peoples. Like polite but persistent kamikaze pilots, mosquitos knocked to come in the netting door which brought a slight breeze into the muggy Singapore youth hostel in which Jenny found herself, once more unpacking her far too heavy rucksack. Her mother had helped her pack.

'If you roll it like this, love, you can get more in.'

'Great, cos I've got these bottles of anti-frizz to get in too.'

'What's that... five, six bottles! I do think other countries will have hair products too; you won't be able to stand with that on your back, let alone walk!'

'I'm going to get fit, Mum, that's the plan!'

'Don't overstretch yourself, love... in any way.'

Her mum had run out of stalling practical advice and thus was verging on getting emotional, and only managed a "take care" before the tears came.

'Oh, Mum.'

She sat with bowed head under the top bunk relieved to both shed her load (three anti-frizz bottles left still) and to be at her next "home". The immediate sounds were the ever-present mosquitos, but over the "zzz" harmony was the cacophony of hooter traffic that wasn't targeted explosive car rage as in London, but an incessant high-pitched banter. Jenny suddenly felt far from her dear old mum and also the rhythms of London, the clear "car-contained" signals of irate motorists and huffs of impatient queuers still in line. Here, the noises and chatter ran riot together but were belied by smiles everywhere, but which to trust? This was suddenly all a new overwhelming feeling – being here out of her comfort zone – but this was the first day of her lone adventure and she needed to get brave and go explore, otherwise what was the point?

Six months in Israel had been a safe, idyllic pastoral dream. Even the air raid sirens felt unreal, and bundling into the shelter with secreted Shabbat wine yet another party. Five a.m. cold dark arisings, but then semolina with jam breakfasts in the canteen after three hours of grafting either picking bananas in the emerging heat, or on the tractors weeding and baring souls with fellow kibbutz volunteers. And, on days of "promotion", peeling vegetables indoors in the busy kitchen in her own world with the guttural Hebrew around her buffering her thoughts. At the end of the day, blue boiler-suited work clothes were swapped for people's own personality clothes, aching bones warmed by the sun, dipping in the pool. Then, sundown strollings through the sweetcorn rows, eating them raw and pretending she was in love with Hime and writing poems again like a lovesick schoolgirl. For Jenny like most people her age, any age, she just wanted to be loved, but she was also greedy for the thing other adventurers referenced as "life". Jenny had to tear herself away and go confirm the dates for that onward ticket, otherwise she could see herself just staying... and staying.

So, from Israel, she had joined an eccentric Englishman and a motley group of international travellers on the train carriage called a "bogie", which had made her laugh and then, on realising she was now with grown-up travellers, she coughed into her hand. She then worried they might think her infectious so quickly dropped her hand and grinned inanely for some time. She vowed to work on her first impressions.

Roland had bought and converted the "bogie" to lead tourists around his beloved India. They slept on narrow wooden benches which, during the day, they all sat on and turned their faces to the open windows, ready to bob back in again at stations where curious brown hands would want to touch their whiter skins. There was no kitchen as all food was available at the stations they passed through and ablutions were made in the tiny makeshift shower with a trickle of icy water. Although freezing, Jenny stood longer than most, as she had acquired a coral infection from snorkelling in Eliat and, so, scrubbed it vigilantly. In this moist climate, she was terrified of it getting worse and her persistent dream of losing her passport had a new companion: amputation, but this was what adventure was all about, wasn't it!

Jenny was filled with the wonder of India passing in all its differences: Delhi, Jaipur, Agra, Kovalam. At one station, a beautiful, say, eight-year-old girl, had flung back the door.

'Chai, chai.'

On entering their carriage, she was silenced by the nine pairs of foreign eyes appraising her. She took a seat and primly pulled her ragged skirt to cover her bony, brown knees and sat with her back erect, staring out of the window, fleetingly "one of us", until she alighted at the next station, swallowed back into her own world. Jenny had been struck at the self-assurance of a child and a child with "seemingly" nothing.

Two months had gone already and Jenny was back in Delhi but grateful for the windbreak of friendship she'd had with her thus far. Her onward travels were completely alone but, spurred by the self-assurance of "India girl", she packed her rucksack once more: passport, check.

So, sunglasses on – which helped her feel hidden and safe, and of course it was very sunny – out through the gauze and into the heart of downtown Singapore. First stop, to reward her bravery Raffles, for a Singapore gin sling, naturally.

Jenny soon learned the art of the tattered book as a shield. A shield to unwanted attention, a shield to any attention. She had always tried to "shrink" away from any limelight but, at five-foot-ten and of "solid" build, she wasn't easily overlooked and, thus, had always been the one pushed forward to buy the underage fags when she didn't even smoke.

Now armed with her Lonely Planet Guide with noted irony, she was able to soak up the differing atmospheres of beach, bazaar, and next stop, Bali – more beaches and bazaars – then to Perth, Australia. And, thus, looking forward to toilet seats (toilet roll even!) and clean sheets on comfy beds – and arriving feeling relatively unscathed.

THE FOURTH ERA

1987

The year the first criminal was convicted using DNA evidence.

20
Claire

The holes were opening up again for Claire. Tony felt the brunt of her restlessness and as much as he tried to placate her, he annoyed her. As he worked from home, he was there to prepare tea as Claire got through the door and so he really tried to take note of both the time and fridge contents but seemed to come up short with both.

'Bloody hell, Tony, do I have to do everything? I feel like your bloody mother.'

The obvious next step, having already moved into a house with a spare bedroom, was actual children to put in there. Not particularly maternal but not wanting to ignore programming, Claire had persuaded, that is told, Tony that "it was time" and so they embarked on "project baby". Miraculously, as it seemed to many lucky couples and Tony's delight, his "swimmers" reached their target pretty effortlessly. Claire was soon reading the two blue lines as positive, bringing up her porridge and suddenly happily fat with a new purpose and on maternity leave. A trip to share this with the parents was reluctantly deemed necessary.

As they pulled up outside the house of Claire's childhood, she noted even more changes. The front garden was now hard standing for her dad's new work van and, down the side of the house, she could see a bicycle shed overstuffed with trikes, bikes and all manner of plastic wheeled animals. Just little differences, but they irked.

Claire had loved the former myriad of rosebushes in the front garden that gave off a heady scent as you approached the door (now repainted pillar box red for some reason) and she remembered she hadn't been allowed a bicycle until she was ten – her dad said it was "too dangerous". She especially missed the purple and pink fuchsia bushes whose flowers her dad had told her were bells for the fairies to ring when in trouble, and that a fairy always came.

Claire determined the visit would be short, it really wasn't home anymore. So, once all hugs and kisses were negotiated, Claire tried to signal the brevity of the visit and model this to Tony by sitting on the edge of the sofa, which proved impossible as it possessed the squishiest, most enveloping cushions. So, from this pseudo-comfortable position, Claire needed to ensure that the visit was temporary in other ways, thus she launched into:

'We have some news!'

'Are you okay, love?'

Claire firmly shut off this avenue of her mum's worries.

'YES, Mum.'

'Oh, love, are you...?'

'Going to have a baby? Yes.'

Her mum burst into tears, leaving her dad to gather the important facts.

'Oh, congratulations, you two, well done. I mean, that's wonderful news, when?'

Tony very proudly stated:

'You'll be a grandad on April 10th, Jeff!'

To be brought down to Earth by Claire:

'Well, that's the due date but who knows... I was early, wasn't I? We'll let you know, as they say!'

Claire's mum gathered her emotions enough to dispense Jeff off to find something to toast the news with. Whilst she asked about nursery colours and which knitting patterns to start, Claire began whisking Tony away. This was even before the tea trolley was wheeled out, much to his disappointment. He had enjoyed basking in a bit of parental love and Claire had even momentarily enjoyed the unusual giddy heights of undivided parental attention from her own formerly pre-occupied family. She was "somebody" in their eyes at last, with another "somebody" all to herself – well, with occasional support she presumed from Tony. But this had been enough of an "in" to allow her parents, and so they sped off home as Claire told Tony she wanted him to help her finish stripping the old wallpaper in the spare room, the nursery.

This was "her" baby and Tony had to work harder to support their new family now. She was "done" with other people's aches and pains and broken bones. She wanted to devote herself to this tiny bundle of precious, perfect, forming bones. "Soppy" Tony had wanted the "surprise", hah! of discovering whether their child was Olivia or Oliver. Claire had her way as usual and, at the sixteen-week scan, needing to be in control, needing to know, she primed the sonographer to tell them. Clearly new to her trade, she had taken a worrying age to at last hone in on the tiniest member, her Oliver!

As gender neutrality was a thing of the future to Claire, it didn't affect her decorating of the blue nursery with Elmer frieze and the drawers full of diminutive dungarees. Claire had never felt so fit – physically or emotionally (there had been a few wobbles before this perfect era which Tony had obliviously ridden). Incubating this new being meant her diet and self-care had a reason to be attended to. The alcohol which had been a feature of their early married lives was banned to Tony's disappointment, but to Tony's relief, Claire took charge of the cooking once more to ensure the healthiest diet. Aqua natal and pregnancy yoga classes filled up her last trimester, along with baby books and even planning ahead reading: *How to Parent a Teenager*. Claire was going to be the best parent her little Oliver could have. Thus, she wore her pregnancy well and all holes seemed well and truly about to be filled.

21
Jenny

Perth, her final destination on "project adventure", was a welcome drier heat and it was good to hear accessible language around her again. Buoyed by this familiarity, she quickly got herself a job at a yacht club with a backdrop of bobbing boats and expansive cloudless blue skies, accompanied by the soundtrack of clanging mast riggings, jostling each other like children liberated through school gates. It augured well.

Although she had never pulled a pint in her life, the steady filling of "jugs" of lager and mopping the swilled excesses was a wonderfully stress-free lifestyle, hypnotic with repetition, with a backing track of anodyne radio chat shows, giving her time to think – well, at the beginning. This was the first time she had to put roots down, just long enough to save for the return journey and decide what the next era looked like. The job had come with a cabin in the yacht club marina. It was just big enough for a bed, shower cubicle (complete with requisite mould and resident spiders), a single gas ring and a chest of drawers to put her remaining bottle of anti-frizz on.

Australia might have been a wonderful experience if she had chosen a less sexist arena to earn a crust and form friendships, which was what she was now really craving. With her travel buddies she had an instant and supportive connection: "Where are you from and

going to, and where is the best place to grab a shower/best Pad Thai?"
All adventuring together.

Suddenly she felt exposed and alone as all her fellow bar staff had
their own friendship and family circles and yet another "Pommie"
could sort themselves out. The feeling of exposure didn't just stop at
her friendlessness but at her perceived "availability".

After months of sun and traipsing sights, Jenny arrived tanned,
honed and looking the best she ever had. Unfortunately this resulted
in unasked-for and often drunk, thus insistent, male attention. As an
only child with a widowed mum and as a girls' school then female-
dominated college graduate, the male species remained an anathema.
Even after a few forays into relationships with said species, she was
none the wiser.

Jenny's relationship history thus far had been a mere bagatelle
of a couple of dates accompanied by, usually, unsatisfactory sex
with namely: Colin, a fellow psychiatric nurse doing the rounds of
her fellow nurses; Leo, not his real name but assumed for when he
was a published poet (which was never going to happen in Jenny's
experience of his simpering sonnets to her); Bob, a policeman who
proposed far too early for anyone's comfort; and was it Andy, with
the motorbike which kept on breaking down or was that Pablo
on holiday in Lloret de Mar? Anyway, none of them had any real
foundations of shared interests, beliefs and a love of Labradors
which may have qualified them as a relationship in Jenny's eyes. And
then, here she was with this hunting pack of undiluted testosterone
cascading like said bagatelle up to her position at the beer-swilled bar.

Wednesday nights seemed to be the bar's Friday nights, so by the
time Saturday arrived, there had already been a long rowdy build-up
to the weekend and Jenny dreaded having a Saturday evening shift.

She had never mastered witty putdowns but had got slightly better at ignoring the repeated obscene slatherings.

Nonetheless, when a regular who felt he had a claim on Jenny lurched over the bar to display his prize to his drunken mates by trying to "snog" her, she was very grateful to the nearby guy who intercepted:

'Sorry, mate, she's with me! Are you going on your break now, love?'

Dazed but grateful, she had the nod from her boss and she stepped outside.

'Thanks for the rescue. That was quick thinking in there.'

'You're English! I'm from Peckham, London.'

'I know where Peckham is! I used to live in Lyndhurst Way!'

'No way! Very posh!'

'It was a house share with millions of us.'

'Worth millions more like! Sorry, I didn't know whether you needed rescuing or not.'

'No. I mean, yes, I did. He's just one of many drunks who get too lairy here.'

'Lairy! Now I know you're posh!'

Jenny felt she had a little bit of home to tether her on this huge unmanageable continent and she held on tight. They arranged to meet up on her day off and spent it at Cottesloe beach, sprawled on aligned towels on the hot sand. He solicitously applied factor thirty to her sun-kissed but still Anglo-Saxon skin and she let him more often than was necessary; she liked the feel of his firm hands working her skin.

They had several beers on the beach and then walked to his hotel room nearby to rid themselves of sand and freshen up before supper, out at a nearby restaurant. Of course, as Jenny could see looking back he meant it to happen like this. Once in the shower, Darren, having promised he wouldn't come in as there was no lock, did just that and came in, already naked.

'What!'

'Move over!'

'No, I'd rather not.'

He had mimicked her voice.

'I'd "rather" not! Don't go all posh and frosty on me. I said, move over.'

'No! Don't…'

She couldn't separate her responsibility from his. She had let him touch her body on the beach, hadn't she? So, of course, he thought it was an invitation. And they were both tipsy. But she had clearly said no. No, as he entered the shower cubicle. No, as his mouth bruised her evading lips and her nostrils filled with the stench of his suntan oil soured with his sweat and cheap aftershave. NO, as he pinioned her flailing arms against the clammy, mildewed tiles. NO, as he rammed his cruel body against her sore sunburned skin and then screamed NOOO as his knees pulled her refusing legs apart and NOOO as he entered her.

Moments – and a lifetime – later, he left the shower and sat on the bed, at least having the temerity to look shamefaced when, after a forever of trembling shock, she dragged her clothes over her wet skin and had to pass him to run out of the room. The hotel receptionist gaily shouted 'Gday!' as she ran out of the door and was promptly sick on the kerb. They had seen it all there before and what had just happened was possibly just another tawdry inconsequential sexual act. But it wasn't to her.

She turned the word "rape" around in her mind, not daring to let it sour her tongue by speaking it. Anyway, she had no one to tell. No friends locally; she couldn't call her mum, tell her boss, anyone – and she knew she never would. But every time she applied suntan cream thereafter, she held her breath so as not to remember that particular smell.

Back at work, the grubby language, the belching and the constant approaches prompted a heightened, albeit a contained, inner recoil. Jenny didn't realise she was doing it, but she began to eat to quash these uncomfortable feelings that the approaches evoked, and as she grew a fatter armoury, thankfully the attentions disappeared as the pounds piled. She never saw him again, mercifully.

She had overheard a conversation about a Darren having run out of money who had gone back to England and assumed it was him.

And anyway, having accumulated enough dollars in her rucksack, visited Ayers Rock and been duly and rightly affected by the Aboriginal traditions, she decided her own dreamtime – the inter-relation of all people and things – badly needed addressing. She was homeward-bound.

THE FIFTH ERA

1988

The year of *So Emotional* by Whitney Huston.

22
Claire

Of course, Claire's bag had been packed since month six. All the unfamiliar accoutrements of this imminent journey: breast pads and paper pants carefully folded, checked and re-checked. And the "first babygro" wrapped in blue tissue paper, imagined and re-imagined a million times with the occupant's tiny limbs being nervously and gently guided into his first clothing. Tony was a heavy sleeper, so it took Claire several "yellings" to alert him to the fact that "it was time". He had had many "briefings" re full petrol tanks and different routes to the hospital, dependent on traffic and time of day. This was 4:07 a.m. and, despite his usual slow entry into any day, for Tony, he was relatively alert.

'But you're only thirty-seven weeks!'

'Stop panicking!'

'I'm not but—'

'I was early; we thought he might be too.'

The journey went well, without too many speed bumps, as Claire's contractions were becoming strong. Claire was practising her deep breathing with the birth tunes on the car's radio cassette: *Pull Up to the Bumper* by Grace Jones being Tony's only addition, but even that didn't seem to distract her from the deep place she had with much practice gone to.

On arrival at the labour ward, Tony was delighted to be made redundant, but the enormity of the situation hit him and, like so many fathers, he had to be given a quick seat. Once in hospital and seeing Tony buckle, Claire too became disturbed by the reality of the inevitability of proceedings. Having spent the last few years micromanaging her life, and then Tony's, to make it safe and to work for them, now the panic was rising as she was going to have to hand some control over for once. However, her assigned midwife, Adele, although just twenty-something was no-nonsense and obviously very practised with mums such as Claire and jollied her speedily through, from her arrival at the delivery suite to the final stage of labour, all going almost to the birth plan. Unfortunately minus the birthing pool, but fortunately minus Grace Jones.

Several hours later, Claire was still hanging onto some semblance of control, managing to breathe into her "happy place". So, she didn't see the swift urgency with which Adele attached her to a continuous monitoring machine after listening again for the baby's heartbeat, but she felt Tony's hand squeeze that bit tighter.

'Claire, your baby isn't happy in this position so I'm just going to help you turn onto your left side for a bit, okay? Here we go… that's it, well done…'

The next thing Claire felt was a slim arm reach across her and an alarm went off. Although suffused with gas and air, she became aware of more and more blue scrubs around her. She thought maybe she was hallucinating and that there was really only Adele, her dependable midwife, who was having an Indian take away with her medic boyfriend tonight, or was it a Chinese? Yes, a Chinese.

She tried to convert the blue scrubs into the blue babygro in her overnight bag ready for Oliver but Claire couldn't ignore the beeps and hurried footsteps, and Adele's calm blue eyes became urgently darting.

'You're doing fine, Claire, keep breathing that gas.'

More voices joined the fray:

'Baby's low enough.'

'Forceps!'

'Crash bleep the neonatal team!'

She felt the cold metal of the forceps and then her baby, eel-like, slip into the world. Tony stood as still as stone and she had a momentary image of a petrified tree.

She had been pushing and pushing and pushing as they said and so lay back exhausted awaiting the cry.

The cry didn't come. Then she registered the alarm in Tony's eyes as the baby, her Oliver, was whisked away to a ring of blue, feeding sharks.

'Head in neutral position.'

'Five inflation breaths.'

'Chest rise?'

Claire held hers, reality dawning.

'Yes.'

'Heart rate?'

'Absent.'

Claire was a dark sea away from this unit of blue – the fevered activity of cardiac compressions, drugs being drawn up, airway inserted, airbag inflated, then the waiting, watching, all hoping to save this new infant:

'I don't think there's anything else we can do...'

'All agree?'

Adele crossed the sea and approached the bed with tears in her eyes.

'I'm so sorry, Claire, Tony; your baby was born with no signs of life. and we have been unable to save him. Your baby has died. A beautiful baby boy.'

Claire heard someone in the room scream, it could have been her. Then a renewed searing pain overwhelmed her... and everything went black.

23
Janet

The loss was like lightning all around and waiting for ensuing thunderclaps when they had that call from Tony telling them about Oliver's birth and death all in the space of one call. And then he said Claire was in a bad way and refusing visitors. Even them. Janet wandered from room to room tidying, picking up lost socks, even fluff she never usually noticed. When her legs wouldn't walk anymore, she sat on their bedroom carpet and went through her "presents" drawer and took out bundle after bundle of tissue-papered baby clothes, hugging each tiny babygro in turn and letting the tsunami of sobs loose.

She had kept some of Nigel and Claire's baby things, even the tatty special "blanky" of Claire's. The tantrums that flared when Janet had tried to prise it away for washing and now, here it was laundered and "Febreezed" and "wrong", still with the faded blue elephants but without the right smell – as Claire would have agreed for once. Poor Claire. This set Janet off anew, but she couldn't afford the time to be lost in old reveries; a new little baby girl had entered their lives and needed them.

They weren't set up for tinies, in fact, they had told the fostering people that they'd do primary age only, but this was different.

Jeff had already borrowed a travel cot from the neighbours and had put it in the bedroom next to theirs. This had been Ella's room, but she was delighted when told she was to be promoted to Claire's old room, as it was bigger and was at the front so she could see who was coming and going. She especially liked spying on the brothers from number seven playing football in the cul-de-sac, as the eldest, Laurie, was "fit as". And a new baby sister, however temporary, was finally something to boast about at school.

Janet knew a newborn wouldn't need much and she was possibly only to be living with them for this emergency but, still, she couldn't help nipping out and buying a few mobiles and an Elmer elephant nursery frieze. She had pasted this quickly on the wall whilst Jeff was out collecting Ella so he couldn't change her mind or pop this excited bubble of hope rising up amongst her grief.

RIP Oliver. And now here was Olivia, meaning peace; Janet hoped so.

24
Jenny

There was nothing quite like being sat in her dad's old Ercol armchair, feet on the pouffe, gin and tonic and Edam and crackers on the side table, and her mum's crinkled, kind face opposite her in the matching chair, welcoming her back. Both of them drinking in much gin and all news in person now, not the sparse news conveyed in spasmodic, flimsy, blue airmails from far-flung poste restante.

'I can't deny I'm delighted to have you home again.'

'And I'm delighted to be here, Mum. I don't think travel's for me.'

'You had some great adventures though?'

'Oh, yes! But there's something about being with someone who really knows you inside out that can't be found on the run.'

'On the run?'

'Mum! I don't believe it! You're using my own psychiatric techniques on me!'

'Get me! Sorry though; just trying to get a feel for how you really are?'

'Fine, Mum, honestly, just need to take stock and plan the right next move.'

After a couple of restorative weeks of those arms and Anaglypta walls around her, Jenny's work ethic and compelling "purpose in life" had her signing up for a graduate social work course at Bournemouth University. It made sense.

She still felt she "wanted to help" but in a less acute setting and hadn't she chimed with the social model of psychiatry most? To her, it made perfect sense that if people lived on the seventeenth floor in abject poverty that they may be a bit depressed, so yes, she could help in this way.

Aided by the bank of Mum, she got herself a flatshare and a few items of furniture and moved into Winton the day before term started. Not a natural student, Jenny just wanted to fast forward these two years and get "out there".

A variety of placements and her slightly more grown-up dinner parties with her sociable housemates, Lisa and Brona, got her through the less welcome lectures and essays about ecomaps and genograms. Before long, Jenny was throwing her mortarboard in the air with glee and determination to make this next era a happy and, importantly to her, a useful one.

Her fellow students, flatmates, or even her knowing mum didn't discover her bulimia – or they never questioned her fluctuating weight, long periods in the bathroom with the radio on (George Michael, full blare) and biscuit barrel troughing.

'We've run out of milk again, girls, I'll go!'

And off Jenny would run to the corner shop, ostensibly to buy the milk but really to replace the cereal she'd had handfuls of in the middle of the night or biscuits to refill the biscuit barrel she had bought for their shared biscuit supply. Jenny was particularly weary of constantly replacing packets of biscuits. It was a tiresome and complicated process. In order to leave them as if untampered with, she had to remember where the plastic wrapping had been folded down on countless packets of bourbons, custard creams and, her worst offender, chocolate chip cookies.

There were too many close shaves.

'What are you doing hiding in the dark, Jen?'

'Just looking for the paracetomol. I have a headache; sorry if I woke you.'

'Phew, I thought we had mice! I could hear what I thought was scuffling and scurrying... eughh!'

She constantly berated herself for these undercover acts and hated herself that sooo much energy was wasted on the fear of potential discovery. After too many ridiculous alibis at the ready, she had an epiphany! The contents calculations of a large biscuit barrel were not as exacting, and thus more forgiving than the pesky packet problem. So, she finally sourced that biscuit tin with soundless lid removal and slightly less angst ensued.

This dirty hidden secret had first started during the intensity of psychiatry – the eating to blanket unwanted emotions and the subsequent purging to regain control. It had then easily resurfaced in Australia, but the weight had sheathed and hidden her frame, so, what had become a protection lurched to the extreme of equally distressing invisibility. Thus, she had begun making herself sick again to deal with her hated fat. This habit had taken hold; a needed friend to counteract an emptiness she still felt. But this friend stole the enamel from her teeth and all control around food. Jenny felt it was time to address this before starting her new job.

25
Claire

Claire lay in bed alone, curled around the plaster imprints of Oliver's perfect tiny hands and feet. She had managed formerly to keep Tony in the dark that his wife's mental health problems were an actual "thing", until a rare post-wedding visit to Claire's parents to share the wedding pictures seemingly in another lifetime.

'Well, I must say, you both looked very tanned and happy. What a lovely setting, right by the sea too. Who were your witnesses again?'

'It was just two other guests in the hotel.'

'Oh.'

'I told you, Mum, we just wanted a day without fuss.'

Claire surprised herself with the pride she felt for her husband who, unusually, felt the need to speak up to defend his new wife and navigate this new in-law territory as best he could:

'My parents obviously missed out too, but they are not as understanding as you.'

Janet couldn't help herself.

'We think you're the understanding one, Tony!'

Claire's mum had found an opportunity to take Tony aside, asking him to help her with the tea things, and when Claire tried to shadow them was rebuffed as firmly as her mum dared with her. For the sake of peace, Claire, for once, did her mother's bidding but lingered by the kitchen door.

'I just wanted a moment with you to say how relieved her father and I are, oh, and happy of course, that Claire has finally found someone to cope with her, well, her "fluctuating emotions" shall we say. You seem like a great foil for her.'

'Well, I think I'm the lucky one. Claire puts up with my "boringness"; maybe that's why we're a good match.'

'Well, that's wonderful, whatever the "recipe" as long as it works!'

To Claire's fury, her mum couldn't help fishing by adding,

'And I'm sure all that silly self-harming is behind her now – with you by her side.'

After gulps of realisation hidden by a thin smile, Tony was just about able to summon a response, as Claire came in wearing a thunderous expression and Tony's formerly hidden diplomacy skills made a timely debut.

'I'll do my best; I'm sure like any couple we'll ride any storms together... eh, Claire? Er, this looks lovely cake... Janet.'

'Oh... well, I thought as I didn't make you a wedding cake I'd make this one now; you can keep a tier for the christening.'

Janet prattled to soothe tensions as usual.

'I'm only teasing; all in good time, eh!' And another squall was averted.

Regards the riding of these storms, as time went on, Tony found keeping his head down and out of the way was the best approach, and he had become very fit from all the running he had taken up as a consequence. Claire explained the scars on her arms as past teenage angst and, whenever plasters or bandages from supposed "work injuries" had appeared, he chose not to go there.

But now he had to go there.

This was his wife at her lowest. But Tony couldn't cope either. He had needed to share his grief at losing their son, but Claire had shut him out, irrationally blaming him; she refused to see any family at all, or to go home, even though the doctors had discharged her.

After the final visiting time and a particularly vicious attack on Tony which resulted in Claire throwing her cup of tea in his face, he snapped for the first time, and called her parents to take her home. He had enough on his new familial plate.

Claire's parents couldn't cope with her either. All they had at their disposal were crumpets, sea air, homely comforts... and love, and hoped these would help heal her heart and the new wounds on her arms. They had contacted their social worker and explained their situation and Kevin, a rumbustious four-year-old new in placement, was rehomed. However, the now permanent presence in Claire's family home of Ella, now a moody teenager, just served to alienate Claire further from her parents and plough her deeper into her anxieties.

'How long is "she" staying?'

'If you mean Claire, well, this is her home too, Ella.'

'I'd rather have baby Olivia here. I'd help with her.'

'Well, you know that can't happen. Maybe when Claire's better. She needs to be on her own and in her old room for now. I'm sorry.'

'She hates us all, me especially.'

'Nooo. It might seem like that, but she's just hurting and her mind isn't thinking right at the moment. And she is probably jealous of you with your whole life a clean slate in front of you.'

With the memories of the care she had received at The Maudsley, one Saturday afternoon when the rest of the family were returning sandy and loud from the beach, Claire planned the timing of cutting her arm with the same precision as the cut itself and got the escape she wanted. She was admitted to their local psychiatric unit that day.

26
Jenny

Jenny had veered away from any psychiatric placements as she had that experience covered and so, for her course, was placed in autism, counselling, hospice and dementia services. Therefore, this appointment at Bethlem Psychiatric Outpatients was her first renewed experience of this local facility, but this time not as a nurse. Or The Bethlem Royal Hospital to give it its full name, and here she was once more flicking through its renowned history in a pamphlet in the (muted green, of course) waiting room:

"In 1247 the Priory of Saint Mary of Bethlehem was founded, devoted to healing sick paupers. The small establishment became known as Bethlehem Hospital. Londoners later abbreviated this to 'Bethlem' and often pronounced it 'Bedlam'. At some point, the monks began to accept patients who had symptoms of mental illness rather than physical disability or disease. It is certainly true that by 1403, 'lunatic' patients formed the majority of the Bethlem's clients – and so England's first, and perhaps most infamous, mental institution was born.

"The hospital regime was a mixture of punishment and religious devotion – chains, manacles, locks and stocks appear in the hospital inventory from this time. The shock of corporal punishment was believed to cure some conditions, while isolation was thought to help a

person 'come to their senses'. At the same time, it was a religious duty to care for and feel compassion for people afflicted by madness."

It was strange being on this end of proceedings. Jenny didn't know at first how to behave, having "crossed that line", but thankfully psychiatry had come a long way and she realised there was no point in holding onto a professional carapace. She needed to bare all the toilet bowl details of her life and be helped. Twenty sessions though! After faking, unconvincingly, that it was what she was expecting, Jenny had to face the facts that the therapist was taking this seriously and she, Jenny Turner, ought to accord herself with the care she had given others – and do so too. This was going to be the hardest part, resigning herself to being a "patient", one of "them" and having a "therapist"; well, that was going to take a lot of getting used to too. However much she knew mental health was a continuum, she had hung onto the fact that she was on the other safer end, not quite the "sorted" matching handbag and shoes end, but near enough.

And, secondly, this was the "biggy", that she was indeed "worth" helping. Yes, she had to start believing in herself but that was the nub of the problem: herself. Thankfully, Sophie, her therapist, had her feeling comfortable and opening up from the outset.

'I can't seem to find where I start and finish, if you know what I mean. Not that I even have any edges at all, at twelve and a half stone!'

'Do you often make jokes at your expense?'

'Yes, I s'pose I do...'

'Tell me more about these missing "edges of you"?'

'Well... everyone else seems to have a real sense of self... but I feel as if I'm looking for an approximation of me to copy, so I can fill in the missing bits. Like doing the edges of a jigsaw first, you get the outline first, don't you? I want an outline.'

'What are these "missing bits"?'

'That's just it, I don't know, but, oh… I, well… I think I'm being self-indulgent. I should just get on with life and "be" happy without questioning all the time.'

'Do you think you are being "self-indulgent"?'

'Sometimes.'

'Do you think you are entitled to be sometimes?'

'Well, no, I s'pose, I came from a family that were public servants and so I feel I am here to serve, not as I say be self-indulgent. I guess I'm still looking for my purpose.'

Sophie let Jenny sit with her thoughts a while.

'Tell me, what made you seek help now?'

'I'm tired of being this way, feeling life will be all right tomorrow – when I'm thin – I want to be happy this minute.'

'What stops you?'

'Me! I really am my worst enemy.'

'And a "friend" would act differently.'

'Yes.'

'So, we need to help you be a better friend to yourself, as I'm sure you are to others?'

'Yes, well, I think I am.'

'Right, well, I hope we can start healing that friendship today.'

'Thank you.'

At that moment, the rest of Jenny's defences toppled down and she sobbed into the proffered tissues but managed to sniff and gulp her way to the end of the rapid, and forever, one-hour appointment.

'But the only way I can regain control is through making myself sick.'

'And you start the bingeing when…?'

'When I'm feeling out of control, too emotional about something.'

97

'To stop feeling those emotions?'

'Yes.'

'So, what is the worst thing that can happen if you did go home now and eat a whole packet of biscuits?'

'I'd get even fatter and hate myself even more.'

'And you'd make yourself sick?'

'Yes. And I don't want to keep doing that. I know it can't go on.'

Jenny strode to the bus stop ironically feeling somehow lighter, and with her new food diary under her arm she had the promise of a healthier way of control.

27
Claire

As Claire awoke, she had to peel crusts from her infected eyelids and the daylight seared into her "scritchy" eyes. All a bad metaphor for her current state. She thought supposedly having post-natal depression was more than enough to cope with. The familiar cool hospital linen and blue waffle blanket planted her firmly in her predicament. Then she heard a scream – it was hers.

'Claire. It's okay. Do you know where you are?'

'Yes.'

'And why you're here?'

'I killed my baby.'

Claire turned her face to the wall and willed her whole body to join her eyes in their sealing. Tony had sowed the idea, but she knew she had carried out the act, had made her body clamp down on her baby's head, squashing his brain in her bones. Tony was the devil's accomplice and so, whenever he dared to visit, she thrashed out at him, spitting like a cat. That's what she was now, an animal, yes, a hamster who had eaten her own offspring, but Tony had served her precious baby up and told her to destroy him. She sniffed the hospital covers, the newborn smell, unconjurable now. The scent had disappeared into the hell's ether three weeks ago; snatched from her with his tiny bones and a hospital label hastily attached to his floppy wrist. In case he should be confused with another half-eaten newborn. Not just Tony's, but other voices joined his now to taunt her:

'Don't eat that!

'You need to shrivel and be tiny bones too.'

'Oliver is sitting waiting in your belly; he will never be digested but churn inside until you die and release him.'

Claire had been moved to a side room opposite the nurses' station and was on suicide watch. Days passed numbingly. The drug round, the only marker of time. She became adept at pretending to swallow her tablets and with her mouth open to display they'd gone, could store them in a wisdom tooth extraction hole to dispense with her own way – down the toilet, biding her time.

Back in fourth year, she had unusually bunked off school away from teenage life choices of geography or history – what did it matter – and had strolled along the coastline; her school dinner money spent on greasy Chinese spring rolls and the penny arcade, testing her luck. Well, she wasn't ever lucky. But she could still be sneaky and choose her moment. When the new student nurse was checking on her supposed sleeping body, and the rest of the staff were busy or on a meal break, she seized her moment.

The old Golf Monthly magazine from the dayroom came in very handy. Scrunched up in her armpit, with her arm pressed to her body, it pressed on the brachial artery, closing it off, just long enough to stop her pulse, causing the nurse to panic and presume her dead.

'Help!'

As the nurse ran in scared circles, Claire also ran, but purposefully for the unlocked door and out into the main Kings Park Hospital. Being dressed in her own clothes that morning was seen as "progress" and indeed it was. She flew unnoticed out of the main door and into the world beyond, hurtling into a woman about her age standing lost at the bus stop.

'Hey!'

28
Jenny

'Oh! Sorry, I was miles away!' A young woman about her age looked up at her, mumbled something that could have been an insult or apology; Jenny ever diplomatic went for the latter and helped her to her feet.

'Are you okay?'

'Yes!'

'Are you sure?'

And the woman ran off as if she had a different bus to catch than Jenny's, which pulled up at that moment. That teasing thought of recognition pulled away from her, much like the sea dragging sand away. On the twenty-minute journey, Jenny was able to sit back against the tattered upholstered tartan seat and just "be" for the first time in a very long time. Her inconsequential thoughts wandered from bus furnishings to whether she could remove the stray hair from the person's shoulder in front without them knowing. All ebbing and flowing without the anxiety of food obsessions. Surely it couldn't be that easy.

Her usual corner shop haunt was closed; the owners had gone to Tenerife for a bit of winter sun, so Jenny picked up a supermarket basket and took her time amidst the aisles, choosing what she actually fancied for tea, rather than the low-calorie meal she had always felt she deserved. Not the best cook – ready meals were her saviour and a mac cheese and bag of salad felt, well, almost balanced so she put in a single large cookie. Maybe this was the way to go, small temptations, small steps.

Her dear mum called at the usual time of 7 p.m. and Jenny found herself telling her about her long-kept, dark secret and was not surprised that her mum half realised.

'You obviously didn't want me to know but I could never understand "why" though, love?'

'Nor do I, Mum. Maybe because I don't "measure up".'

'What!'

'I just always seem to want to be like someone else – or actually be someone else.'

'But, why, when you are amazing as you?'

'But you have to say that!'

'Yes, but it's true and you have to find a way to believe that.'

She felt bad leaving her mum clearly crying but covering it with false brightness and had to write the exchange in her food diary, as the resultant emotions made her want to grab her coat and head to the offie for chocolate. Yes, upsetting others was a trigger. She was so rubbish at confrontations. She'd thought leaving the emotional tumult of psychiatry behind her would help her find an even keel, but any ripple of emotion could rock her sensitivities and have her reaching for "forbidden foods". Writing all this down took time – and in this time the emotions ebbed away and thus the urges. This was progress.

'How was this week?'

'Okay. The diary helped.'

'Tell me an example.'

'Well. As I said, I've only been in post for two months, so I'm feeling my way still, and there are lots of times when I doubt myself...'

'Go on.'

'Well, like on Friday: I had an appointment with a really bullish family who is sending their mother with dementia into care. I don't think they've made the right decision about the home; they've just gone for the first available slot. So, I needed to discuss it with them, and on my way I pulled up at a garage to get a packet of biscuits, chocolate, or anything, and had left my food diary on the passenger seat. I saw it, made myself fill it in, and by the time I'd done that I'd identified how I was feeling.'

'Which was?'

'Out of my depth, irritated with the couple, not able to help, but I calmed down and the urge to binge had almost gone.'

'That's great, Jenny, well done. And the meeting?'

'It was a bit tricky, but I felt better as I actually didn't "swallow" what I wanted to say but said it quite evenly I thought. And it was okay. They agreed to rethink.'

'Great! What about the feelings... and eating then?'

'Well, I did suddenly feel, "Woah, what have I done!" And wanted to binge, I won't lie.'

'And did you?'

'Well, the garage had closed by then!'

29
Claire

Bedraggled and exhausted from the endless traipsing, wearing only her pregnancy jeans and an old hoodie with no money or means to get any, the rain and a hitched ride led her back to her parents. She was going to get money from them for a private detective to find the Mastermind, to bring them down, alongside Tony.

Claire's mum was getting the weekly shop in from the car when she saw Claire approach, dropped the bags and ran to her.

'Love, you're freezing, what the—'

'You've got to help me, Mum.'

Her mum led her into the front room, shouting to Jeff to 'come quick and get the fire on'.

'Claire! Why aren't you at the hospital?'

'Jeff, not now.'

'Mum, you've got to help. We've got to find them urgently before they take anymore.'

'Who, love?'

'They call themselves "The Fairies"; they're evil, not storybook ones, real ones that steal babies and replace them with changelings. Only I wouldn't accept the changeling, but they still took Oliver.'

'Oh, god, here we go again!'

'Jeff! Go and get some tea, would you! Oh, Claire, you poor love, you're safe now. Nobody took Oliver, it's so terribly sad but—'

'Mum, you're not listening! You've got all these changelings too; they are evil. You need to swap them back and we've got to get a private detective. I've got money. We can trace Oliver. Tony's in on it; you've got to help me.'

'Of course I'll help you, Claire... always. Just have some tea and get warm and we'll sort all this.'

Days of unceasing fairy rantings ensued. Her parents had arranged for Ella and their other two foster children to have emergency respite care elsewhere, as they felt Claire could have been a danger to them, such was her obsession with the "changeling" thing. Even with them gone, Claire's state of mind wasn't improving; they had come to the end of their tethers, and admitting defeat, reluctantly led, or rather forced, Claire back to the hospital, whose staff had daily been trying to encourage such a return.

A second section under the Mental Health Act was implemented on her arrival and ECT was broached with her as the best course of action to lift her "post-natal psychosis". Of course, Claire wouldn't agree to that. A huddle of bobbled jumpers, beards and some fresh-faced innocents gathered around her bed with mumblings of "hallucinations, confusion, delusions".

She was definitely NOT deluded. They were if they thought she wasn't going to take the other murderers down with her.

'Claire, we've spoken about this before. I'm very sorry but your baby boy, Oliver, died. He was stillborn; it was nobody's fault. You are ill and we need to get you better so you can go home and join your family.'

'I have information. You've got to let me out; he'll do it again.'

'Who is giving you this information, Claire?'

'Huh, I'm not telling you. You're probably in on it too. You need the babies for your experiments, and now that you're running out of babies, you're using me.'

'Do you mean the ECT, Claire?'

'Yes.'

'Remember, you've had it before?'

'Yes, you stole my brain.'

'You were depressed previously and it helped, and we think it will help you feel better once more.'

Tony and her mum, after guilty discussions, signed the consent and mistakenly tried to explain this to Claire, who had to be held down as she went to attack them both.

'Devil's spawn! I hate you.'

'I'm so sorry, love, we just want the best for you.'

Her mum stood, hands held out to Claire, sobbing silently – years of tears of helplessness where her daughter was concerned. Tony could only stand bewildered by this seeming stranger capable of such a complete unpacking of herself and was terrified for both of them and the future.

'You're in on it. You acted all innocent, but YOU killed Oliver and now you're planning on killing me to cover it all up.'

The nurses intervened and Claire once again was sedated and wheeled to the aptly named rainbow suite, where, once asleep, electric currents were sent through electrodes attached at special "vantage points" across her skull. Claire had a series of controlled seizures and woke ten minutes later, groggy with a slight headache, but unaware of the seismic shift beginning to change her thought processes from baby killer to bereaved mum.

30
Tony

Tony had no one to turn to. His parents were grieving for the grandson they had never seen. They could offer little support from afar and as they had never met Claire, couldn't offer advice as to whether this new Claire was here to stay or just a temporary interloper, and were clueless as to how he should progress his family life.

Clive, like his few other colleague buddies, steered him off any difficult topics that were out of their realm of experience, or indeed interest. They had all sent cards and said the right things on Oliver's death, but they thought Tony, when he wasn't too busy with this new family stuff, should be looking forward now; getting back to talking about football results and the odds on whether Mike Tyson was going to knock out Michael Spinks or not. Certainly not discussing ECT; that was the stuff of Gothic novels surely and, so, not for them.

Tony rang his granny who had retired to be near her best friend in Wymondham in Norfolk, which Tony always teased her about.

'You've found the right retirement place then, Gran. I gather it's pronounced Wind-em!'

'Yes, Glynis and I can trump together like true old ladies here!'

Granny T. was originally from Llandudno and said of her migration:

'You can take me out of Wales, but you can't take the Welsh out of me.'

It made Tony remember that as a little boy, she used to say she had the River Conwy running through her veins. One summer when he had gone to stay, she'd been peeling potatoes for the obligatory Sunday roast and had cut her finger. Tony had been so shocked that she had bled red just like him and was surprised she wasn't as disappointed. This gullibility stayed with him and made him question, more than most, what was true and right.

'How are you, Gran?'

'I'm fine, Tony. Oh, what a lovely surprise. To what do I owe the honour?'

'Sorry, Gran. I've been meaning to ring, but things still aren't good.'

'It'll take time, lad.'

'It's not just losing Oliver, Gran, it's Claire.'

And Tony had gone on to seek his Gran's advice about whether he should sign the consent for her ECT or not.

'I've got to go there this afternoon, with both Janet and Jeff; we're meeting with her consultant and I still don't know what I'm going to do.'

'Done the pros and cons list, like I always tell you?'

'Yes, but this is even bigger than Australia or not.'

'Is she going to get better without it?'

'That's just the point. She had it before and it worked.'

'So, what's different this time?'

'The fact that she said she'd never have it again and she just wants to go home.'

'But you say she's still not right?'

'Far from it, I trust the doctors but...'

'But...'

'I know she will hate me even more than she does now if that's possible.'

'You have to do it for her recovery, love, and then later see what your future together brings.'

'Yes, you're right, Gran.'

'Oh, I'm sorry that you're going through this – just weather the storm, love, weather the storm. Life will come good at some point.'

The torrential rain smearing his windscreen and the snarled traffic approaching the crossroads couldn't have been more symbolic for Tony. He knew that this was probably it for his marriage as he finally took the left turning for the hospital entrance.

31
Jenny

It was Jenny's last meeting with Sophie, and she would miss her. Not that she knew anything about her really and that was so strange, for Jenny was a "connector", someone who knew at the outset others' star signs, if they liked Bowie or Def Leppard, and whether they were a dog or cat person. She had always known that need for prized human contact, but Sophie had enabled her to know, question and also accept a lot of other aspects of herself, formerly un-fathomed.

One was her need for approbation and how easily she could have her opinions changed from "of course, via Coventry is quicker" to "avoid Coventry at all costs" by an assertive other, and how she felt nobody would ever truly love her apart from her mum.

'So, you have all the tools now, Jenny.'

'Yes, thanks to you!'

'Take some credit for once, Jenny! This has been all your hard work. When you first came here you were judging your self-worth solely in terms of your weight and now...'

'Yes, I know. I am actually feeling better about "me".'

'And those "edges" of you?'

'Not quite as fuzzy, I think.'

'And able to face those triggers?'

'Yes, even the biscuit aisle after a bad day!'

'Good to hear!'

'Remember, whenever those feelings get too strong, acknowledge them, name them, don't eat to blot them out, keep your food diary going and the regular "treats", and come back to me if you need to. I have a feeling you won't.'

She rang her mum that night as usual and heard the enlarging Leylandii dilemmas with her neighbours. And updated her re work – her caseload, confidence and enjoyment growing in equal measures – saying she was filled with a sense of being in the right person at last; life was going to be okay.

At work, she was becoming fond of so many of her batty old clients, in a professional, "boundaried" way, of course! Especially Delilah, who had been a cleaner to royalty and she felt sure they'd have to institute a gagging order to stem her stories. But then again, Jenny had always enjoyed struggling with what was a delusion and what was reality and felt sometimes that actual belief was all-important. She reminded Jenny of Ashanti, a patient at The Maudsley with hypomania, who was convinced she was the new messiah. Jenny felt she had no right to judge and, at a staff meeting, had argued that it was indeed time for another such visit, and that definitely a female might lead with a more useful approach than walking on water. Possibly Ashanti could well lead the homeless to shelter at Longleat Safari Park, as she proclaimed!

Yes, Jenny was enjoying making a difference in the lives of her elderly clients by fighting for the right placements with new-found conviction. Janice, her supervisor, had asked her if she would consider mentoring a social work student and was clearly anticipating her staying. So, Jenny bought herself a new mattress (a double) to celebrate. Life was indeed on the up!

THE SIXTH ERA

1989

The year the Berlin Wall came down.

32
Claire

Living back at home at the age of twenty-seven wasn't in Claire's plans, and neither in her parents', who were still finding it difficult to negotiate Claire's volatile emotions. And Claire was finding the easy happiness of the rest of their "new family" (with the return of the little ones) nauseating to accept. Foster children were meant to be the difficult ones, so why was it she who was the petulant child in the house? Claire knew her mother watched her every move, alert for any warning signs and triggers, and she regularly overheard her parents checking in about her:

'Jan? Well, did you see her arms?'

'No, she pulled the towel right round her.'

'Can't she see what she's doing, not only to herself but to <u>all</u> the littluns… and us!'

'That's just it, she never did understand other people's views; you've got to finally realise, love, she's…'

'She's what?'

'Oh… different, that's all, and she only has us now.'

'Well, I'm desperate for a beer; how long do we have to keep this up?'

'Go out with Terry then; we can't have any here, we just have to be patient.'

'How many more bloody times! She's got to get a grip herself!'

Luckily for everyone, Claire decided herself that it was indeed time to get that "grip" on herself. She had always managed to stay in work, had been an excellent physio, and, hallelujah, they had a maternity cover vacancy at a GP surgery only an hour's journey from her folks. So, after a brief interview, adroitly circumnavigating her psychiatric history, she started the following week.

Then, after the contracted four months, a relieved mutual farewell brought Claire to her <u>new</u> job and first "own home"': a long-vacant upstairs maisonette in a quiet side street in Westbridge. She could see a beech tree from her sitting room window which obscured the concrete flats opposite, thus creating a more tranquil scene than actually existed. She felt safe, suspended in the air, above a very quiet elderly couple, who didn't use the shared garden space except when they went out, hand in hand, to put birdseed out. And she only saw them on bin days to wave at, so all in all it was a good bolt hole for now – as Claire didn't know what "next" entailed. Tony had uncharacteristically moved very quickly with the separation, selling the house, dividing up the "spoils" and seemingly that era was over. She had only Oliver's plaster hands by her bed to remind her she had had a family of her own, once upon a time. The rest of her life from before was dead to her now, she knew that much. In a fit of, was it, pique, hurt or cruelty, Claire had said she didn't want anything else from their shared belongings either; they didn't "mean" anything to her now.

Returning to her sparse flat every weekday, at least she was too exhausted from seeing patients to care about the "emptiness". However, weekends told a different story and now winter was ending, she had no excuse other than to hunker down with a book, gazing at it unseeingly, she felt she had to "do". After white-washing her flat to bring in light, she set her sights on the garden. It too was lightless, and Claire felt compelled to obliterate "dim" from her life. She had always felt dim in comparison to her fellow students, and the few friends she'd had, who had all been Teflon coated – repelling all bad thoughts, all bad experiences, and were exuding of charm and golden glow. She looked up "dim" once more: unseen, lustreless, seen indistinctly; the synonyms weren't any more favourable: rayless, caliginous, murky, overcast.

She knocked on her neighbour's door and asked if they minded if she tackled the overgrown garden. They invited her in and therein started a regular visit of Saturday afternoon tea, and a tamed garden offering a mix of dappled shadow and basking sunlight. *Out damned "dim"*.

THE SEVENTH ERA

1990

The year the first 'in car sat nav' was launched.

33
Jenny

Jenny didn't want a long-distance relationship, she wanted it on her doorstep or preferably on her still unexercised mattress. So, she compiled a favourable but not outlandish description of herself and sent it to the local paper's singles column.

Always one for "signs", the first reply she opened had a witty reply and, although he sported a rather debonair image for her usual taste, as he lived ten minutes away, Jenny decided he was the one. At a safe crowded wine bar for a first date, he peered over a huge bunch of non-garage flowers, and Mills-and-Boon-like Jenny tumbled into his flirting blue eyes and didn't regret her hunch.

'What a relief you don't look like a serial killer.'

'And you're not a cougar like my last date. Phew, good start, eh!'

'How do you know? I could be sixty-six and good at make-up.'

'No, I like "natural" and you look natural, with gorgeous blue eyes.'

'You too, I mean the eyes. Oh, god, I'm awful at this first-date stuff! Can we restart? Hello, I'm Jenny...'

Suddenly her life was transformed: dinner at his, dinner at hers, dinner out and back to his again, the pounds were piling on, but she was happy. At last, she knew what a relationship felt like, this all-consuming absorption with each other, and if he didn't like dogs, well, this was grown-up stuff and not childhood dreams, so some compromises were inevitable.

Tom gave her a gym membership for her birthday and suggested they work out together. Jenny had never worked out in her life; only swimming sedately with her head up, so as not to have to tackle the resultant wild hair (as she'd never wear a swimming hat; that looked either far too old / Costa del Sol retiree or furthest from her nature, that is, far too competitive). However, Tom seemed serious about this joint venture, so she tried to be. Physical Education lessons at school held for Jenny those bad memories which many shared, of hiding in the fog at cross country but still being spotted, and having to do extra loops as penance and returning hours later, red-faced, sweaty and, frankly, dying. The shiny gym equipment and her new Lycra felt aeons away from Mrs Tunstall's whistle, but Jenny soon realised it created the exact same inadequate feelings, sweat and beetroot complexion and she felt she was a disappointment to her athletic partner.

'Come on, Jen, put some more effort in, you'll soon see the benefits!'

She never did see or feel those benefits.

34
Claire

Although her once whitewashed flat now had mildew and cobwebs worthy of "performance art", the garden was Claire's haven, providing a balm to alleviate her heightened emotions.

Handling the soil, she'd read, could be mood-lifting and it wasn't just the microbes that were helping her, it was the actual results of her endeavours – she'd splashed out on a cherry tree and that first blossom had been particularly significant. To "blossom": to develop good, attractive qualities... well, she could but hope.

This was at last a resting place for Oliver's ashes. Of course, she had taken ownership of those, telling Tony he probably wasn't the father anyway. And she had read that mothers around the world feel like their children are still a part of them long after they've given birth.

Apparently, during pregnancy, cells from the foetus cross the placenta and enter the mother's body, where they can become part of her tissues, so Claire felt that in her madness she was somehow lucid and that part of Oliver did indeed live on inside her.

Her new friends, Beryl and Eric, stood and said a prayer as she scooped the ashes mixed with top manure around the tree's roots, and patted Oliver gently down to sleep.

She had placed an old garden bench under the tree and the couple had taken to enjoying the sun on their faces and chatting to her as she toiled – pruning roses, taming honeysuckle, savouring every thorn and scratch as if she was Jesus himself. Slowly, the couple began to trust their strange young neighbour with long-held secrets of their lives.

'She's not interested in our dusty memories, Beryl.'

But Claire surprised herself by nurturing this frail duo and wanting to salve their life wounds; she had found people to care for and who needed her at just the right time.

'Go on, Beryl, I really do love hearing how it was.'

'Well, do you know, we had a cigarette machine put in our little post office? I didn't want it, especially as Eric smoked then and I thought it would make him smoke more.'

'And did it?'

'Well, no, but it wasn't long before all the local lads tried to have one over on us and say they'd put money in and hadn't got their cigarettes, remember, Eric?'

'Yes, love.'

'I put one over my knee once; he must have only been thirteen. His mother came up later and gave me what for, and I gave her what for back, then ten minutes later, she came back and apologised. She thanked us for stopping him smoking as her husband had died of, what was it, love?'

'Asbestosis.'

'That's it; more trouble than it was worth that machine.'

'Remember those early days when we sorted the mail in the back shed, Eric.'

'No, we didn't do that, although lots did.'

'Yes, we did!'

'Oh, okay, we did.'

'Did we show you our own special ink stamp? We were allowed to keep that.'

'You showed her, Beryl, several times.'

And so it went on.

Saturdays were a time for "posh afternoon tea", best china and sinking into their old sofa, dodging certain springs and the ever-present cat hair. Claire wasn't a baker so bought shop scones when it was her turn, but Beryl was a star baker and magicked cloud sponges worthy of *Bake Off*. That was until one Saturday when Eric fixed his eyes imploringly on Claire when she took an expectant large bite of Victoria sponge. The consistency was there but the sugar wasn't. Not a natural "empath", it took Claire quite a few bad bakes to realise something larger and more vital than a cake ingredient was amiss. Eric was grateful for this and it wasn't until Beryl went walkabout one day, that he confided in Claire about his wife's failing memory and asked her for help in finding her.

Beryl was found, as she then often was, on the coast road heading for the ice cream parlour, and with Eric's knees playing him up, Claire was often the one to coax her back after a "ninety-nine". Claire had never had grandparents, and as she had abandoned her own parents, siting their abandonment of her, Beryl and Eric were the perfect private pair, demanding only appreciation of cake and occasional "retrievals". And she had a purpose.

35
Jenny

Life, Jenny believed, had to be meted out fairly; although Jenny realised hers <u>was</u> fairly blessed and the "meting out" didn't always work out – there were no wars in suburban Kent and she wasn't sleeping rough. Apart from the bulimia glitch and being a bit lost career-wise for a while, she now had everything she dared to wish for. Jenny was convincing herself that she was truly happy, and something surely had to go wrong. Of course, it already was, but it took Jenny longer than her mum and friends to realise what that "something" was.

Tom had secretly bought the show home in semi-rural Meopham, complete with blackout curtains and all the white goods. It was the one that they had visited on a supposed "nosy", and then he asked Jenny to move in with him. Although it was miles from friends, family and work, Jenny couldn't resist the romance of it all and of being so "wanted" – and, anyway, who wouldn't want to live in a house with a waste disposal sink! The bloom of freshly painted magnolia soon wilted with such a long work commute and it was so exhausting keeping the house cleaned to Tom's high standards. He worked so hard, as he often told her "for their future" that it felt churlish of her not to just knuckle down and be grateful for all she had wished for: her prince and their castle.

THE EIGHTH ERA

1991

The year the USSR was officially dissolved and the World Wide Web came to life.

36
Claire

For someone who wasn't terribly good at "relationships", Claire's fondness and care for Beryl and Eric surprised her, and she became very protective towards them both. If the bin men left their emptied bin too far up the road, she of course brought it back but felt the need to stalk the bin lorry to rebuke them.

The housework seemed to be too much for them and after a few cups of tea with ingrained stains unveiled by sipping, Claire managed to, as unobtrusively as possible, wield a cleaning cloth and toilet brush. Although Eric clearly realised Claire had seamlessly inserted their shop of ready meals into hers, he was too proud and too grateful to comment, for fear the kindness stopped.

Little did he know that Claire liked having a trolley semaphoring loved ones, rather than a lonely basket to fill. Both Eric's knees and his lungs were getting worse and no amount of physio from Claire could get him mobile enough, which left Beryl to wander too far and too often. Unable to take matters into his own hands, Claire seized those same matters and soon had an appointment arranged with a social worker who was to come out and assess Beryl and Eric's capabilities for remaining in their own home. Claire had realised some time ago that they couldn't remain there, but unfortunately, Eric was a little, or a lot, behind this particular curve of realisation. However, he trusted Claire as a friend and respected her professional integrity enough to allow this young social worker into his home, his fortress of fifty years.

Claire had bought a lemon drizzle cake and laid the tray with the cutwork tray cloth Beryl had embroidered years ago as part of her trousseau. The doorbell chimed with a half-hearted, low-battery, lowkey welcome and Claire went to answer it. As she opened the door, she was making a mental note to replace the battery – it wasn't used much and, as she had her own key, she hadn't noticed it. And a woman of about her own age stood with bright blue dangly earrings swinging beneath a halo of blonde frizz and either side of a wide, warm smile who arrested such thoughts. Her gut turned, she knew her from somewhere, deep in the past, but where?

'Hello, my name is Jenny Wells, social worker, is this the right house for Mr and Mrs Todd?'

Jenny... Jenny. Of course. She looked older naturally, but there was no mistaking that hair, that smile, and that "comfortable" figure; she looked as if she still gave good hugs.

'Hi, yes, you have, come in. They're expecting you. I'm their neighbour and friend, Claire.'

'Pleased to meet you, Claire.'

Jenny was undoubtedly good at her job. She was glad for her that she'd left psychiatry; she had seemed too "naïve" somehow for that job, wanting to "fix" everyone, but dementia care was a world of innocence and gentle action that she could see suited Jenny. She had won Eric and Beryl's trust and after a politely nibbled slice of shop-bought lemon drizzle (Claire noted she was clearly still on the diet), all were chatting easily about the beautiful garden outside, Eric's job as a postman, Beryl's as a postmistress and their early starts for umpteen years, mostly just the two of them. Claire was worried that Jenny wasn't picking up on Beryl's frailty of mind as Eric was so adept at covering for her and leading her to safe topics where she could shine, but Jenny, having gained their trust, then gently quizzed Beryl to glean her orientation to time, place and circumstance.

'This a lovely home you have here but I'm a sucker for a garden. I won't make you get up, Eric, so, Beryl, could you show me your "estate" please!

Genius. Claire stayed inside with Eric and by the time Jenny returned clutching garden spoils of green strawberries and indiscriminate weeds, Beryl clearly had begun to demonstrate her need to be cared for "professionally". Jenny said all that garden appreciation had made her thirsty and asked Beryl to get her a drink of water, which of course took a while and then Beryl returned empty-handed. Eric's face crumpled as a child's does knowing that the summer holidays were ending.

Claire felt proud she had brought this kind social worker to guide her precious friends through this most difficult juncture in their lives. She enabled Eric to trust in Jenny's solutions for a safe future for both of them and very soon, although not soon enough for Beryl's wanderings and too soon still for Eric, they were all visiting homes together.

37
Jenny

Every elderly client lodged a myriad of worries but also a special place in Jenny's heart. However, now she had Tom at home balancing her life, he made her switch off, paint their nest and enjoyably turn the earth and see what she hoped was their forever home and garden take shape.

She had been surprised to realise Claire was the same Claire (although a slimmer structure around those doleful eyes) whom she had tried to dissuade from having ECT all those years ago – and was delighted she had been "right"; she had obviously not been "mad" but simply sad. And it could so well have been her in Claire's shoes, or rather ECT electrodes, as well she now knew. Everyone just needed the tools to be resilient; some had them, others had them given, whereas others, like Jenny herself, needed to save and shop around for them!

Claire had accompanied this lovely couple on each visit and clearly had become their "surrogate daughter or granddaughter". By the second visit to homes, Jenny had plucked up the courage to say she recognised Claire, who she was sure had worked out the connection too. She'd waited until Eric and Beryl were joining a seated exercise class in the dayroom to get a "feel" of the place, before suggesting they grab a coffee in the staff room and chat, ostensibly about the home's suitability, although the overly-chivvying, pearl-strung manager had already got Eric's back up, so it wasn't a likely success:

'I think this is a no – you?'

'Definitely!'

The way Eric harrumphed and straightened his tie when she told him they had "all sorts" there from a judge to tradespeople! He'd got her measure and it was never going to happen.'

'Still, it's great to get a chance to talk... Do you remember me?'

'Of course. It was hardly a forgettable part of my life however hard I've tried."

'Sorry, I—'

'Don't be. You were the kindest person there.'

'Oh, dear, was I? Thank you. Well, how's life treated you since?'

Jenny suddenly felt the need to prattle, which was always her downfall when she was a psychiatric nurse. She had never done the meaningful silence well, always interrupting with a positive statement. Jenny grabbed a Jaffa Cake from an assortment left for guests.

'You'll see I'm still on a diet, must be several hundred since then!'

Claire smiled, reading this woman's nervousness.

'Life's been okay. I qualified as a physio after all and just been plodding on really – all that behind me.'

Jenny could feel the tension leaving her; she hadn't realised how much she had wondered about Claire until that moment.

Now, unabashed, she questioned Claire about life now.

'And are you working now?'

'Yeah, I'm working still as a physio, in a GP practice now; quite cushy.'

'Oh, great!'

'And, you, it seems you've found your niche too?'

'I genuinely love my job now. When we met I was finding all that overwhelming; me being responsible for someone's mental health was a joke!'

'Married?'

'God, no! Although I am living with someone, we've got a little semi in a quiet close in sleepy Meopham.'

'Sounds riveting!'

Jenny laughed long and loudly and Claire felt as if the sun had come out from behind a cloud and was shining down on just her.

'And you?'

'What? Am I cojoined in marital somnolence? No, I never felt the need. Happily single, no kids either.'

'You always did have a way with words!'

'I actually live about five minutes drive from you, in the buzzing metropolis of Shotswood!'

'No way! You'll have to come round for supper.'

'I'd like that. Saves me cooking!'

Cedar Trees had been the third home they visited and, much like one of those TV property search programmes, Jenny was getting to know her clients' tastes and needs as each visit ensued. "Cedars" was the smallest and didn't have the glossy magazines in the reception, or the most salubrious location and the paintwork definitely needed attention, but it was "right" for Beryl and would be right for Eric too. They had volunteer drivers who collected the more immobile relatives daily to visit their loved ones; volunteers mostly who'd had relatives at the home and knew how much such contact mattered. Beryl and Eric had not been apart for fifty years (except for two nights in hospital when Beryl had their only son). This swung it for Eric and he finally accepted that he could no longer keep his beloved Beryl safe and this home could, and they promised she could have ice cream whenever she asked for it.

On the second visit to Cedars, Eric and Beryl joined the activity co-ordinator leading a pottery class and, again, Jenny and Claire disappeared for a cuppa and catch up. Jenny enjoyed the tales of Beryl's ice cream missions told with Claire's acerbic wit. Apparently (or so Claire said), the coastal ice cream parlour had added a "Beryl" cone to their offerings as Beryl enjoyed the ninety-nine with raspberry sauce, hundreds and thousands, complete with treble flake, and was adept at helping herself behind the counter if she felt they were a bit short on any particular topping! Eric settled up with the parlour weekly when Claire took them all out for a seaside fish and chip supper and a "Beryl" to finish!

After Beryl moved in, Jenny kept in touch with Eric and oversaw Beryl's care for a while, so she often bumped into Claire and enjoyed a good sing-along with Geoff in the dayroom, both catching each other's mirthful eye when they were the only ones singing. Geoff still had a lot to learn about song choice and *Amazing Grace* wasn't the catchiest to get everyone to join in! Jenny told Tom about this new acquaintance. She'd been thinking of suggesting to him that Claire come round, as a new neutral and thus "approved" friend, because her other mates grated on him.

'I was thinking about inviting my friend, Claire, to supper. I think you'd like her.'

'Why?'

'Well, she's funny and—'

'Do we need amusing?'

'It's just we haven't had anyone round since we moved in together and Claire is the only girlfriend I have locally. I do think you'd like her.'

'Anyone who was crazy once is bound to still have it in them. I'd say steer clear. Anyway, we're busy.'

So saying, he gave Jenny "that look" and nuzzled her neck, and all conversation was forgotten again.

This started Jenny's secret visits to Claire which became more and more of an escape.

38
Claire

Claire found she looked increasingly forward to Jenny visiting on her way home from work and often cancelled her last patient, so that she was there in plenty of time to have the kettle on, as Jenny was always in a rush. In part, she was jealous of the man in Jenny's life who seemed so attentive and was often texting Jenny to find out her "ETA".

Claire would have found him too demanding, but Jenny was clearly sold on what was to Claire this extreme interdependence. However, her own confidence grew as she knew she had also claimed a place in Jenny's heart and, when Jenny's visits lengthened to a glass of wine (which required "stories" told to Tom re her lateness), she knew she was the winner. In fact, it was easier and easier to get Jenny to stay just that little bit longer and they enjoyed creating the scripts of these stories together.

One night, both were sitting in the garden with the Autumn sun warming their faces. It felt almost like being on holiday, especially after a glass of Sancerre; it was a Friday after all. They had an assortment of cheese and nibbles to soak up the wine, so Jenny became braver and accepted a small top-up, but then panicked as she went to the loo and spotted the thieving clock (which had stolen an extra hour and a half) and her phone flashing, berating her with thirteen missed calls.

Claire always veered toward the more macabre excuses and with great detail:

'Hey, how about one of your elderly clients was being battered to death by a fellow resident... with their ivory walking stick in an argument over whose urine-sodden chair was whose and you had to be interviewed by the police.'

'Ivory walking stick! He'd think I'd morphed into Agatha Christie... Oh, god! Think. Think!'

Jenny ran for the door and plumped for the less prosaic approach: she turned on the car radio as she hurtled home and listened to local traffic reports, finding road closures that she could cite for her delay.

Claire sat bemused, finishing up a second bottle of Sancerre, pondering on Jenny's departure. She didn't feel able to judge what a "normal relationship" was, but she didn't gauge much happiness from Jenny's talk of Tom. In fact, Jenny was unusually tight-lipped about him and she didn't glean much at all. Their friendship seemed to satisfy them both by being lodged in that present moment of "having a laugh", usually at others' expense, with Jenny always absolving her own offerings of "gossip" with a "but bless them!"

39
Jenny

Tom had had a difficult upbringing and Jenny, who needed to believe in a reason for everything, thought they were meant to be together so she could "save him".

He was also under a lot of stress at work and Jenny began treading on eggshells to anticipate the increasing "bad days" at the office and tried to distract him with his favourite meals. However, seemingly never a great cook, she had apparently deteriorated into an inept one who either under or overcooked. It was never Goldilock's porridge and "just right". Many meals ended up in the bin and she was partly relieved as she had been trying to lose weight, to get into the overtly feminine clothes Tom preferred her in.

Sadly, old habits of bulimia took hold again and every tense homecoming was relieved by a biscuit binge and subsequent "bath" where under cover of running water, she would bring it all up again. Jenny knew it was all her fault, as Tom was clearly overstretched and she had no right to be feeling low herself.

'Jen, you know, I'm running myself ragged for one reason only.'

'But I don't need this fancy house or any "things"! I just want us to be as we were at the start, happy.'

Tom's tone could switch rapidly as if he were a proficient actor reading an audiobook. Now he was using one from his sarcastic range:

'Well, I thought we were happy right now, my mistake!'

'Yes, we are, but—'

'But! Oh, here we go. I knew you'd be grating in my ear about wanting kids soon and how I'm not providing.'

'I never... I don't want—'

His look silenced her once again.

'Don't lie to me! If you're not pregnant by me soon you'll get pregnant by one of your leftie colleagues you seem to spend so much time with.'

'Not this again, I—'

The actor added a different tone and also a physicality to his performance:

'Again!'

Jenny sidestepped the bunched fist and tried to stare him out; sometimes it worked and he just crumbled. Whichever crescendo finish, it was always high drama.

'See how you make me behave? It's just that I love you so much, I'd be nothing without you...'

She often worried that he might carry out some of his recent suicide threats and could talk to no one about it – she had seen none of this coming down the road from the seemingly perfect beginnings. Ironically, counselling people by day to be honest about their loved one's state of mind, she could not take her own advice, and Polly-Anna-like tried to find more and more ways to make Tom happy.

THE NINTH ERA

1992

The year that rioting by local youth broke out across cities, including Bristol, and a shipping container filled with 28,000 rubber ducks was lost in the Pacific Ocean. To this day, they are still being found around the world.

40
Janet

Olivia's fourth birthday was two days away and she was to have her first proper party at "Aunty Jan's and Uncle Jeff's". They had offered as they were more geared up to host ten rumbustious little beings than dad Tony, so he gladly accepted. Olivia was with Aunty Jan at the kitchen table decorating paper plates with sticky stars and shapes, when the phone rang.

'Mum.'

'Ahh! What a lovely surprise. Claire!'

'Aunty Jan, look!'

Olivia had finished another plate and was keen to share her efforts.

'Claire, love, give me one moment.'

Jan plonked Olivia in front of the TV, something she rarely did, and shouted to Ella to sit with her whilst she took a phone call.

'Sorry, love, children everywhere as usual here. You have my full attention now. How are you?'

'I'm fine, Mum. I only rang to say that I'm off travelling around Europe again so won't be in touch awhile.'

'Oh, right... How long's awhile, love? We don't hear from you much anyway.'

Claire's tone had grown even more vexed and exasperated in just the few words they'd exchanged, and Janet knew, like a frightened bird in her palm, she would have to create a calm sanctuary to hold her a moment longer, so she added,

'But I know how busy you are. I always fancied the Northern Lights. Do you think you'll get there?'

'Maybe. How's Dad?

'Oh, he's actually playing golf today; he'll be so sorry to have missed you. But I think the walking is helping his chest. And business is steady; he's got a good new apprentice. Nice lad. One of the Emerson boys from up the road, if you remember them?'

Janet noticed she was superstitiously crossing her fingers as if that could bring a long and easy mother-daughter chat.

'No. But that's good. Anyway, I just thought I'd see how you were before I go.'

Janet resignedly uncrosses her fingers, holds in a sigh and catches a rising sob.

'Oh... okay, love... Send us a postcard, eh? We'd... all... like to see where you are.'

'Nobody sends postcards anymore, Mum.'

And with that, she was gone. Janet placed the receiver gently down and squished between Olivia and Ella on the sofa watching *Bananas in Pyjamas* – for quite a while.

41
Claire

Weeks went by with only a brief text message from Jenny saying she was busy and would be in touch soon. Claire, although struggling with feeling so seemingly abandoned, busied herself with an online creative writing course; she had started feeling she needed a hobby and had been encouraged by Jenny who said she had a gift for fiction.

Little did Jenny know Claire's whole life had been walking a fine line between the difficult truth and her fantasy fictional life. She felt she could write a world travelogue with the number of countries she had purported to visit, both on annual leave from work and excuses for absenteeism from family celebrations. Last year had been particularly good: Christmas in fictitious Finland, with new lover, Laurence, a classical musician who'd injured his bowing hand and they'd gone there for rest. Whenever her mother demanded photos, she always trotted out the truth for a change that "she hated having her photo taken". And Claire avoided any inclusion in the out-of-work socialising with this busy travel schedule.

She had also "been"' to all the Scandinavian countries, supposedly visiting spas, Christmas markets and, of course, the Aurora Borealis, just to gloat at her mum. That area appealed partly as she saw herself as the dark-haired one in Abba and Jenny the curvaceous blonde, but also, unlike her real destinations which were hot, she felt she may be able to breathe in the imagined colder clearer air, and that the odd leap from a sauna into an icy plunge pool might clear her clotted head at last.

A book on Scandinavian traditions she'd found in a Sunday bookshop wander proved a rich source of content for her "holidays" and she found plenty of their quirks to pepper such tales (which she scripted in advance) to make them all the more authentic when regaling her colleagues:

'They have mackerel for breakfast. Euughhh! It's to fuel up for the day. I stuck to the croissants. But that coupled with their habit of chewing "snus" – tobacco mixed with salt for a nicotine fix – ensured I stayed away from all possible romantic encounters. Imagine their awful breath as a result of such weird habits!'

Then remembering:

'Anyway, I am still getting over Laurence.'

And:

'Scandinavians have a "no shoes indoors" policy, obviously time to get cosy – well, at home, I just trudge mud in from my garden regularly, so this was a hard one for me. And I was reluctant to have my holey socks on show. Scandinavians must spend a fortune on whacky socks!'

'But there's one habit that we should adopt: everything stops for the Winter Olympics and they cross borders for cheaper alcohol. Yeah, when I was there, I did a quick trip to Copenhagen from Malmo in Sweden just to get some more wine!'

And something else great about them:

'They don't brag. I loved that about them. I hate boasters.'

But it was their habit of leaving baby strollers outside shops that intrigued her the most and the one she didn't include in her tales. Most Scandi societies are thought safe and this, coupled with their belief that leaving babies out in the cold is good for their immune system, means that it is very common to see prams seemingly abandoned, but there is no baby snatching. Claire thought and certainly not for the first time: *how easy it must be...*

42
Jenny

Jenny remembered those long-ago Sunday night feelings when Mondays would herald a spelling test or a worry if her best friend, Lauren, would choose someone else to sit next to on the coach trip to Bosham Ruins. She would give anything to be back there with that young stomach-churning than sitting in her car, steadying her breathing and her nerve. And here she was, aged thirty-two (when life and such anxieties were meant to be under control), outside the quiet, blank-faced house which belied all the angst inside. Tom's car wasn't there, but that didn't mean anything; he often parked elsewhere, then ambushed her when she opened the door, or "surprised" her as he described it. Today was one of those surprises.

As soon as she turned the key and opened the door, she felt his presence. Jenny had never liked zoos, seeing the captive animals pacing, feeling their pain but also sensing the potential danger if they should escape and wreak their frustration on her. Her very own black panther (sometimes aptly known as the ghost of the forest) came out of the shadows and wasn't to be appeased that evening.

'Oh, hello, love. I hoped you'd be back early. I've bought us a lasagne for tea and—'

Knowing as soon as she said it that even Champagne and caviar wouldn't work that night.

'Liar! Where the hell have you been?'

To defend herself was pointless, so she had to choose either the upbeat pacifying approach or the more muted acquiescent one. As if there was ever a choice; whichever one she opted for she would wish later she had gone for the other. For now, she chose the upbeat one.

'I can rustle up something different if you like. You know how good I am at rustling! Or order us a Chinese?'

'You haven't answered my question, bitch! Where have you been?'

'Well, I went from here to the office for supervision then to meet a lovely new family in Langley whose mum—'

'Don't patronise me; tell me the fucking truth for once.'

Jenny was in the usual conversation cul-de-sac; she had no right answers. She moved to the softer furnishings of the sitting room whilst she still could and slumped into the preposterously named cuddle chair, still with her coat on.

'I was at work, Tom, honestly.'

'Honestly! You don't know the meaning of the word. Do you think I'm stupid?'

'No.'

Tom approached her – his body corkscrewed to get in Jenny's face.

'I didn't hear you?'

'No.'

He snapped back and paced.

'I've said you can give up work, but no, you just want to punish me by complaining to all your colleagues and getting sympathy. And whatever else you get there, eh?'

Then he was back in her face with the same old accusations, and they danced the same old choreography of his paranoic falsehoods, Jenny's mollification and the same old resultant finale.

'I don't believe you. Slut. Who is he?'

'There's nobody else – just you, Tom, please.'

Sometimes the please helped, sometimes it just inflamed the situation. This time the coiled spring was not to be appeased and his fist found her stomach, the usual initial landing place. Then there was no boxer dance and resetting of position; it became a one-sided brawl of continued body blows and, this time, knuckles ricocheting to the side of the head, then for the first time, to her face. He caught her nose with his right, ringed hand.

Tom reeled backwards sobbing his: "sorry's", his: "it's because I love you so much", his: "I will always love you's", his: "I can't live without you's", whilst Jenny calmly sat with her mauve paisley scarf turning red as she mopped up the blood, until her legs could take her to the bathroom to assess the damage. She didn't recognise the Jenny in the mirror, not just because of the cut and swollen nose, but because she couldn't meet her own eyes. Although extremely painful, Jenny didn't think her nose was broken. Thus, armed with paracetamol and ice packs, she went to bed early once more, knowing at least that night she wouldn't be disturbed. On such nights Tom usually took himself off to the spare room to sulk until the next time.

Apart from deflecting the few invitations and enquiries from friends that were still bothering with her despite her persistent "no's", Jenny just went to work, then straight home and bore it all for far too long.

43
Claire

When she opened the door to Jenny and her usually beaming face was replaced with an unrecognisable one, Claire knew she should have interfered sooner. Jenny's usually dancing eyes were dead but most striking was the purple arc over one eye, never a make-up shade Jenny would have applied. She, unusually for her, folded Jenny into her arms, then headed to the fridge for the wine and reached for the wine glasses but chose tumblers instead. This was serious. Priorities sorted, she only then clocked Jenny's three bulging cases abandoned in the doorway and brought them in.

She'd never met Tom, had never been allowed into that hallowed prison. But Claire vowed then that she would from now on be Jenny's protector. Especially as, on that same long, sad night, all of Jenny's painful secrets surfaced like rising bile: her rape when she was in Australia and recently her bulimia which had reared its head again, prompted by her chaotic emotions around Tom.

The symmetry wasn't lost on Claire of Jenny being her rock all those years ago in hospital and now they were together again – together against men and together against the world.

Claire knew enough about domestic abuse from training sessions at work, that it wasn't about a "final straw", but she couldn't help asking Jenny: "why, after that particular beating" she managed to leave. She hated herself for being jealous about the answer:

'It was Christie at work who just asked me how I was that day, the way she said "really?" when I said I was okay. She really looked into my eyes as if she knew. Then, when Tom started on me that evening, I just knew it was for the last time. It was as if she was there behind me.'

So, Claire was determined to demonstrate that she was the one and only true friend that was there for her, for all time. After a few months, when Claire had allowed herself to believe that Jenny was staying, that she really was her housemate and she felt Jenny was healing enough, Claire started dropping hints about a girls' night away. So, there followed, not just one, but regular city breaks, spa weekends and anything far removed from a Buddhist retreat as it had to be full-on and hedonistic, and they certainly achieved that.

For their first break, Claire had thought a murder mystery weekend might prove "cathartic" and be an escape, as never were there two women who needed to escape more. They arrived at a very posh hotel in Surrey with manicured Capability Brown grounds and wall-to-wall antiques. They were tempted to check the underbellies of some pieces in their room for authenticity, fearing they were too clumsy for the real thing and needed to know the full cost implication of breakages, but realised neither was an aficionado of the Antiques Roadshow so vowed to just be careful.

Once unpacked and changed into their wedding outfits (it was to be an imagined wedding reception), they met their fellow conspirators and wedding guests at the pre-arranged afternoon tea. They had been sent identities and short biographies of their new selves, two weeks before the gathering. Jenny was Sonia Cohen, a famous art collector and cousin to the groom, and Claire was Zoe Short, a friend of the groom and sister of the wedding caterer. They mingled with fellow wedding guests, heady with the delight of deceitful pretence; even Claire had transformed, by being Zoe, into a raconteur socialite but was ever watchful and intervened if any enemy male approached her Jenny.

Many cucumber sandwiches later, they were joined by a very rowdy group of guests – clearly, the actors had arrived "onstage". They were privy to a row that escalated and then suddenly one of the "guests" keeled over. After snatching a guest's last vol-au-vent, the victim enjoyed a very voluble and dramatic death. The search for the murderer began!

In the hubbub, Claire and Jenny were separated but met up in their room to exchange all the clues they had gathered. Claire learnt more from eavesdropping than Jenny had from tending to the "dead" body, as it all seemed so real at the time! Jenny said she already suspected Zoe of having access to the catering and thus the canapés, which "dead Vanessa" (ex-girlfriend of the groom) had choked upon. Claire explained that they weren't suspects just the actors, but Jenny was fully immersed and took some convincing!

'Do you think you could kill though, as Claire, I mean?'

'I've often wished people dead, but not really. I'm dark but not that dark! You couldn't; you're too forgiving!'

'Oh, I think I could say if I had children and someone hurt my kids.'

Claire was used to letting her guard down with Jenny and only Jenny but realised she had to be careful even with her.

'Well, I think it's the caterer but I'm sure it's not over yet.'

At the three-course evening meal, the main characters played by the actors spent time at each table for each course, dropping clues and answering questions and, lo and behold, during the serving of dessert, someone else keeled over! This actor, clearly keen to get home after a six-hour stint, didn't make such a "meal" of their own demise and a barely audible whimper was heard nearby, so Jenny called: 'Murder!' Both Claire and Jenny had had a couple of glasses of wine by this time and were tempted to keel over too. They restrained themselves and their giggles and retired with more wine to go over the evidence thus far, plus an envelope of further clues which had been slid beneath their bedroom door.

At breakfast, Detective Schmidt, with the help of the assembled guests, ran through the possible murderers and their motives. Claire and Jenny were delighted that they had guessed right. It was Claudette the caterer! Their guess was made on gut instinct and the best alliterative name and not the very complicated denouement, as explained by all the actors gathered. All suspected causes of death of arsenic in the absinthe, antique candelabra wieldings and strangulation by tasselled tiebacks were dismissed. Claudette had simply been suffocated by a pillow when she had gone to bed exhausted after the buffet – which Claire and Jenny felt was a bit of an anti-climax, and if ever called on to be murderers would opt for a more definitive act! They also thought the murder victim had the cushiest job, and if ever they were asked to be part of a cast they would plump for that part, preferably after drinking too much poison.

They left after another hearty breakfast and many congratulations to the cast vowing to go on another such weekend soon. Claire was delighted it had been a success but decided maybe that she would take matters into her own hands and invent identities of her own for their future escapes, as there had been far too much socialising with other guests for her liking.

Jenny was clearly up for more such adventures. A few months later such an opportunity arose. Claire had reduced her work hours and thus needed to occasionally raise some extra cash. She took on private clients in their own homes not wanting her privacy invaded. A drummer in an almost famous band who wanted his repetitive strain injury kept a secret, hired Claire for a series of treatments and casually invited her to his next gig, as it was in a nearby warehouse but told her opportunistically to "come in disguise". Little did he know Claire would take him seriously and the gift he had given! Claire demurred, never intending to go, but as the very Saturday approached and Jenny and she were at a loose end, she suggested they went along as clairvoyants, mingling in the crowd together and telling fortunes.

So, she and Claire "mingled" with the guests, reading palms and gazing off into the distance with ever-practised air, tuning into supposed "vibrations". They hadn't felt bad as they considered, all in all, they had given a great service: predicting health, wealth, happiness and the occasional message from "Bill, or was it Bert? Or possibly Brian?" from beyond to all who would listen.

At the end, Claire couldn't resist reading Jenny's palm and Jenny by this time was a convert; she lapped up that her life line was long and her love line showed someone always in her corner looking out for her.

44
Jenny

It was mostly embarrassment that she had made such a wrong choice, which kept her from telling her mum for some time. However, of course, her lovely mum had already guessed, even before Jenny turned up with a car full of more belongings to store there – and accompanying bloodshot eyes.

She made it easy for her over Jenny's usual gin and tonic, sitting in her dad's armchair, chomping on her usual Edam and crackers and spilling all, alongside her crumbs. No "I told you so's" but her mum clearly was relieved that the relationship was ended. Jenny heard for the first time about her own mum's past beaux and felt they had entered a new realm of the mother-daughter relationship; one of parity on all things emotional.

Jenny felt as an egotistical child, as is true of all children, she'd never wondered about her parents' previous loves and whether her parents' marriage was lucky to be okay enough; it was easier to believe that it was. Jenny's mum had apparently nearly gone to join the Hong Kong police prompted by a broken heart from the "love of her life", only to meet Jenny's dad on the rebound and had been persuaded to stay and "settled" for marriage with him, instead of life's adventure. The relationship which was originally based on a shared understanding of police life, friendship and then a love of their only child, had grown into something deeper. Jenny's mum, although wondering about that different path, had never regretted plumping for the more predictable option.

Thus, her own advice, forced out by her daughter, was dual: Jenny was urged to seize all the wonderful opportunities life had to offer, but in the seizing, not to overlook the quiet more dependable treasures beneath her nose. After several nights sitting in the same chair of confessions and absolutions, wolfing her mum's restorative shepherd's pies, Jenny was refuelled with hope again for the future.

45
Claire

After yet another pathetic call from Tom pleading for Jenny's return, Claire determined to cheer Jenny up – although she was astounded by how cheered she seemingly was.

'You're a bloody space hopper the way you bounce back.'

'Are you commenting on my size again? You scraggy bag of bones!'

The two friends had soon fallen into the easy banter of equable housemates, berating each other only when the milk or more usually the wine, ran out. Claire said to Jenny that she was grateful for the rent Jenny was paying, but secretly she hugged to herself the far more valuable reward of unexpected warm, dependable companionship.

Claire was confident this burgeoning friendship was now "established" so felt ready to plan a proper holiday – a mystery week-long break – the most "out there" of the trips thus far. This new social life was the stuff of Claire's dreams and she cherished being able to keep Jenny safe.

Emboldened by their "script" development sessions from the "Tom era" and their psychic outings, Claire handed Jenny her new escapist identity and they headed off to Bournemouth to sit on the front, with seagulls, eating their chips.

According to plan, they revelled in astounding the whole beachfront when they left their walking sticks, stripped off their crimplene slacks and headscarves and emerged thirty years younger running giggling helplessly into the sea. Crimplene is a difficult fit on wet salty legs so even more heads turned as they made their way back to the bed and breakfast trouser-less, with grey wigs back atop bespectacled but beaming faces. Their host, clearly devoid of humour, suspiciously watched their every move in and out of their shared room. At breakfast, when Claire told him they were lesbian performance artists rehearsing for a new art installation, he clearly couldn't get out of the dining room quick enough to report back to his wife. Jenny leant against the kitchen door eavesdropping: him explaining the reason for their "weirdness", and this resulted in the first of many wet knickers long before her pelvic floor was the problem. Jenny being Jenny always felt the need to leave huge tips to assuage her guilt at kidding these innocent people and the cheap breaks were never so cheap for her.

Each day, the two "oldies" bedecked in spare olive and beige crimplene worked through a veritable variety show of antics. These included: loud farts in Westover Gallery on a chaperoned tour which enabled prolonged contact with a group and repeated wind opportunities and, later, leaving false teeth (a gleeful sweetshop discovery) with their tip, to a bemused maître d' in an upmarket restaurant, where they'd asked for their steak to be cut into small pieces because of said teeth!

Jenny told Claire she felt happier, freer and more alive in this recreation of herself than she had pretending to be the dutiful partner to Tom. This proved to be Claire's cue to pry into this hitherto closed topic.

'Oh, Claire... I keep doubting myself and you know me, I do easily doubt anyway! But he's so convincing.'

'What do you mean "is"?'

'Well, I obviously haven't seen him…'

'I hope not! But he's still ringing?'

'Yes… Don't look at me like that! I was going to change my phone again, but it's such a pain telling all my contacts.'

'He's got a nerve! Can't he take no for an answer?'

'That's just it, he can't; he's sick, Claire. Hyde just keeps winning over Jekyll.'

'Don't give me that guff! You'll be saying it was your fault next!'

'No, but I know you won't agree – and most people wouldn't… but I went along with it. I was ripe to be a victim; he sensed that when he met me. And I thought I could help him.'

'Oh, Jenny! You can't save everyone! But you've got to save yourself… promise you won't be drawn in again?'

'I promise. Makes you wonder though. How many selves we all have within us to explore - not just Tom.'

Claire pledged with another pinky promise that she would endeavour to find lots.

THE TENTH ERA

1993

The year *I Will Always Love You* by Whitney Houston was number one in the UK charts.

46
Jenny

Tom, knowing Jenny's schedule, knew the best time to catch her was on the homeward journey. He continued hijacking her world with his myriad selves, none of whom Jenny wanted to encounter ever again, but found herself pulling over to talk to him, bizarrely often into the same layby; surely an analogy if ever there was one. It was either:

'Hello, bitch. You think you've moved on by moving away but don't think you can get rid of me that easily.'

Or for Jenny the worst of the many evil approaches:

'Jenny, please talk to me. You know we're right for each other. Nobody understands me like you do. I know I fucked up and I'm getting help now. I really am. I don't know how I'll go on without you. Just say you'll meet and hear me out; somewhere neutral if you like.'

Jenny listened to each call and restated in a flat weary tone, various versions of:

'I did love you, yes, past tense; you abused that love. / There is no going back for us. / You need help, Tom, so you don't abuse anyone else. / I'm going to put the phone down now. / Please don't ring again; I'm moving on and so must you.'

Jenny would then sit in her faithful, battered Fiat for long enough to calm her breathing, so her hands were still enough to grip the steering wheel and her legs trembled-out to drive to what was to her home, her sanctuary, for now. She wondered if Claire was aware of these exchanges as she always seemed to greet her with an extra-large glass of wine on such homecomings.

Determined to do the "moving on" thing, Jenny overturned her darker thoughts and promoted the hopeful ones to plan a weekend away for her and her stalwart pal. They had revisited many confidences of late; Jenny about Tom's sadistic cruelty, the rape of course (which she had vowed to tell nobody) and her bulimia, and she had been surprised to hear that Claire had formerly battled with her weight too and felt inspired by her friend's overcoming of all her many former struggles.

Without Claire's dark flair for such excursions, she had gone online and sourced a murder mystery meal and used the characters and plot as an outline for a trip to Bruges, safe in the knowledge that Eurostar had been a hit for them both last time both in terms of captive audience and captive barmen. Jenny knew "outsiders" would find their behaviour childish but, to her, it felt importantly "other", and knew she shared this newfound "out of body experience", literally, with Claire. Others took drugs; they swapped identities.

She had decided on Loretta Choker as Claire's pseudonym and Olga Onaslab, which she thought lent itself to a heavier-set Russian princess, aka Jenny. One of Jenny's families was getting rid of a lot of their mother's old clothes (on her move into the nursing home) and asked Jenny if she knew what to do with them. She certainly did. This particular woman was almost Jenny's size and Jenny had already vowed to dress like her when older and completely barking. Thus, with a few eased seams in her diamante top and a few safety pins in Claire's silver lamé sheath dress, they were ready for the Orient Express aka the Eurostar.

Jenny had supplied their own etched crystal Champagne flutes (also courtesy of the mother's family when Jenny had, of course, overshared her life and plans). Brim full of prosecco and work freedom, Jenny and Claire immersed themselves in their new identities, sharing the thoughts of the supposed murderer in the hoarsest of stage whispers so the neighbouring seats were privy to their detective thinking:

'Vot a vay to go.'

'I vant to drowwwn in Champagne!'

'Zomehow I don't feenk that vould verk for us; we're immune!'

'Detective Slurper said—'

Both choking on their own slurps of prosecco:

'Detective who!'

'I said, Detective Slurper revealed that she died of poisoning.'

(The accents slipped occasionally)

'Should we avoid the buffet?'

'At all costs.'

Wherein they tucked in heartily and still as noisily into their own picnic which Jenny had themed, less successfully, managing only cod roe for caviar and bricks of pitta bread for blinis but had felt chocolate was world food – so they mainly lined their stomachs with crisps and Galaxy bars. Their neighbouring passengers, obviously needing a rest from such overt tomfoolery, had escaped to the restaurant carriage.

Loretta and Olga had a wonderful journey and, although applause and bows were missing, they left the carriage at Brussels undeterred. Both marvelled at their new-found enjoyment of blatant pantomime, when previously both had shrunk from such spotlights.

They retained their air of grandeur staying near the Grand Palace and even managed to join in the Ommegang, Brussels's medieval pageant, merging into the costume finery on show with every item of bling Jenny had brought with her. Although this was only held annually, they felt it flukily took place especially for them, on the Sunday as they were leaving. All thoughts of whodunnit were erased by the dramatic pageantry and, to be honest, by the volume of alcohol consumed that weekend, so they really didn't care who had murdered whom.

Jenny was very relieved it had been such a success and became rather attached to Olga's diamante top, so that it became her go-to party outfit, as Jenny was determined that parties were back on the agenda again. She had found a George Bernard Shaw quote: "Life isn't about finding yourself. Life is about creating yourself." And together they vowed this was to be their new mantra.

47
Claire

As she was alert to any sign of tension in her friend, Claire noticed Jenny's shoulders occasionally still dropped an inch or two. Fuelled by Jenny's horrific stories held like a chafing stone in her body and determined to stop any interruption of this more carefree existence, Claire paid a visit. She pulled up at a Stepford Wives suburban white box, just as Jenny had described:

'Tom?'

'Yes, who's asking?'

'I'm a friend of Jenny's. I have a message from her; may I come in?'

Tom led her silently into a white immaculate kitchen, again just as Jenny had described, but noticed the image was askew: plates were piled high in the sink with tell-tale takeaway cartons in an open bin.

'Excuse the mess, the hired help's not been. Coffee?'

Claire could see he thought he'd switched to charming mode.

'No, I won't be here that long. I just wanted to make sure you understood Jenny has moved on.'

'Oh, has she now!'

Claire didn't want to linger longer than necessary so walked disdainfully over to his overflowing bin.

'Yes, and if you ever contact her again there will be something nasty in a takeaway or perhaps something flammable in your bin.'

'Says who!'

'Don't ever abuse or underestimate her, or any other woman, ever again. I know what you are capable of, but you have no idea what I am capable of.'

'You could be anyone.'

'Exactly... you'll never know. By the way, this is from Jenny, call it a farewell present.'

She placed the package, ostensibly from Jenny, on the breakfast bar and left. It contained Jenny's old door-key and a record snapped in two: *I Will Always Love You* by Whitney Houston.

Although she had scripted this, practised her look and how she would deliver the lines, she was now trembling from the adrenaline coursing through her body. Her legs just about managed to convey her to her car and work the pedals, until she rounded a corner so she could stop and regain control over her heightened emotions, and her limbs.

THE ELEVENTH ERA

1994

The year that the Loch Ness monster was confirmed as a hoax.

48
Claire

It was Claire's happiest period since (in her "former life") her cocoon of pregnancy, and it held almost as much promise. She felt she could rely on Jenny's friendship entirely. This was a first-ever, and in her head started testing the "bestie" word and then started dropping it into the conversation at work: what she was doing with her housemate who was her "best friend" that weekend and how her "best friend" had bought her the new handbag/pen/ whatever item might be at hand. She did this just to get the concept over that she, Claire, was worthy of a notable best friend, one who liked – no, loved – her enough to buy her presents that were perfect, as she knew her inside out.

She even found herself divulging certain bits of her past and of her mental health struggles, but only bits and only to placate Jenny's curiosity and cement their friendship even further:

'So, it must have been weird, your parent's fostering at first, right?'

'Still is.'

'Go on...'

'Yes, nurse!'

'Sorry, just interested. I had my mum and dad all to myself.'

'Exactly, I did too until Mum got it into her head she had to "give back" and I was fifteen when we had our first foster kid.'

'Tough?'

'Yeah, my brother was eighteen and off to uni, so he wasn't affected but I felt shoved out prematurely.'

'Cuckoo in the nest.'

'Yeah, exactly! I told my mum that. I'd looked it up: when the cuckoo lays its eggs in another bird's nest and the baby cuckoo hatches, it turfs out the other baby birds one by one. How cruel is nature, eh?'

Claire suddenly realised she was entering realms that could unravel more past than she wanted.

'Wine?'

'Of course! But what did your mum say to you then?'

'Like always she made excuses to suit her way of thinking. She never "got" me. My teenage feelings were too difficult for her and not as important as all those cute, littler kids.'

'How many did you have?'

'Emergency at first, so one after another, and then Mum started to get too attached and said she'd rather do long-term fostering. My dad just went along with it all for a peaceful life.'

'And was it?'

'I s'pose till I was at uni and not coping and then they realised too late that just cos I'd left the nest didn't mean I didn't need them anymore.'

'But you don't see them now, did you—'

'They don't love me, just put up with me, so there's no point... not good memories there.'

Then Claire clammed up.

'That's all you're getting, Mrs Psych!'

'Have you ever thought of fostering, I mean, not yet obviously!'

'Bloody hell, no, why, would you?'

'I think I would. If I couldn't have my own, that is.'

'Saint Jenny!'

'No! From a selfish point of view, I can't imagine not having kids, but, shit, am I relieved I wasn't pregnant with Tom!'

'I s'pose it wasn't meant to be there.'

'Is this the Claire Hetherington I know talking about FATE!'

'I'll get that wine.'

And Claire went off to plunder their never-ending "cellar", which had begun as one assigned cupboard in the kitchen and now was the understairs cupboard too; the hoovers and anything remotely useful were easily relegated to the garage.

The answers for Claire were still often found in wine and the subsequent hangover raised questions too – about home.

49

Janet

Their newest foster child had been filthy on arrival and now they couldn't keep her out of the bathroom. So, after years of struggling with just the one, Jeff had given into Jan's pleas and with the help of many mates in trades, had built a two-storey extension. It housed the longed-for second bathroom, a fourth large bedroom that could accommodate two or even three single beds and a large playroom/family room downstairs; even though all the kids were always to be found around Jan in the tiny kitchen, dunking their fingers in cake mixes or raiding the biscuit tin.

The only downside to more space was more cleaning and although Jan had just a lick-and-spit approach, it still added to the time spent on housework which could be spent cooking and caring. Her head down the new toilet scrubbing whilst the children were at school, she almost missed the phone ring and was puffed by the time she answered it:

'Mum? Are you okay?'

'Oh, Claire! How lovely, sorry, I was cleaning our new toilet; we've got an extension. Dad, Johnny and Chip built it. Get us, eh! It would be great to show it to you.'

She knew she was gabbling and so drew breath.

'How are you, love?'

'Fine. Work's busy but I'm managing to get some mini breaks in.'

'On your own?'

Janet kicked herself.

'No actually, Mum, with my best friend, Jenny. We've had quite a few European city breaks.'

'Ooh, lovely... Rome?'

'Not yet but we went to Venice.'

'Did it smell?'

'No, that was years ago, Mum.'

'Oh, that's good. Did you go on a gondola?'

Why couldn't she talk to her own daughter – what rot!

'Yes, even though it was extortionate. How's Dad?'

At that moment Jeff came in with a blare of children's voices released from desks and order, to run riot on Victoria sponge and garden freedoms.

Janet put her hand over the receiver and hissed at Jeff: 'It's Claire.'

Jeff took the phone whilst Jan ushered the noisy brood out of Claire's earshot.

When she took over from Jeff again, Claire was obviously winding up the conversation.

'Dad sounded well.'

'Yes, he's good, missing you, of course; we both are.'

There she had done it again and the precious phone call petered out. Jan joined the kids in the garden and without tasting, wolfed down even more cake than they did.

50
Jenny

It was on an extremely "winey" wine bar night out with her colleague, Christie, that Jenny had her arm twisted. With her fiancé, Ben, Christie was going to set her up on a blind date at their recently renovated one-up-one-down. Seemingly, with all their own ducks almost lined up, they were keen to entertain in their new home and help Jenny at least get "a few feathers" of her own, which was very kind.

Jenny had gone for jeans, casual, but added a striking turquoise velvet top which she felt both suited and lifted her and her outfit. She rang the doorbell with difficulty while juggling a fruity red wine and non-garage flowers.

A beaming stranger caught the flowers as she with her usual clumsiness went to shake hands, forgetting hers were already full, and thus the ice was broken – but luckily not the wine – and a romance was forged, despite Jenny almost dismissing him for having fair eyelashes and invisible eyebrows. John led her into the tiny open-plan living area, where Christie and Ben pretended to be too busy cooking, ostentatiously turning their backs and, whisking for effect, leaving the new lovebirds to get to know each other.

'No! I live there too, whereabouts?'

'Oh, in Upland Street, it's off—'

'Norland Gardens, yes, I know. I live at 28 Norland Gardens!'

'No!'

'I live at 184 Upland Street.'

'I jog past your road every day!'

Tick.

He was a chartered surveyor and was charming about the improvements that Ben and Christie had made to their house. As they toured every skirting board, re-laid pipes, tightened faucets and, lastly, the new casement windows John had advised Ben to get, it gave Jenny the chance to scrutinise his every gesture and expression, all of which "passed muster", whatever muster meant!

Tick.

The meal was immaterial and certainly hadn't needed all the "preparation", a simple "decanting" and reheating was all that was required, but both Jenny and John (gosh, they sounded like a car sticker already!) were oblivious as conversation skittered from shared travels, a love of Labradors (biggest tick) to a shared distaste of all things right wing.

The usually garrulous Christie didn't get a word in edgeways Jenny realised, but she gathered from her smug farewells that she didn't mind too much at all. In fact, Christie was already claiming the new couple as her own triumph as they teetered together down the path.

'Can I give you a lift? After all, I pass your door!'

'Well, thank you kindly!'

So, the new double mattress did see some action again and it was a far more meaningful occupancy than Jenny had anticipated. However, she wasn't too worried about the wear and tear, as John and she soon split their time equally between both of their mattresses, with spare toothbrushes also featuring in both bathrooms.

Tom and that period of her life weren't immediately obliterated, so John had to jump a few hoops to "prove" he wasn't another perpetrator of domestic abuse. Jenny tried to trip him up with various emotional obstacles and tried very hard to push him away; she had gone out of her way to be her worst self. Jenny was sick in his car after a work's do, where she had flirted with his boss and got paralytically drunk, had pointed out (almost) all the terrible things she had done in life from the bulimia, to actually punching a drunk Australian on the nose (who'd tried to hit on her in a London bar when those Perth days had come flooding back). She'd held back about her rape, not able to go there with anyone else.

John had been unperturbed and had said he'd decided he was "up for the ride" wherever it led them. And Jenny had to accept it. Every time his square, serious face looked down, it was as if she operated strings; a comment from her and his head would pull up with a bashful smile tweaking around the corners of his mouth, which jumped into those warm hazel eyes – and, well, she was smitten all over again.

Jenny's mum seemed to find John charming too, and he loved her; the biggest ever tick. Rather than the stress of forced first chats in Jenny's mum's house, John had suggested he take them both to a National Trust garden nearby so they could meander and talk among the hydrangeas, before having afternoon tea.

Jenny almost felt superfluous as they compared favourite architecture and when John admitted to a love of Glenn Miller, she thought her mum would fight for his hand in marriage too!

51
Claire

Jenny wasn't the only one who made John jump through hoops, however, the hoops Claire held up had giant barbs on them. Not trusting her own judgement anymore, Jenny asked Claire if she could invite John to supper early on in the relationship and as much as Claire had wanted to keep Jenny to herself, she couldn't say no. Although she had never seen Jenny with Tom, she instinctively knew this was different with John; Jenny was totally herself and not the tautly sprung, cautious version Tom had caused her to become. Well, almost herself. Claire couldn't help but sneer at her new giddiness as she brought in more wine from the kitchen and saw the love birds break apart from an embrace. She joined them at the makeshift camping table and felt she was that *third wheel again*. Claire realised she was battling jealous feelings.

'So, John, as Jenny's best friend...'

There, she'd said it in front of Jenny now too.

'It's "incumbent" on me...'

She'd show him she was clever and, therefore, could see through his refuelling her glass and being soo polite; she'd wait to trip him up.

'Thank you, yes, a little more... So, I heard you were engaged?'

Jenny nearly spat out her wine.

'Claire, it's like having my dad back leading a CID interrogation. How did you know that?'

She had done her homework; it was quite easy digging dirt on people if you needed to; she'd had plenty of practice with Tom's pit of a past.

'My fame goes before me, or rather a lack of it. I was engaged at nineteen, first love and all that and, sadly at that time, believed in no sex before marriage and so wanted to hurry things up!'

Jenny leant over and kissed him as naturally as Claire had ever seen her behave.

He scored points with Claire for not asking how she knew but was clearly ready to be so open that the spines, of his very open book, were practically bent back on themselves. He was evidently very invested.

'Luckily, you've changed now! So, how did you "hear", Claire?'

'Oh, I got talking to a colleague whose partner is a surveyor and it somehow came out.'

Of course, it hadn't happened like that; she'd had to use her overtime pay to hire a private detective for a personal background check and gleaned a lot from their tactics, although not much intel for her money.

John was too immersed in the present to worry about the past and so the conversation skittered onto other topics.

The comfort and solidity of everything rebuked Claire's own experiences but she sat and ate her homemade lasagne and a disaster of a pavlova that prompted laughter not embarrassment. She wanted to drink in, not just more of the fruity red, but the ease of this loving couple, so happy in their own skins. It got to 2 a.m. and they were still regaling Claire with their hurricane camping disaster story and Claire found herself reciprocating, telling John some of the repeatable insider details of some of their jaunts. John seemed genuinely rapt by her wry retorts and, for once, didn't feel like a gooseberry. So, in her own post-meeting analysis, she had to reluctantly admit to herself he was "maybe" okay.

It had been thirteen years in between Claire being nursed by Jenny and now this "friendship" and she, unused to being curious about others' lives, found she wanted to know everything there was to know. If she wasn't to have her own relationships, well, she supposed this was what they called living "vicariously". Claire was very black and white with people and decided to back John for now. This would be imperative, she realised, if she was to keep Jenny as her friend. But she'd keep a wary eye and be there for her when, undoubtedly, hopefully, they would break up…

52
Jenny

Even John's proposal was perfect; not because it was all Eiffel Tower and rose petals which she would have hated (she'd had enough fake sugar coating with Tom), but because it was unplanned and somehow more "solid" (unfortunate analogy)! John had been mending the leaking toilet in her shared house, yet again. Jenny was sat on the bath edge, laughing at him for having his arm in her u-bend and quipping salacious remarks, while spraying deodoriser to mask the "un-fragrance" of the tiny bathroom.

'Well, maybe we should get our own u-bend?'

'I'm not into sex toys, Mr Wells; you should know me better by now!'

'Huh!'

Then he got uncharacteristically shy.

'What?'

'I meant, I've had it with mending this toilet.'

'I'm sorry...'

'I think we should have our own toilet, in our own bathroom, in our own house.'

'Wow!'

'We "get on", don't we?'

'Well, I'd say it's a bit more than that!'

'Exactly; this isn't the ideal scenario but...'

He moved from lying by the toilet to a kneeling position and Jenny squealed.

'Let me wash my hands first...'

Jenny held her breath.

53
John

John had bought the ring months ago. Jenny and he had a Sunday afternoon wander around antique shops and she had lingered over a particular sapphire ring. He'd tried to memorise its placement in the cabinet as well as an approximation of the ring itself, but didn't trust his own eye to have remembered the right one. So, a whole twenty-four hours later and taking a long detour between site visits, he was gulping at the numbers but writing the cheque anyway for what he hoped was the right ring.

Never a natural romantic but hoping his actions such as mending her car's exhaust umpteen times, vocalised his love. John thought that maybe Jenny would expect him to step up for a proposal of marriage. So, the following Saturday, the skies were a perfect blue and as Jenny was a lover of literally anything on the blue spectrum, he booked an afternoon visit to the nearby butterfly house where he was assured there were plenty of blue admiral butterflies. To add to the blue theme, he had a bunch of cornflowers in the boot to give her on the picnic which included blue cheese to be eaten, maybe not by a noticeably blue lake, but it definitely had peacocks nearby. The ring was safely in his pocket and he pulled up outside Jenny's house, brim-full of emotion and unusually lost for words.

Jenny met him at the door with her characteristic huge grin and kiss, then whisked him inside.

'Are you ready?'

'Nearly. Just before we go, can you have a look at our toilet; it's leaking and I'm worried when I next sit on it I'll find myself plumb-eting into the kitchen – get it, "plumb-eting"!'

'Haha, very good. Sure.'

Her sheer, vital happiness had floored him; John couldn't hold onto his secret for much longer:

'Jenny, you amazing, kind, clumsy, gorgeous, hare-brained woman, will you marry me?'

The blue ring was the right ring, thank god. And, once every last trace of u-bend aroma had been scrubbed away, they did get to see blue butterflies. And who knew peacocks like blue cheese as part of their high-protein diet! Jenny commented on the reality and laughter of it all; auguring well for their future. John heaved a sigh of relief and vowed to get a plumber in, in the future.

54
Claire

Jenny was increasingly staying over at John's. Claire knew it was wrong to feel "jilted" but couldn't stop herself from mooning about the house. The evenings after work and weekends felt even longer than they had pre-Jenny living there. Her only distraction was words. She looked up "dark vortex" feeling that was what she was caught up in: "a powerful circular current of water – usually the work of conflicting tides". Yep. However, these tides abruptly stopped and pooled into the deepest of still wells. Eric needed her, of course, but even though she popped something in the microwave for him every evening and stayed to watch Neighbours (although goodness knows why he was so interested in surfer beach bums in another universe), there were still too many hours before she felt it was bedtime and her own high-pressure weather system still needed to settle.

Under the pretence of clearing up (Jenny was as compulsively messy as Claire was ordered), Claire spent evenings sorting, but really trying on, Jenny's clothes. She wanted to see what a Jenny self might feel like, how she may behave and convincing herself it was just like all their other new identities – only this one was real.

She stood for hours in front of the long mirror in the hall, the one Jenny had bought her to bounce light around the hitherto dark space, impersonating Jenny's full-throated laugh with her head held back:

'Claire, you crack me up!'

And trying again and again, throwing her head back in Jenny's inimitable style:

'Claire, you crack me up!'

But she didn't feel the laughter inside.

Claire then laundered and replaced all Jenny's clothes neatly in her drawers, well, nearly all...

55
Jenny

Her mum was overjoyed, of course, and Christie too who, now pregnant with their first, was on maternity leave and keen to use her "final days" being part of the planning for the wedding that, of course, she had created! Neither wanted a big affair as they had found a doer-upper in Brodhampton and wanted to spend their money on cement and windowpanes rather than sugared almonds and hired suits. The ceremony was at the local registry office, attended by Jenny's mum, John's parents and brother, Andy, and his fiancée, Lara, Claire, Christie and Ben, of course. Christie, being days away from "popping", added to the excitement of the day. Then, it was back to John's parents' house. They had downsized locally but still had room for a small marquee in the back garden to accommodate the coronation chicken, chocolate wedding cake, fifty or so gyrating friends and the Motown band Jenny had set her heart on.

The honeymoon was four nights in the Lake District; it poured with rain, in July! But undeterred, they giggled their way around all the lakes in unflattering plastic ponchos, sending rude postcards to all their friends using half-remembered addresses, but, otherwise, very bound up with being newlyweds, drunk on cider by day, wine by night and love at any time of the day or night.

THE TWELFTH ERA

1995

The year that Forest Gump won the Academy Award for Best Picture.

56
Claire

Her friendship with Jenny had evolved from coffee and chats at Cedars to their now monthly costumed trips and being housemates. And so, the evolution continued. When Jenny moved out, thankfully the suppers with both Jenny and John and invitations to larger gatherings of curry nights, random fancy dress cocktail do's and Hawaiian shirt barbecues came. They were very social and Claire became accustomed to this new way of life. Having such friends and being introduced as "special friend Claire" gave her an identity at last. Jenny and John tried a few times to set her up. Once, with a colleague of John's who happened to be passing through on a Saturday night at supper time with a bottle of wine in hand!

Or, when out altogether sourcing box hedging for both their houses, they stumbled across an old school friend of John's, who suggested a cuppa and catch up in the garden centre café. He then blew his cover when he knew Claire's name before being introduced and an awkward scone tea ensued.

Therefore, both knew better than to set her up with anyone else for a while. Claire had been very clear she was no longer "on the market" and neither pried why she had "shut up shop" as John so plainly put it.

THE THIRTEENTH ERA

1996

The year that Dolly the sheep was born.

57
Jenny

Having, at long last, been comfortable as Jenny for some time, she felt ready to "expand her edges" and "become" a mother. John had been very happy to be led as to when they started a family. After all, he had a very secure job and the "nest" was ready enough, but he hadn't felt the compulsion Jenny suddenly felt. Little did she know her expanding waistline which she was used to was, in fact, already a new life and not the chocolate digestives. They were both equally poleaxed and delighted.

Jenny told her mum hours after her positive pregnancy test which was still clutched in her hand and, not one to follow convention, shared the news with most friends way before the superstitious twelve weeks. Birthing plans were drawn up, John was commissioned to build their very own birthing pool (of course) and the labour symphonies were almost compiled. The baby name book was pored over on the ever more frequent trips to the loo, as she changed her mind daily from going traditional with Archie/Alice or more outlandish with Chantria/Chad. It took her a long time to get passed D in the alphabet.

However, there was no need to reach "E" at all. Neither of them bargained for the seismic loss they felt when Jenny miscarried at eleven weeks. At first, they thought it was just another small monthly bleed she'd had, disguising the beginnings of this never-to-be pregnancy.

Months of existing followed and joy was hard to find. Although Jenny with her glass at least half full and often to the brim, did try very hard, especially when Claire in her inimitable style to "buck Jenny's ideas up" said "at least she hadn't gone to term". She tried and failed to go along with that particular "glad game". Thus, when a couple of months later her period was late for the second time, she found herself fizzing with excitement, flicking John with urine splashed from her own triumphal pregnancy stick held aloft like the Olympic flame; one with a distinct clear blue line this time – always her very favourite colour.

58
Eric

Eric manoeuvred his walking frame to prop himself at the kitchen sink. He hated Claire doing his washing up on top of everything else. She'd got him one of those frames you could park your bum on awhile; "Like a shooting stick" she'd said when trying to persuade him to accept it.

'Thanks, but tell me, when am I going to go bloody shooting!'

Besides, he liked to stand there and watch her at weekends, hard at work, out in their shared garden. She was a soul possessed when she was hacking at the rhubarb or pruning the wisteria but a tranquillity he rarely saw in her seemed to still her when she was quietly weeding or repotting one of her many seedlings. He wondered at these "nurturings" and also those he benefitted from. He knew she was too proud ever to admit any failure in relationships or talk about her past at all, but he'd seen a greedy longing in her whenever they were out having a ritual "Beryl" at the ice cream shop when rapt little faces received their first ninety-niner. She would moan about the mess they inevitably left, but Eric could see this was a front and wished some other human could earn her loving but thorny heart, and maybe even another precious baby like her Oliver could be created to fill her life.

He knew he didn't have long and indeed didn't want to live much past one last Christmas. At night, he lay awake listening to his heartbeat, marvelling at its insistence, but registering its thready ebb and flow and the accompanying tuneful wheeze of his lungs. He was finding the very act of getting out of bed exponentially exhausting each day, let alone walking his stooped frame from the bus stop to the Cedars door, being ridiculously too proud to accept lifts from the volunteer drivers. He knew it was daft, but felt sure his dreams of Patrick were his own son calling him, readying him for their reunion. He was fairly certain Beryl didn't have long left either; she barely woke when he went in each day. So, yes, he was in a hurry to go with Beryl to the "beyond" with all memories returned.

But he had an inkling that it was inevitable Claire's friend, Jenny, was to have another important person in her life and thus would be moving on soon. So, he didn't want to leave Claire alone just yet, and as he knew too well, Christmas pudding for one was the loneliest meal.

And he had a few last bits of life admin to do. He'd put a deposit down on a burial plot for himself and Beryl and he needed to go in and sort that. Then there were his Hornby trains; he'd heard they could fetch a bob or two. Sadly, there was no little Eric to pass them on to. He wasn't going to get maudlin but felt it was imperative to leave Claire in as good a way as he could manage practically, if not emotionally.

She'd have to tackle that bit herself – he never was one for talking. Beryl had been the talker, had managed to "read" people so well too and seemed able to fill in missing facts that Eric couldn't ever see were missing. Like her saying she had an inkling that Claire was holding onto a great sadness and fear. Eric had said:

'Of course, she is! You, narna, just like us, she's lost a son!'

'There's more to it, Eric. I've got one of my feelings.'

'You read too many agony aunt columns, you do!'

'No, I catch her sometimes when we're out where there's people, families like. There's this look on her face.'

'So, she's not allowed to have a look now!'

'You always take her side. No, it's as if she's watching life from afar, frightened to step into it lest she gets swept along to someplace she doesn't want to be.'

So, all he could do was let her know, in his will, how much she meant. But he'd get her a few Christmas presents first, probably some bulbs for Spring; there was still plenty of time...

59
Claire

Claire knew as a friend she should act pleased – no, delighted – for Jenny, but she couldn't. When Jenny called all breathless with excitement, Claire knew with certainty there was an added rift about to happen in their friendship – a bigger hole caused by a new little being.

Sure enough, Jenny was pregnant again and safely through that first trimester. Claire had seen the "writing on the wall": the "Pregnancy Weekly" on the coffee table again, the sample paint pots and even bloody crochet patterns on there too. She hadn't told Jenny about her babies, her Oliver, about Tony, about her hospitalisations, anything, only sharing her "other lives". She was so good at "fabricating new truths", formerly for her parents, and lately for everyone, even herself. Sometimes she could hardly discern her own fact from fiction. However, it was a necessary device to keep her present self together.

Claire had been enjoying being part of their lives' fabric until now, when she knew this was about to all change again; the fabric was being rewoven. She had been there; the world shrinking to a bump and moving limbs dancing on your very soul, with no one else mattering. And Claire had grown used to "mattering" to someone again.

At that very time, she had that phone call she was dreading. Eric had been hit by a car as he stepped out to cross the road on his way to the Cedars. It was made all the more ironically sad as their only son had been run over by a car; that's why neither Beryl nor Eric had driven since.

A male doctor, so young he was barely shaving, greeted her:

'Your father—'

'He's not my father. I'm a friend.'

'I'm sorry.'

Claire got there in time to be asked about the "do not resuscitate" decision but not to hold his hand for that last breath, as Beryl should have.

To be truthful, Claire would have gladly agreed to a "DNR" plan for herself and, indeed, would have suggested it for a few other people, but Eric wasn't one of them.

'No, I don't know his "wishes"! We never had reason to discuss it.'

Claire knew exactly where this conversation was going, and she didn't want any part of it.

'As I said, Eric has had a very serious car accident which caused a number of broken bones but, more importantly, internal injuries... which he is very unlikely to recover from.'

'He's a fighter; he visits his wife in her nursing home every day. I know he'd want to live.'

'I don't doubt your love and care for him, Claire—'

'I'm a physio, I can nurse him back, I can!'

'Well, as a physio, you'll understand that the ventilator is the only thing keeping Eric alive at the moment.'

'No!'

'Yes, I am so sorry...'

Then began the silence of kindness and finality.

'Would you like me to take you to him.'

At this, Claire got up and ran out of the hospital and kept running and running until she was out of breath and had to navigate her way back to where she had left her car, not only hours but aeons ago.

After answerphone messages from the hospital couldn't be ignored any longer, weeks later, Claire returned to collect a plastic grey hospital bag reminiscent of one she had many years ago. But this one contained Eric's paltry personal effects: his shirt, always a white-ish one – this one a little greyer and frayed at the collar – his crewneck which all but covered his tie (always knotted at his recently increasingly baggy neck), knee'd trousers, shined black shoes, door keys, a wallet with a picture of Beryl, his bus pass and little else – and his socks. It was those holey black socks now crusty with dead sweat that unlocked the violent torrent of tears somehow.

As the new kith and kin, Claire found she coped best by flinging her grief into sorting out Eric's "estate". How grand a title for a Parker Knoll recliner, a few sticks of other well-worn furniture, no antiques but a lifetime's collection of Heritage Railway magazines and Beryl's embroidered antimacassars. How sadly and so soon the flat was sold, monies released to be consumed by Beryl's care and new neighbours moved in. And Claire began to keep her curtains closed against this unwanted new presence.

60
Jenny

Never healthier or happier, Jenny was the archetypal blooming pregnancy: swollen, with a taste for lamb chops, greens and gravy, followed by apple crumble and custard most nights; her bulimia was beaten back to another lifetime. Work had finished, the nursery friezes were pasted and tiny, pristine babygros folded and refolded as carefully as origami, cocooned in tissue paper, waiting. Maybe it was the empty waiting hours or the high-kicking hormones, but something made Jenny a bit maudlin, and against her professional judgement, she found herself visiting Beryl. Claire, for some reason, didn't and was seemingly avoiding Jenny too. Perhaps it was to balance the great fortune she felt, growing this new life against a backdrop of stability at last, that these visits happened so often.

'Where's Eric?'

'Probably gone to get you some shopping, Beryl. Look, I've got you some more wool.'

'Where's Eric? Where's he gone?'

'Picking up his Railway magazine no doubt, and some more ice cream for you I bet! It'll be lunch soon; fish and chips Friday. It was always fish on Saturdays at our house, was it yours?'

'Eric!'

Jenny knew to distract and engage her with other conversations and took in some wool and a bobbin to wind it, hoping to engage her once busy fingers with something useful, knowing her favoured sewing needle was long discarded. However, she was going downhill fast, as if she knew to soon follow Eric.

The day of her funeral was depressingly grey. Jenny always felt funerals needed to happen on fine days, not "happy, blue-sky days" but "shafts of sunshine days", that promised more but didn't shout irrepressible enjoyment of a missing life. The local church was sparsely occupied, with a few older people and staff from the home and possibly some former neighbours she thought she recognised from Eric's recent funeral. Claire was absent.

A thin rendition of *Amazing Grace* by tuneless Geoff from Cedars (he'd found a place for it at last) and Beryl was speedily despatched behind the swished closed curtains, and there was "tea" at the home. But Jenny wanted affirmation of life and went full-on glittery Christmas shopping knowing that, soon, she would be too waddly, too brimful of new life.

61
Claire

Claire had always hated Christmas, especially now she was estranged from her parents and ex-husband, and now had lost her proxy family, Beryl and Eric, whom she would have fussed and been fussed over. She couldn't count on Jenny offering any Christmas invitations as she was too bound up with her imminent cuckoo in the nest.

However, Jenny did surprise her with a visit and a present to put under her non-existent tree; she had always been embarrassingly thoughtful. However, there was obviously an ulterior motive for her visit, which became clear after the niceties were done with. The funeral:

'She wouldn't have cared, or Eric.'

'True… I just thought you might want to say goodbye, for you?'

'I said goodbye loads of times.'

Claire sat with the hurt of this accusation, but couldn't tell her friend that on her recent visits to Cedars where she had been prepared for Beryl's "shoutings" for Eric, Beryl had instead in her escalating confusion taken to calling her "Mummy" and it had torn at Claire's heart. With Jenny, she could be present and future, and certainly didn't want to think about that particular part of her past, that she had shut a trap door on. A door that only opened at night, when sleep was elusive and a child's cries tormented her.

'I know you have problems with feeling abandoned; I just wanted—'

Claire cut her off:

'Abandoned? Where <u>do</u> you get this tosh from?'

'I know, I'm sorry, I just worry you're "going under" again.'

' "Going under"; no wonder you had to leave psychiatric nursing!'

'I didn't have to... look, we've both "looked over the edge"—'

'Hah! "Over the edge"; there you go again!'

'Well, you know what I mean... me, firstly, alongside patients... and then inching a bit closer myself... And you—'

'And me'?'

'I'm your friend and I care about you. We've never talked about <u>your</u> mental health really.'

'And we don't need to now.'

'I told you about my bulimia.'

'This isn't a trade-off situation.'

'No.'

'That "psychiatric sausage factory", ECT, post-natal depression; it's all behind me.'

Jenny was incredulous:

'What!'

'What?'

'Wow! You just said you'd had post-natal depression. I didn't know, so you have a—'

'NO! That part of my life is closed to me, and to you.'

'Oh, Claire, but I want—'

'No, Jenny, you may "want" all you like, but you don't understand – <u>I</u> want to forget.'

Jenny was clearly still taking in the news that Claire had had a child and sank into the chair that clearly hadn't been offered. Claire softened momentarily.

'I admit I did need help then – that's it. I was unlucky.'

'Wow! Claire, you can at least be honest with ME! Are you going to run from other meaningful relationships all your life?'

'Possibly. Anyway, why did you come?'

'Well, that seems, well… Ohhh, I'm not going about this in the right way. I actually came here to ask you to be godmother to my child… Is that insensitive now, sorry?'

'Me? You want your baby to have a mad mentor?'

'Claire! I NEVER think of you as having been "mad"… just sad, especially now I know—'

'You know nothing!'

Claire couldn't handle the implicit pity on top of the gaping wounds being wrenched open. Wounds that she had so diligently packed with falsehoods for years. She had trusted Jenny as her one equal in life, and Jenny had stepped over that line… and ruined it.

'Why, thank you, Saint Jenny! I think it's time you left now!'

At that point, Claire opened the front door and ushered a tearful and very large Jenny out slamming it after her, to underline her fury.

Claire had always found the sound of Eric's TV drifting up through the floorboards comforting, but at that minute, the new neighbour's baby dared to cry and Claire was down there for the first of many angry inflated complaints. She knew she had terrified them and was pleased.

For some reason, she called home and then, of course, instantly regretted it.

62
Janet

Olivia had brought home her end-of-term workbooks to Janet as she was staying with them for the weekend, so her dad could go Christmas shopping for her in peace. Janet felt bad she was viewing them before her dad, but Olivia was so keen to share them that Janet couldn't deny her. Olivia's "personal workbook" all but punched Janet in the stomach. Under the perennial heading "My Family", Olivia had drawn herself in the middle with her dad's hands on her shoulders and her hands in each of hers and Jeff's hands, with lots of blurry children circling them as if they were running. And, in the top corner, was a female who Janet presumed represented her mother. This figure had her back turned and she was writing a letter: Dear Olivia.

Janet would normally use such pictures to get each child they'd ever fostered talking about their family but at that moment, of course, the phone rang and Olivia sprang to answer it:

'Hetherington family, who's speaking please?'

'Claire.'

'One moment, please, I'll get Aunty Jan.'

Olivia put her hand over the mouthpiece as she had seen her Aunty do and said:

'It's Claire.'

Janet, taken aback, flicked her hands at Olivia as a gesture for her to leave the room immediately, which she did but not before leaving Janet with a deliberately hurt expression.

'Hi, love.'

'Hi, Mum.'

'Oh, love, it's so good to hear your voice... How are you?'

'Okay, Mum, just thought I'd call and say Happy Christmas. How are you and Dad?

'Oh, this is so lovely. Dad's okay; he's still enjoying work and his beloved golf, of course.'

'And how are you? Still busy with the fostering then?'

Janet, already unnerved, didn't tell her that just that week the adoption papers had come through. Ella was now officially theirs and, at nineteen, was growing up into a kind and capable young woman. All her harum-scarum days were over. Janet wondered if Claire knew somehow but thought it was probably her own guilt piquing; it was Christmas that made her call, just as Claire said.

'Just a few, aged six to nine, so keeping Dad and me out of mischief. But none of them are here Christmas and Boxing Day, if you were thinking—'

'Sorry, Mum, you know how it is...'

Janet wanted desperately to know "how it was", but said instead:

'Okay, love, but you know we are always here for you – should you need us.'

'I was trying to remember that Christmas we had at Grandma's in London. Did we go to Hamleys and get teddies, or have I imagined that?'

'Yes, we did! Fancy you remembering that! You must have been just three at the time. Do you remember, we went to a very posh hotel for afternoon tea and you were sick in Grandma's lap as you'd eaten cream for the first time!'

'I still hate cream... What are you having for Christmas lunch, the usual?'

'Of course, even with just the two of us. Nigel's lot are going to Christine's parents this year, but Dad still wants the works! What are you having?'

Janet didn't ask "where" – still trying to keep Claire on the line.

'Don't know yet. Probably a pheasant.'

'Fancy!'

'Yes, well, I better go. I'm sure you've got lots to do with all the little ones and I'm really busy with... everything. Bye then. Happy Christmas.'

Janet tried but couldn't hide her sadness.

'Bye, love. Happy Christmas to you.'

And Claire was gone again. Olivia slunk back into the room. Janet pulled her close and apologised for being so abrupt and suggested they made Welsh cakes for tea.

63
Jenny

Born on Christmas Eve, John and Jenny rejected the more obvious Hollys and Marys, but quickly settled on Eve, to be known as Evie. They felt it was a name to work all year long, as each day could be a new eve for her, and she was definitely their new dawning.

She looked like a miniature John with those beautiful fair brows and lashes and what was soon to be his wide generous smile. A "good baby" but nevertheless all-consuming, Jenny found herself soon describing Evie as so many months old, rather than weeks – *when did that happen?* And still no visit from Claire. With the "naming ceremony" on her mind and also her friend's own state of mind, Jenny decided to call unannounced. With baby Evie stirring in her car seat, she stood at Claire's front door rocking the seat with her foot, willing her to be quiet. The door, as so often is with maisonettes, was actually at the side and she could see straight into Claire's back garden, or rather she couldn't anymore, as there was a huge fence (it must have been the "maximum" allowed) occluding her view. Although Claire's car was parked outside and so she was most probably in, the door remained unopened.

Several sleepless nights later and not just caused by Evie's very "on demand'" feeding, Jenny, after a third failed attempt to get Claire to open the door, resorted to tracing her parents. With an unusual surname, Hetherington, and knowing where Claire grew up, they were an easy find, and, when Jenny wrote to them leaving her telephone number, she received a call within the same week.

'We're just glad she's got a close friend at last – she's been very "distant", shall we say.'

'When did you last see her?'

'Seven years now. She did ring just before Christmas and I got my hopes up. But we know not to ring ourselves... We write with photos of all the family – we're just waiting to be let back in.'

'Oh, I'm sorry, I didn't know; she can be very private.'

'I'll say! She was happy once upon a time, you know. Or so we thought. Until that first time she cut herself, well, you'll know she then got admitted to hospital.'

'That's so sad.'

'But having been a psychiatric nurse, you'll understand all about post-natal depression.'

'Yes! I only recently found out she'd had a baby.'

Janet hesitated. She was so bad at secrets but bit her lip and moved the conversation on.

'And even then, they hadn't diagnosed her. We've recently wondered if it's borderline personality disorder, but we've never been able to have those sorts of conversations with her. Her dad and I, and James, her brother, we've all struggled and, well, she won't let us help.'

Borderline personality disorder! Jenny felt so dense. So much of Claire's life and behaviour made sense now. She wrote to Claire saying she needed to talk to her and would turn up at the surgery if she didn't let her in when she next called. Next time though, the door opened and, thankfully, Claire emerged with an equally abashed expression. Phew, they were still friends and, although Claire was cool about her precious Evie, Jenny understood and was careful as the visit grew into hours, to feed as surreptitiously as she could and underplay all cooing.

She broached the subject of being the other "special" person in Evie's life. It wasn't to be a full-blown christening but just a "welcoming" of their little girl into the microcosm of their immediate family and friends, in preparation for her later entry into the big wide world with these chosen people on her side. Claire agreed. Jenny left feeling happier that a permanent rift had been avoided as she was now well aware of the fragility of Claire's trust. She hadn't mentioned her new-found "intelligence".

The ceremony was brought forward to the Easter weekend as Claire was taking a sabbatical abroad with a little of the monies left to her from Eric and Beryl's post office savings account. The sun shone, Evie gurgled, and Claire assumed her best sociable self and even seemed touched that John and Jenny had chosen her name as Evie's middle moniker. Jenny had liked the name's meaning: "clear", as she felt her life hitherto had been far from that and she wanted her own daughter to have more "clarity" about who she was and where she was going than her mum!

Jenny reluctantly returned to work part-time, but once she was back, found she had actually missed being her work self and thus relished the sharp relief of each role. Evie was happy in the hospital's nursery. Jenny got a promotion, enabling John to take a chance and go self-employed taking on commissions to restore his beloved older properties; all were in their element.

THE FOURTEENTH ERA

1997

The year that Princess Diana died.

64
Claire

Claire had indeed gone abroad, but only for a few weeks to Sorrento for some winter sun and to escape her infuriating neighbours. She intended to lie low and hibernate for a while to plan her next steps. However, on her return, she found she didn't want to move from her maisonette after all, but she did want the family underneath her gone.

She became fixated on HER cherry tree which she could see from her window but which was obscured from view when she was in her own divided garden so that the tree and, therefore, Oliver, were denied her by the ugly, lurid, orange fence panels put up to segregate their lives. In Claire's view, she was very entitled to lodge all the complaints she did about the Cresswells, her enemies; after all, they were "based" on truths. Claire found the baby crying and, in particular, the drone of their baby food blender, as well as their new puppy yelping, their music and loud conversations VERY disturbing and thus "excessive". So, with the help of her diary recordings of these "disturbances", she was able to lodge at least four complaints with her local council.

When she had complained about their cruel pruning of the cherry tree and the subsequent lopping off of all overhanging branches so she had no part in her tree – well, that was a declaration of war. After six months more of these fractious times, she spotted a

"For Sale" board outside the property and her heart soared. She had won and, furthermore, she had enough income helped by Eric and Beryl's money to buy downstairs too, re-uniting the two gardens and Oliver's cherry tree.

She knew she had to box clever because if the Cresswells knew she was interested then they may well not accept an offer from her. It was a stressful time, as every time a prospective buyer viewed, Claire had to somehow be doing something equally as obnoxious as her neighbours had purportedly done to her. So, she found herself frying onions at all times, accompanied by heavy rock, or playing taped sounds of Alsations barking, which all added to the "attractive" atmosphere. She also perfected loud outbursts, ostensibly arguing with a partner, which varied depending on her mood from:

'You're not bloody knocking down another wall! The ceiling will collapse, you cretin!'

To:

'Oh, here we go again! Go on, piss off with your floozy.'

This one was accompanied by bin-liners of clothes being emptied out of the upstairs window, narrowly avoiding potential buyers.

It seemed that the ploys were working, and it was time to contact Jenny and confess that she was "back" so she could enlist her help with Operation House Purchase, and she supposed... go through with the naming ceremony thing.

65
Jenny

Delighted that Claire had come back from Eritrea, however heroic she'd obviously been by volunteering there, she had been worried about her being in such a place in her vulnerable state – especially as she seemed unwilling to discuss it at all. So, Jenny readily agreed to be the "front woman" for the house purchase to "root" her friend in this new venture. John, in his chartered surveyor role, was able to get a few thousand knocked off the price for blown double glazing and, very soon, they were helping to take down the offending fence that divided her new large garden. It was celebrated as much as the Berlin wall falling; well, almost, three bottles of prosecco anyway, as Evie was at John's parents for her first overnighter.

It was great to see Claire repairing her hard work in the glorious garden, and cuttings of lily of the valley and Agapanthus went back and forth, as both women were in their elemental elements. And, typically attuned, they bought each other identical garden planner books to plan their own future landscaping. John crafted a garden seat (to replace the old rotting one of Beryl and Eric's. It fitted around the cherry tree's broadening girth and all three would sit there with a cuppa watching Evie crawling around in the "wildflower" area. It became a regular haven for both women and little Evie with Jenny dropping by for horticultural advice, their usual gossip exchange and the shared marvelling of Evie's development.

THE FIFTEENTH ERA

1998

The year Anthony Gormley's landmark sculpture, the Angel of the North, was erected at Gateshead.

66
Claire

The years seemed to be slipping through Claire's fingers and apart from her glorious garden marking the seasons, all days, weeks and months were the same. Evie was the only mercurial part of her life. Claire had taken to having her for a few hours on some Saturday afternoons to give Jenny and John some alone time; she marvelled at her ever-shifting milestones. At eighteen months, she would sit up in her pram and gabble away, as if in the very Scandi, Claire had pretended to be studying. This little being equally charmed her as she looked knowingly into Claire's eyes, and unnerved her.

One sunny Saturday, she had put the snacks Jenny had packed for her (the bottle, Pom Pom Bears and banana) in the basket of her new buggy and had set off for the park. Evie had fallen asleep almost immediately. As Claire watched her she felt an overwhelming need to hold Evie skin to skin – as she never had before... Claire sat on the first park bench she came to. Evie didn't stir as Claire held her inside her blouse, her beatific face buried in Claire's still ample bosom. She basked in the sunshine, sharing smiles with other mums and shy dads as they went past pushing buggies as if she were one of them. Emboldened by this proprietary feeling, Claire did more circuits of the park then kept on walking and walking, well aware her Evie time was nearly up – but those smug Scandi mummies came to mind, as they all too often did when the empty ache within her gnawed most strongly.

She thought how easy it would be to quickly return home before Jenny and John arrived to take her back. She'd grab an overnight bag, bundle Evie into the car, stop at the local shop for more nappies and milk powder, draw out all her money and just go, the two of them, no note.

Evie awoke at that point and Claire jogged home, her pace quickening with every cry and every addition to her galvanising plan. Work was used to her sudden absences, so she'd call them with a new excuse, but that was for tomorrow. For now, it was important not to leave any clues as to her whereabouts. They just needed to disappear – and she was practised at that. It was already approaching the arranged collection time. Claire was panting as she rounded the corner ready to abandon the overnight bag and just get in the car and go, saving precious minutes.

Claire rounded the corner to see Jenny and John's car outside and them, pretending not to have been panicking, hovering at her front door. She slowed her pace to collect her fireworks of thoughts, opening with:

'My, I'm not late, am I?'

'Not at all! Sorry, you obviously didn't get my message?'

'Message?'

'Sorry, yes, I messaged you saying Maureen's been taken into hospital again and she'd never forgive us if we didn't take her favourite granddaughter in with us to see her!'

'Oh, right. I was jogging to get her to sleep as we've had quite a busy afternoon. She's been fine; had her bottle and all her snacks. Well, I better not keep you.'

She bent down to caress Evie's downy head.

'Bye, Evie, see you soon.'

'Thanks, Claire, you're a love. Sorry, we can't stay. Supper Friday?'

'Yeah, sure.'

And Claire barely moved from the sofa for the rest of the weekend, rerunning the "what ifs?".

On a non-Evie sunny Saturday, a cream envelope plopped through Claire's letterbox. Wondering how to spend her day, she had started by making a percolator of strong coffee in the kitchen and took the letter with a large mug to her bench of all great things: reading, garden surveying, drinking wine and Jenny gossiping. In the light of her recent dark thoughts and self-castigations (regarding sins nearly committed), she had been secretly trying positive affirmations; very "out there" for her. So, this letter had to be good news, yes?

"The judges were very impressed by your entry and would like to commend you on your work. You have been invited to the magazine's head office for a celebratory lunch with the winners of our short story competition and your fellow runners-up."

Well, that would do!

She did tell Jenny, not to boast, but to get her advice on what to wear. Jenny of course translated this as an invitation to go shopping and she found herself in possession of a new navy linen trouser suit and lemon blouse, "But I hate lemon!", and a lemon handbag which she'd never use again but which Jenny insisted completed the look. The solicitude of her friendship evoked a rare but goring guilt in Claire, of almost kidnapping Jenny's daughter, which overrode her distaste and the lemon handbag joined the items by the till.

However, Claire did feel very confident in her new apparel when stepping into the foyer of the magazine's offices. She clocked a gaggle of mismatched people who were standing shifting like a nervous giant amoeba at the reception (an anachronism she knew wouldn't make it into her "phrases book", but it amused her). As she was directed to join them, they were all shepherded into the glass lifts.

Next to her, she could smell John's aftershave – Polo Sport, she thought it was – and before she knew it:

'Is that Polo Sport I can smell?'

The smell's owner turned as much as lift confinement allowed and said:

'Yes, you must have a good nose!'

At which point the lift opened to spill them out.

'Yes, I see you do have a very good nose, sorry! Are you winner or runner-up like me?'

Spoken by a very tall well-built man of around her own age.

The afternoon passed in a blur. Claire had started this new script with a bold opening and thus managed to continue to be a more open version of herself. Helped by her lemon handbag, of course, Claire found she was agreeing to continue the celebrations post the very disappointing, but good for gags, limp buffet and onto drinks and then dinner with the wonderfully smelling David.

Dinner finished too early, so there was time for more drinks before Claire's train home and, in fact, there was time for sex and more sex in David's hotel room and for her to apply some Polo Sport to her dishevelled self, to cover any obvious "sex smells" on the journey home. What a day! She clutched her lemon handbag to her and wondered at her easy lie of being on the pill. Would it come back to haunt or succour her?

67
Olivia

More than a tad overweight, Janet puffed up the stairs with her fourth laundry load glad for her knees that this was the last. Imogen's had been first and Janet had pushed her sequinned crop tops down into frothy tutus, challenging the overstuffed drawer to shut. At eleven, Imogen was at that quixotic teeter between self-conscious teenager and carefree child; not that Imogen had ever been carefree. Next, was Amar, a sad seven, who had been an emergency only a few days ago, so too soon to have acquired much laundry. He shared a room with Ted, who was a regular "respite", to give his poorly single mum a break and Ted a much-needed outlet for his eleven-year-old boisterous steam. Ted loved his mum fiercely, but Janet saw how much he needed these weeks away, as demonstrated by his, the largest, pile of laundry, now newly free of football field mud, fish scales from river trips and a whole bottle of ketchup. Lastly, Liv, as she was now called since:

'Olivia is dead to me and you from now on!'

And this was declared at age seven; she was now an even more grown-up ten.

Janet knocked and waited to be asked in. Jeff and Janet had agreed on allowing all their troubled charges the right to privacy in their own rooms from whatever young age, as most had little such control over their own lives previously. A "come in" was croaked. Liv had tonsillitis and so was the only one home. Her dad was having a busy few weeks and so Liv was back with Aunty Jan and Uncle Jeff. She was sitting up in bed with the hot Ribena doting Jeff had just brought her. Janet put Liv's laundry pile down. Already into fashion and, thankfully for Janet and Jeff's Christian morals, it was modest: Liv favoured plaid shirts and distressed denim dungarees worn with one strap down and one up, of course. All a relief for Janet's laundry schedule, as everything could go on together at forty degrees.

Liv mumbled thanks and firmly closed her Agent ~~Olivia~~ Liv diary. 'Want anything?'

'Can I have some chocolate ice cream for my throat, with extra sauce?'

'You must be feeling better!'

Whilst her Aunty Jan got her the ice cream, Liv went back to her diary. It was both a daily record of her life thus far but also a collection of clues and hypotheses (she had just looked this new word up) about her beginning in life – and, most significantly, her mother.

She took another sip of her Ribena and slid under her *Disney Mulan* duvet cover. She had really wanted a *Madeline* one but, apparently, they didn't exist; she hadn't complained.

Madeline was her early heroine and she had styled her personality on the brave orphan. A voracious early reader, she'd read all six books and often imagined she was Madeline in this her "second house" , which was like a modern-day orphanage. Although, of course, she knew she had it a lot better than Madeline:

"In an old house in Paris
That was covered in vines
Lived twelve little girls
In two straight lines."

Liv's well-fuelled imagination often ran away with her and she would tell "tall tales", as Aunty Jan called them, to get attention at school. These were mainly about her mother:

"She's an actress on location in the Bahamas in a film with Ryan Gosling. I'm going out there in the summer holidays when they have the party at the end; it's called a wrap party and she's sent me a really grown-up purple dress to wear for it."

"My mum's a vet and she's out in Africa working in a safari place. I'm going out there soon and she's going to take me to meet all the big five: elephants – my favourite and hers – and lions, leopards, buffalo and rhinos. We're staying in a tent with a lookout place really close to them all."

Then, when her school friends realised these travels hadn't happened, other stories had to be found: "Mum's really upset I can't join her as I don't have a passport; it's lost." And: "Mum got bitten by a tiger and is in hospital out in the middle of nowhere."

In the back of the diary were the "Facts Known So Far" section and the "Hypotheses" section.

Under "Facts Known":

- My name is ~~Olivia~~ LIV Knight, I am ~~six, seven, eight, nine~~, ten
- I was born on February 10th 1988 in Alderchurch Hospital
- I live at 23 Almond Crescent, Huddershall, and at 3, The Limes, Brimstoke
- I live with my dad in Huddershall but stay with Aunty Jan and Uncle Jeff a lot
- They are not really my aunty and uncle
- I have brown eyes and brown straight hair

- ~~I have a pet rabbit called Blossom which stays at Aunty Jan's and Uncle Jeff's~~
- I go to school at Saint Joseph's, Huddershall
- I have no brothers or sisters; I am an only child
- I have a birthmark in the shape of an artist's palette on the inside of my right arm
- I am allergic to penicillin
- I am allergic to spinach, cabbage and broccoli

And under "Hypotheses":

- I was found in a carrier bag left outside Aldechurch Hospital and my dad was lonely so kept me. Could be true but Dad still doesn't date anyone.
- I am really the daughter of someone royal, but they won't get me until I'm an adult as they don't want me being photographed. But I think they'd have got me more toys and money for Dad to take us to Greece on holiday.
- Dad got someone pregnant and is too ashamed to tell me. He still doesn't have a girlfriend, although Samantha from his work seems nice.
- My mum ran away when I was born, as she never wanted children and wanted to be a famous model. I can't see any famous models who look like me.
- My mum ran away when I was born because she didn't love Dad or me enough. But why won't Dad just tell me?
- Something else happened really scary like an alien abduction or she was murdered.

'Here you are, love. Two scoops of ice cream and a lake of sauce. That should keep you going.'

'Thanks, Aunty Jan.'

'You okay up here? Not too lonely?'

'No, I'm just going to write in my diary and then read a bit more of your *Anne of Green Gables* book. She's an orphan too.'

'You're no orphan, Livvy Lou.'

Janet kissed the top of Liv's head, breathing in her shampoo shine still present under the sweaty bed head and leaves her be.

THE SIXTEENTH ERA

2001

The year it was found that Dr Harold Shipman may have killed more than 300 patients since the 1970s.

68

Jenny

Never consistent about anything, Jenny just "happened" to check her breasts one morning whilst lazing in bed, reacquainting herself with her body after the rarity of sex (as Evie was at the in-laws). Yes, it was definitely a lump, but was it moveable? She hadn't a clue, but it seemed to get bigger every time her fingers found it, time after time, until, sitting in the GP's surgery, she was sure Dr Perry himself could see it growing through her top.

Suddenly fast-tracked, Jenny tried not to pull others onto this hurtling nightmare train. But she had to rely on both her poleaxed mum and John's parents to babysit when her world transformed overnight from ignorant bliss to breast cancer clinics and new head-scarfed friends.

Jenny always had the feeling life was dished out in dollops of good and bad, as if by some omnipresent dinner lady, who, if you didn't eat all your greens (that is, refrain from obscenities, gossip and hangovers), well, you didn't just miss out on the gypsy cream tart, but you had to stay behind and do penance, for example, have breast cancer. So, she wasn't in the "why me?" category but found herself palling up with those with a similar "that's life" philosophy (even many who had more bad dollops than good) and who shared the worst waiting room magazines, a backrow giggle in the provided yoga sessions and a celebratory cocktail at the end of each "green" week of chemo.

John accompanied her for the first few treatments but, although grateful for his loyalty, wished he would make himself useful elsewhere; she didn't want anyone else to be a party to the strange fearful tedium of clinic days and the polite patient exchanges that never dared go "there":

'All right? Only three more, isn't it?'

'Better or worse than last time?'

'Getting used to it now.'

'Like your new scarf.'

'Julie not here today then?'

And Jenny thought by keeping it separate from home, then home wouldn't be tinged so much by her illness. Her mum offered too but Jenny told her she preferred her to conserve her energy to amuse Evie during the ensuing "red" weeks. This was one positive outcome for Evie and Gaga (Evie had been unable to say Grandma for quite a while and "Gaga" had stuck, to everyone's amusement. Gaga took pride in her new moniker, despite the seeming slight). They developed an even closer bond and Evie would run past her sleeping mother on her return from school to find the latest fairy notes Gaga had hidden for her in their garden. The fairies also hid sweets, made a lot of meals for the whole family, and seemed to tidy and iron without the huffing and puffing Jenny made about such domestic chores.

It was also amazing the friends that came out of the woodwork – with hampers on the doorstep and encouraging texts – and the others that disappeared into the same woodwork, like Claire. Some people she knew felt they'd be tainted with her bad luck, some just didn't know how to absorb hair loss and nausea into the school gate group chat of spelling lists and bedtime routines... and others, well, they just didn't care. She couldn't quite place Claire into any category; she just felt so hurt by whom she had thought of as her closest, her "best" friend. In her own maelstrom of hormonal emotions and flirtations with death, she had no space to "accommodate" Claire's lack of any response at all; she knew Claire wouldn't be at her mother's deathbed; it was an excuse.

69
Claire

The patients and colleagues at her surgery saw her as a competent no-nonsense physio, efficient both with her time and advice, never getting personally involved, perhaps imagining she saved her more emotional connections for outside of work.

Claire wasn't "saving" them at all. Once again, her own struggle with such connections came into sharp focus, knowing she was lacking in her response to Jenny. She couldn't sit next to her and her slow, slow drip, drip of chemicals, or drop around trays of lemon chicken for the family, so she retreated into herself again. At the same time, Tony got in touch; he had met "someone", saying:

"After all, it's been over a decade, our lives have moved on and it's time for a divorce."

Oh, was it? They arranged to meet at a service station halfway between their respective new abodes; his in Seasalter with Samantha – *how simply saccharin.*

'I felt we owed each other this conversation, and I wanted to see how you are—'

'I'm fine. How's Samantha?'

'She understands we had a past, and respects I need to do this.'

'How very wonderful of her.'

'Claire—'

'Yes, that's me.'

'Can't we just talk... Don't you want to ask about—'

'NO!'

'Do you even open my letters or look at the photos?'

Claire got up abruptly, said she needed sugar and retook her seat like a racehorse in the starting stalls.

'Okay, I understand... I hope one day you'll be able to for all our sakes...'

He saw Claire was ready to go again and changed tactics.

'So, tell me, what's been happening in your life? Have you met anyone?

'Yes, plenty, I live in a very busy area.'

'You know what I mean.'

'Is it any of your business now? You presumably want to get married? Is she pregnant?'

'Well...'

'I take that as a yes; bully for you!'

'Claire—'

'Still me.'

'I will always, and if you let her, so will—'

Claire heard no more as, at that moment, her hand moved of its own accord to throw Tony's scalding black coffee in his face and she left with the sounds of his scream, and a waitress and others rushing to help.

On her way home, she passed a travel agent. She doubled back and parked. Her whole body still shaking. She gladly took the spare seat and waited, calming herself whilst the agent finished her call to Costa del Wherever.

'Sorry! How can we help you?'

'I'd like some last-minute winter sun please – anywhere.'

'For yourself or—'

Claire quickly shut that down:

'Yes, just me. As soon as possible. I've got some unexpected leave.'

'How about Morocco, we've got—'

'That'll do, thank you.'

The bemused travel agent booked Claire onto a flight to Marrakesh for the next day. Perfect, as she wanted just such an indecipherable cacophony all around her to drown her own voices in her head. Cacophony: "an unpleasant mixture of loud sounds" – yes, that's what she was right now. She called in sick to work, left a message on Jenny's answer machine saying her mother was dying and left a message on her mother's phone saying a friend was dying and she wouldn't be going home as planned. It was to have been the first time in three years. Since that last time.

Back then, she thought she was pregnant and phoned out of the blue to say she was coming so they could clear the house of any "unwanteds". She had wanted to tell them about this new baby, her "deliverance". They were serving up Sunday roast chicken as usual and were so stunned, that the very rare happening of a forsaken roast occurred. And she miscarried just one week later at thirteen weeks and now… well, she wasn't going. Two gin and tonics on the plane and she felt quietened, for a bit.

However, only two days in, Claire realised she needed to leave. Moroccan souks were no place to cope with stress and even the five-star mini bar had been unable to drown her circus of feelings.

Claire arrived back on an earlier flight with the spoils of manic buying, closed the door on her house and holed up. Formerly, the magnolia walls hosted only one picture, that of Evie in Jenny's arms the day after her arrival all squint-eyed and wary of the world, which appealed to Claire as she shared the same approach. Now, the uncomfortable two-seaters had squishy sequin mirrored cushions, the beds had vibrant throws and the walls had Moorish hangings lining the new broad staircase that linked the two formerly separate flats. Her flat had personality at last, even if the owner didn't. The impromptu trip and these furnishings had emptied her bank account and, as she looked at the bank statement (her only post on the doormat), she realised she was hurtling ever closer towards that known cliff edge.

Holed up, she hoped it would pass but it didn't work like that this time. When she'd gone out to get more wine after a three-day bender, she'd nearly run into a tree. Instead, unaware of where she was driving, she found herself at Jenny's – her mind, she felt, was breaking into a thousand pieces.

70
Jenny

Jenny had lied to John, well, a white lie; something they never did. But Jenny knew he'd be furious with her in her current state fretting about Claire when he thought Claire could take care of herself. For some reason, she never talked with him about Claire's past; she supposed it was because she didn't want him to think any less of their friend, although she knew she was undervaluing his compassion. It had just become a separate part of her locked away with the bulimia, although John knew about that too. Oh, well, there was no time to wonder why, recognising as soon as she opened the door to her wild-eyed friend that she was having some sort of a psychotic episode and she needed to get her to hospital right away.

'You've got to go faster; Tony's chasing me again.'

'Why would he do that?'

'He wants me to kill more babies. I can't do any more. I can't do it; it hurts too much!'

Oh, lordy, Claire really did need help fast.

'It's okay, Claire; you're safe with me. We're going to go somewhere where you'll be away from all that.'

Jenny crunched on peppermints the whole madcap journey to the hospital, both to quell her ever-present nausea and also to crunch down on some of the angst permeating the car. If John had known he would indeed have felt Jenny needed to stay away from her friend, for her own health and that of Evie's too, so there cemented the dark truth of Claire's borderline personality disorder and Jenny's feeling of culpability for her friend's mental health.

'Where are you taking me, Jenny?'

Jenny clicked the lock on the doors and put her foot down.

'As I said, Claire... somewhere safe; you've got to trust me, okay?'

'Okay.'

And, remarkably, Claire fell into an exhausted sleep, only waking up as Jenny pulled on the handbrake outside the hospital.

Jenny knew deep down that ECT hadn't "caused" this but she had a deep skein of responsibility for not challenging the diagnosis of depression all those years ago. She felt that if Claire had been given the right diagnosis and the right treatment from the outset, well, she may have been able to have managed better for all these years.

'Out you get, love. Nobody can get you here, I promise.'

'Promise!'

'Yes, I promise.'

Once Claire was clerked and asleep in a bed in a quiet side room, Jenny tiptoed away. She rang John to tell him Claire had had a small accident, that's why she'd been unable to answer his calls, but she was now on her way home.

She had only been driving for five minutes when she had to pull over and be sick. It was caused partly by the chemo and partly by churning feelings about Claire's situation, but, mostly, by the distaste of lying to John.

71
Claire

It was possibly the strangest Christmas and New Year ever. Yes, there was an enormous tree dressed in the lacklustre way of institutions, jangling jingling music and outside the trees were painted with frost, but the walls were still blank hospital walls, and her mind was a blank medicated mind.

The only visitor Claire had was Jenny, who had come before John finished work for the holidays so that he wasn't any the wiser. They agreed he needn't know, as Claire was still very reticent to share that part of her life. Her parents too were none the wiser, still believing Claire didn't need or want them in her life. Jenny had bought her some paints and a sketchbook and urged her to open them before Christmas day so she could use them immediately.

The art classes were really helping and Sasha, the art therapist, seemed to be sitting inside her mind alongside her and, most incredibly, to be accepting of all the junk therein. Claire had always thought somehow she was missing an essential ingredient making her "less", as if that final seasoning of pepper that lifts a dish, pulling it together, in her had been omitted. Here, she was able to forget that for a while. Sasha had even been the one to hint that perhaps she may have a borderline personality disorder, and from her, it didn't seem like such a bad diagnosis for her particular collection of symptoms.

'I think the way you've described your life thus far you may indeed have BPD.'

'Go on – me sounding like a psych!'

'Yes. You've learned too well, grasshopper! Seriously, Claire, BPD has a negative impact on how someone thinks about themselves. If you have indeed got BPD, well, I hope you'll get the right support now, so life can feel easier.'

'Fire away then. What else?'

'Well, also the way they think about others and the world in general can be pretty negative too.'

'Tick.'

'You've often mentioned you have had difficulty with relationships?'

'Just a tad!'

'Well, that's often a signifier.'

'Don't most people though?'

'Agreed! But in BPD, the relationships are particularly unstable.'

'They've been that all right.'

'Unstable moods, bad self-image...'

'All ticks, yeah.'

'And the impulsive behaviour which often leads to risk-taking and self-injury.'

'Bang to rights.'

'It's not an "accusation", Claire, but it may hopefully help with understanding how you're feeling, getting suitable treatment... and, as I said, well, living an easier life.'

Claire, once more, looked up Borderline Personality Disorder and was comforted by statistics – that one in one hundred people have BPD, so maybe she was one of the other ninety-nine lucky ones and this would all pass. But, then again, it did always pass before but also kept coming back; maybe there was something in this.

In the art room, which was sunlit whatever the weather, Sasha summoned strange playlists that suited each session. *Chopin's Nocturne Op.9 No.2* for watercolours and rainy days, *Guns and Roses's Live and Let Die,* for abstract crazy collages and – she was very partial to a musical – *Can you Feel the Love Tonight?* from *The Lion King* made quite a few appearances for anything from applique to calligraphy. Today, it was *Louis Armstrong's What a Wonderful World.*

'Now, I am going to turn the music off, so we have moments of almost silence in the room...

'Notice what disrupts that moment of stillness for you. Go back to the drawing of your head, where you drew the shape where your brain might be... Ian, great, come on in, here's the head you drew, we've just started... Mark it up into different sections of different sizes. Fill these sections with whatever is taking up your brain space right now and, importantly, what you would like to be in there.'

'My brain isn't big enough, that's the problem.'

'For this, Claire, we're lucky as we have larger paper... here!'

'Thanks.'

Ian sat in the corner shredding his picture, but Sasha slid another piece beneath his nose and carried on.

'Your largest section might be used for your big thoughts – maybe they are the heaviest, or maybe they are big dreams for now, just out of reach but tantalisingly positive – and for smaller sections, you may decide to fill with whims, musings or feelings.'

Ian picked up a pencil and Sasha added wax crayons and paints to his table.

Minutes melded into more minutes...

'Now, you may like to add colour to each section: yellow denoting say... sunflowers and happy thoughts. Whatever and wherever your brain looks, feels like and places it takes you to, this is your time to let it all out on paper and, yes, we have plenty, Claire!'

Claire took out Jenny's gift and was so transported by her task that, until Sasha tapped her on her shoulder and told her she was shutting the art room, she hadn't realised two and half hours had gone by without pain.

Her mind had opened, literally, onto larger and larger pieces of paper. It was like some bacon slicer radiologist had taken slivers of her brain and found tumours but also light. At the end of many such sessions, Claire was gradually accepting that the black, brown and sludge-green crevices were just that, just smaller sections of her mind, and that she was noticing actual orange, yellow and, Jenny's favourite colour, turquoise, occurring more and more in larger sections. It wasn't just Louis Armstrong's vision of the world Claire envisioned but her own garden. She drew delphiniums, lupins and even bright marigolds.

Claire suddenly felt she would soon be ready to get back to that very garden to grow seedlings and maybe even get back to work. Her discharge letter said "depression", so she squirrelled that BPD thought away as no more had been said about it.

72
Janet

Janet was as surprised to hear from Jenny as Jenny was to hear Janet answer the phone, "clearly alive", but both were grateful to share the news of Claire's admission. But once again Janet was denied contact. She had visited Father McBride for confessional more times than usual but that didn't assuage the guilt.

Luckily, home kept her busy and distracted, especially with Ella now relying on her to have Alfie, her six-month-old. Post maternity leave, Ella had managed to take her clients from her salon job with her and set up on her own, hairdressing in people's homes, which was meant to fit around regular childcare but, of course, it was far more erratic than that. Ella needed to respond to clients' whims to have their roots done today!

They only did emergency foster placements and, thankfully, were quiet for a while so Janet was enjoying being a full-blown "granny" at last. Liv was with them more and more as, at thirteen, Tony was having problems dealing with her fluctuating emotions. Always a black-and-white individual, he couldn't quite grasp the black-through-to-white-missing-grey range of Liv's opinions and moods and, relievedly, left that to Janet and Jeff. He was there to provide lifts to youth clubs, money for shopping trips and attendance at school parents' evenings.

Janet particularly loved him reporting back after such school evenings; he was so proud of his clever daughter who surpassed his achievements in all subjects and, thankfully, hadn't had her head turned by boys. He did wonder to Janet about "Sunny" written on Liv's pencil case and confessed he'd been too terrified to ask. Janet said "Sunny" was a six-year-old Palomino mare who clearly wasn't distracting her, so, not to worry. Tony undoubtedly adored her but struggled parenting a very strong-minded child of the very alien, to him, female sex on his own. Thus, Janet enjoyed being the buffer and conduit for many a difficult conversation they brought to her fireside. And they all enjoyed getting the favoured tickets to watch her in every school play, from the nativities to "Annie" and as a recently fearsome "Rizzo" in *Grease*.

Liv, now she was thirteen, was trusted to babysit Alfie for a few hours with Janet elsewhere in the house, of course, but nevertheless, she loved being able to soothe him and make him smile and she learned more nursery rhymes than even Janet had in her wide-ranging compendium. Janet would listen at the door to Liv's sweet voice singing, *Half a pound of tuppeny rice* for the umpteenth time just to get Alfie to giggle on cue at the "pop!" in *Pop! Goes the Weasel*. How easy love could be.

Janet knelt on her now creaky knees nightly and thanked God for these blessings:

'Thank you, Lord, for keeping Tom safe at the moment and also Amar, Anjali, Bertie, Chloë, Damina, Ella...'

(She had learned to do them alphabetically in case she missed anyone.)

'Tisha and Will and all other vulnerable children – may they feel your love. Please pour your blessings on Nigel and Christine for their family, for Jeff's chest and may he not work too hard... May

Mrs Hunter have the strength to leave and Fiona the strength to stay. And, please, please, Lord, guide my Claire and help her find her rightful path… and know we are here for her. Thank you for bringing me Jenny and all my other gifts in life. Amen.'

Jenny was her lifeline, and she became very fond of this implausible friend of her daughter's and met her several times – Alfie on her lap, Evie on Jenny's – both fielding spoonfuls of apple puree and enjoying exchanging proud tales of baby progress before the thorny topic of Claire was inevitably broached.

73
Jenny

John was very reluctant to see Jenny return to work so soon. Thus, Jenny had hated the double life she'd created; sneaking off to visit Claire on either the pretext of work or her own hospital appointments, depending on whom she was talking to. She'd told herself she hadn't actually lied; she was skirting the truth to keep a good friend's secret and, so, John was none the wiser. Anyway, Claire seemed to be getting better, so all of life would soon be the new normal again. She smugly patted herself on the back for encouraging Claire to paint; she knew how much she liked colour in her garden, so had hoped it might link her back to her place of comfort – and it had.

Anyway, Evie was about to have her first proper birthday party and had invited her whole class of friends so there was plenty to occupy Jenny's mind. They had decided that "birth" day that Christmas Eve would stay as that, and Evie would have her birthday on the 5th of January, which was long enough away from New Year hangovers but still near enough to be entering her next year feeling special and not squeezed by others' celebrations. Not that either Jenny or John would ever let Evie get squeezed by anything, not even a sibling if one came along (they had been trying for years, ever hopeful).

So, for more reasons than John and Jenny dare discuss, Evie's fifth birthday party was going to be one to remember.

'Hi, Lucy, go on in. Evie's waiting for you in the lounge.'

Which she was, sitting like a princess on a throne awaiting her subjects, dressed accordingly, of course.

And twenty-three children later:

'Hi, Leo, go on in. Evie's in the lounge; you'll hear them all!'

Party frocks abandoned and pirate outfits donned, with gaudy parrots on shoulders, they squealed outside to board the ship, which dear John had made out of sleepers in the back garden with an upended sail to act as a shield from the surprisingly absent inclement weather. So, after pin-the-eyepatch-on-the-pirate, walk-the-plank and "cannon balls" – which John had to curtail when Imogen got hit hard in the face – she and the rest of the party were distracted by the grand treasure hunt. John had also made a huge treasure chest and buried it under a pile of straw, which they still found wafting in the ensuing breezy days appearing like Davy Jones's ghost. Jenny filled it with their treasure party bags but also clever clues for each one to find out where they were sitting for the pirate banquet. Evie had, of course, wanted her best friends near her, and Jenny knew from other parties who to split from whom, so felt any further dramas were forestalled – as they were, amazingly.

Jenny was absorbed with more pink plastic presents to accommodate, torn wrapping paper and the inevitable egg and cress ground into the sheepskin rug, jelly on the sofa, curtains and goodness knew where else. Then there was the collecting, but reluctant to leave, tipsy, proseccoed parents, grateful to have been off the leash for three whole hours, with someone else hosting the riots; so, wonderfully neither cancer nor Claire entered her mind for quite a while.

74
Claire

By February, Claire was well enough to return to work part-time and life was buoying her along into Summer all of a sudden. It became a new tradition that after each of Jenny's six-monthly check-ups, Claire would plan a girly treat away "like the good old days" she said. Jenny encouraged this quality time. Claire knew it was to "bolster" her and was a chance to be "reviewed by Nurse Jenny" but also knew Jenny needed the escape herself, just as much as ever.

Five going on fifteen, Evie felt that she should join in, so a much tamer weekend was substituted. Claire was confused as to whether she was jealous of this interloper or delighted to be loved as the indulgent Aunty Claire she had settled on being. This dichotomy presented as her flip-flopping from the heart-piercing but immediate gratification of spontaneous child hugs and giggles to the deferred delight of having her friend to herself after bedtime. They had gone to Center Parcs for the weekend; Jenny felt this was an extravagance, but Claire enjoyed using her money to treat them: "After all, who else do I spend my earnings on?"

Their lodge was in the woods to Evie's delight, and it had an outdoor jacuzzi to everyone's delight. The assumed identities were more low-key than usual. As Evie liked being grown up and occasionally going out for afternoon tea with them both, Claire had plumped for the three of them reversing this and all being nearly six and going out to play. Jenny only agreed to "playing" in the vicinity of the lodge as it felt wrong in Evie's company to be "other" than who she was somehow. Also, their other characters were escapes – returning to childhood, seemingly, was not.

Evie loved helping them dress in their costumes of ballet tutu skirts and neon hair accessories, taking charge as the conferred eldest:

'Jenny.'

'Mummy! Oh, okay.'

'Jenny, you can be the monkey in the middle.'

And then a squabble ensued "in character" between Claire and Jenny about who should be the first "monkey"/who was "it" and who held which end of the skipping rope. Evie was soon tired of her aged six adults and said in a haughty "grown up" voice that she was going "off to do her hair and make-up"!

Outfits abandoned and, thankfully, their usual identities reassumed, they had a wonderful time spent mostly in the lazy river or eating burgers. On return, Evie reported to her dad that both had been well-behaved when she'd had a word with them! She also told her dad that Claire needed a husband like her mummy had – and could he fix it! Claire demurred quickly but not before she'd seen John and Jenny lock eyes conspiratorially.

Of course, as she expected, there was a dinner date arranged not long after:

'An old friend of John's is coming to stay, and they'll be 'boring on' about historic buildings, so you've got to come and keep me company. He's here the whole weekend but just help me out for supper – pleeease?'

She agreed to Jenny's delight and her own dread. The Saturday in question came around all too quickly and Claire, annoyed with herself, spent ages choosing outfits, even though Jenny had suggested the "purple fitted dress that shows off your slim frame, you bitch!"

Wearing the purple after all, Claire turned up and let herself in the back door as she usually did now and came across a bearded John opening a bottle of wine in the kitchen; they could have been brothers. Claire relaxed. Okay... so it was an auspicious start with wine in hand and all...

'You must be Claire. Hi, I'm Owen but my friends call me Smudge.'

'Why? That's a cat's name, surely?'

Jenny winced at her friend's barbs out already, but Owen laughed.

'My surname's Smith, hence, Smudge.'

'Sounds like cockney slang.'

John joined in:

'Oh, don't get him started. He's an expert!'

'As you asked! Inky Smudge is cockney rhyming slang for judge and sometimes a photographer.'

Claire was relaxing, just slightly.

'With my luck, Claire would mean something obscene!'

'No, you're safe! "Claire Rayners" – mean anything?'

'Er, you're saying I'm a no-brainer!"

'No, not from all I've heard already! Claire Rayners – pair of trainers!'

'Oh, that's a relief!'

And it all was a "great relief", a wonderfully relaxed evening and as she left, Owen asked if she would be popping round for Sunday lunch, which Jenny leapt on and said she must. Owen had been divorced for three years and was just "emerging"; he had his children alternate weekends and so was busy the following weekend but was keen not to leave a further meeting any longer. As Sunday went well for Claire too, she found herself actually relaxed enough to agree to see Owen later that week.

Thursday, "Owen day", arrived with prophetic storms. Claire pulled up to the halfway meeting point, a restaurant with good reviews. She was far too early, of course, and so had too much time to stew, to reapply makeup in her driving mirror, in poor light, thus bodge it up, and wipe it off again. As Claire was an aficionado of Liza Minelli's school of make-up, that is, "Find your best feature and emphasise it like mad, to detract from the rest of you", this entailed a lot of mascara. Hence, on removing it, she left herself looking as if she'd been crying for hours, which she now felt like doing.

She saw Owen park and look around for her, as she now skulked in the shadows, prevaricating. A few minutes later, she plucked up the courage to follow him in and was warmly greeted by a hug from his wet coat. She slid out of her similarly wet, but unsuitable parka and Owen complimented her on her dress. Instead of this easing her, she saw it as him trying to overlook her disastrous make up and her "prickles" began. With no Jenny and John as her wingmen, she just couldn't do this and found herself spewing comebacks and putdowns even before Owen had the chance to speak. After all, she was the supposed BPD queen of "unstable relationships", wasn't she?

Owen looked bemused and crestfallen. Starters of uncomplicated soup quietly and complicatedly consumed, Claire couldn't remain any longer and, throwing a twenty-pound note on the table, mumbled

'Sorry, this was a mistake...'

And left.

Claire, once again, returned to her empty house and crashed down hard this time. Jenny rang late to see how the date had gone, as she had just got in from her own night out with her new friend the seeming "goddess", Laura. This further compounded Claire's black state of mind and her desperate loneliness.

75
Jenny

Laura, Jenny's friend from chemo, lived an hour away and they met midway between them every month for a meal and a glass of wine in the smart surroundings of The Golden Fleece. The pub was chosen amidst shared black humour of newly growing scalp stubble and it provided a chance to dress up and reclaim their former selves. Each meeting was a necessary offload for both with someone who truly understood, and it became a protective ritual that underlined that they had come through their treatment and were still there.

'How are you?'

'Good.'

'Really?'

'Yes, I'm actually not thinking about cancer all the fucking time!'

'I'll "cheers" to that!'

The gradual friend dance of increasing liberty and intimacy was fast-forwarded by their shared cancer treatment experiences and manifesto of seizing life (although, to be fair, Jenny had always seized life). So, both were brave enough to talk of sharing more than just an evening but actually going away for a whole indulgent weekend, earlier on in the evolution of most friendships.

Even though Evie was growing up fast, Jenny still hated leaving her, but John was taking her to see *Finding Nemo* and then out for "grown up tea" (that is, actually sitting down at McDonald's) not just a takeaway, so she knew she wouldn't be missed! Ten minutes into the journey with the radio on without nursery rhymes, she was singing at the top of her voice feeling so lucky to be alive. Laura was something in HR for the Hilton group and so had got them discounts on a double suite at their Park Lane hotel for their first girls' night away.

Shoes kicked off, as Jenny had blisters already from the infrequently worn "heels", they flopped on the huge beds and gigglingly drank a smuggled-in bottle of Champagne, soaked up with a bag of Doritos. After a quick nap and Jenny's plasters applied, they hit the town for a hugely calorific meal, more bubbles (being sensible with Prosecco this time) and then to claim their seats at the Prince Edward Theatre for *Mamma Mia*. They walked the one-and-a-half miles back to their hotel drunkenly singing Abba's *Here we go again* where they were prompted to shush as they entered the foyer and did their best sober impressions until entering their room.

Jenny remembered to check her phone and texted John to say they were in bed safely and early, and skimmed Claire's four messages to make sure there was nothing urgent – there wasn't.

With more stashed bubbles they had drunk themselves sober and serious midnight conversations arose:

'I couldn't do it again, could you? The chemo.'

'I don't know, as we lie here now, no. But, if it bought me more time with Evie and John, maybe I'd have to say yes.'

'But we're not going to have to.'

'I'll drink to that!'

A two-hour full English breakfast with endless toast and coffee cemented both this deeper friendship and their hungover stomachs. Together, they faced the prospect of going home to Sunday ironing and life.

THE SEVENTEENTH ERA

2002

The year that 'Miss B' – a quadriplegic – was granted the right to die by the High Court.

76
Claire

Claire knew she was on a precipice of change; firstly, the Owen thing and then Jenny's betrayal re the weekends away with Saint Laura, who apparently had "loads" in common with Jenny. She called them The Cancer Sisters to Jenny's amusement, but she wasn't trying to be funny this time. She had been googling "Borderline Personality Disorder" frequently and planned to ask for the new "dialectic therapy", no longer wanting to be this monster whom she had no control over. It emerged too often, and it scared her. And she knew so many others often perceived her as odd.

Another final straw was bumping into Evie, who was out shopping with a friend and the friend's mum.

'Oh! Hello, Evie.'

'Hi, Aunty Claire. You look just like Mummy!'

'Do I?'

'Yes, I know why. You're wearing Mummy's clothes?'

'Oh! These aren't Mummy's; we just have the same taste.'

'Well, you look funny; you don't look like you.'

'I'm sorry, Evie, I'll try and be more "me" next time.'

She smiled at the bemused mum, made her excuses and just managed to get to her car before the shakes overtook her completely. She had squirrelled away quite a few of Jenny's outfits when they were living together, as Jenny never had a clue where anything was;

it was usually on her floor-drobe or in the dirty washing mountain. Jenny was the sort of person who liked to put socks in the washing machine to see if they reunited, not the sort of person who paired socks cuffed together in a mesh bag, or who catalogued clothes – like Claire – so she certainly wouldn't miss the odd outfit.

These outfits had occasional outings further from home where Claire indeed did try and pass herself off as Jenny. She had been upping the frisson of discovery but now had gone too far. She would be mortified if Jenny knew, but it had become a habit of excitement, yes, but also of comfort. As "Jenny" she occupied more space, not just physically, but she allowed herself to be more present in the world, more visible and with Jenny's "armour", she could adopt this likeable openhearted persona. It was, after all, just a natural progression from their dressing-up times away, but Claire knew it wasn't natural and she couldn't keep defining herself by usurping Jenny's identity.

Claire had planned to be open with her GP but when she sat in the patient's seat and saw in front of her this new young face, barely shaving, who asked so jauntily: 'What can we do for you today?' she stalled. Unfortunately for Claire, he was a locum who obviously was expecting tonsillitis, cystitis or any other "-itis" other than a psychiatric condition. She felt wrong-footed.

'Oh, I am having trouble sleeping and feeling a tad low again. I've been depressed before so I was thinking it would be best if I went back on my anti-depressants, the doxepin. It works well for me.'

'I'm sorry to hear that. How's your sleep?

'Not too bad.'

'Appetite?'

'Nothing ever wrong with that!'

Claire was doing her cheery best.

'Are you managing to work still?'

'Yes, I'm part-time now and it's fine.'

'Concentration okay?'

'Yes.'

'May I ask, what work do you do?'

'I'm a physio.'

'Well, then, you'll know the questions we usually ask people who present with depression. So, do you have thoughts that you would be better off dead, or thoughts of hurting yourself?'

'No, doctor, I don't. I just need the tablets for a while to get back on an even keel. I'll be fine.'

Lies all lies, but with that, a prescription was written having promised she'd make a follow-up appointment and Claire collected her tablets. And, yes, she slept better at night, but she felt sleepy and numb most of the time, dragging herself through each week.

One form of treatment was helpful though, and that was her online creative writing course; she could legitimately "be" anyone but herself on paper. At the end of the last term, her tutor had persuaded her to enter her short story into a competition and, to her surprise, she won the second prize of £250 and a commendation from the judges for her dark, insightful style:

"*Once upon a time there was a man called Beck who knew all about suicide and its ideations. I assume he was a man, as they often are; women weren't allowed to be clever then. Maybe that's when suicide became popular with our fair sex. Now, it seems, that male suicide is on the increase, but I deviate which is appropriate for someone of a deviant nature. There I go again. Well, Beck hit the nail on the head about such things and stirred them into the magic pot of suicide ingredients. No tail of newt but black, black dog, crushed spirit and dead, dead babies...*"

When writing this, Claire had looked up the definition of "suicide" and wasn't surprised to see: "the intention of taking one's own life" but was a little taken back at: "the destruction of one's own interests or prospects". So, she was more proficient at this than she first thought...

Her mother contacted her as her father's COPD was worse. Claire always thought it ironic he should have a respiratory condition with her particular respiratory expertise. She made excuses not to visit, yet again, but couldn't resist showing off for once about her writing prize, although she didn't agree to send a copy. She knew they wouldn't be around for much longer and couldn't work out how she felt about that particular loss. After much vacillation, she did relent and sent some breathing exercises her dad could do.

THE EIGHTEENTH ERA

2003

The year the Human Genome Project was completed, heralding possible cures for many diseases in the future.

77
Olivia

At fifteen years old she was already armoured with an arch look and a quippy comeback. Her formerly glossy chestnut hair, brittle by a misadventure, the purple dyed frizz now framed those knowing kohled eyes – of her mother's, apparently; a rare crumb of information (unwittingly given). The whole Goth look was betrayed by her dad's kind, ready smile.

Her Aunty Jan put down the overflowing laundry basket with a sigh.

'Two adults and four children currently; surely the council could help with a new washing machine?' She sat resignedly, folding her busy hands in her ample lap and prepared to fully engage in this conversation that she had been avoiding:

'Dad says I need to get my GCSEs first, but I don't need friggin physics!'

'Liv! Language!'

'Can't I even say "friggin"?'

'No, cos I know what it's replacing! And you, out all of us, have got a much better vocabulary than that. So please use it!'

Olivia, or Liv as she liked to be called now, shrugged.

'And yes, I understand your frustration. I don't think I've ever made use of the block and tackle theory yet!'

'What?'

'It's physics – if I remember! But my point is it's a hurdle everyone has to go over – to your future. And the exams are there just in case you do change your mind later and want to be an astrophysicist, a botanist or whatever.'

'I just want to be a magician or an artist like Dad.'

'Even magicians need to know how many rabbits are in a hat!'

'Haha!'

'And your dad did all his exams first, didn't he?'

'Yes but—'

'It's just another six months, love, that's all. It'll fly by, believe me.'

'I don't.'

'Well, that's your prerogative as a teenager.'

'Prerog what?'

'You'd know if you did your exams.'

'Haha! What's for tea?'

Aunty Jan left the laundry mountain and turned her attention to the potatoes bubbling away on the hob for the shepherd's pie, just as Uncle Jeff arrived home from the school run with foster children: Louis, six; Thea, eight, and Amar, twelve. There was no time to discuss Olivia and her future, until all were tucked into bed at long last and Aunty Jan was able to hug her cocoa in her recent birthday "Best Mum" mug (from a former foster child) and settle her thoughts.

'I just think Liv has a point. It didn't help Claire, did it – forcing her to study?'

'We didn't force her!'

'Well, she was more reluctant than Nigel.'

'She was, she IS more "anything" in too many ways. Anyway, comparisons are odious, as my dear ole mum used to say.'

'Yep, you're right. And Liv is very much her own person. And she's also reasonable like her dad.'

'Exactly. Don't fret, Jan, we've enough on our plates with Louis seeing his mum this weekend. Leave Liv's education to her dad. She's back there from Monday anyway.'

'Yeah, you're probably right.'

'Huh, just probably! I'll take her back – you're seeing that Jenny woman, aren't you, on Monday?'

'I'd like to.'

'Can't understand why.'

'Well, she's been ill and, well, I...'

'Yes, but what is she to you?'

'A link to Claire. She's obviously a good friend and I just thought I'd get the lie of the land to see if she'd let us in at last – all of us.'

Jeff harrumphed and picked up the TV remote to catch the ten o'clock news; the conversation over. But Janet knew he understood.

Liv was in the habit of picking up most information of any interest either whilst feigning sleep on car journeys or presumed deafness due to Sirenia screaming *Into the Eye of a Storm* in her earphones or whilst sitting on the stairs, as she was now.

As she sat craning her neck to get as close as she dared, with one arm clutching the landing bannister and the other perilously hanging onto the worn carpet, she latched onto these new scraps of information to mull later and record in her diary.

Liv had many gaping holes in her past. Her dad was frustratingly unedifying (a word she had looked up and used a lot in connection with her dad) in his curation of these events. She used "curation" accurately too; enjoying English only for this reason: to have the tools to label behaviours in order to understand more.

She had been told she was a "good baby" but thought maybe she had unwittingly learned to be a good baby – knowing, somehow, there was enough trouble going on elsewhere without her adding to it. But this was the problem: life always had seemed "elsewhere". And life was still happening elsewhere, a life that pertained to her but didn't include her – the sense of events untold.

Her Aunty Jan's reaction was always:

'Don't be daft, love, you have an over-active imagination, that's all.'

... and it never felt right.

And nobody, not even her pushover dad, would ever talk about her mother.

THE NINETEENTH ERA

2006

The year that a French woman received the first face transplant.

78
Claire

It was eighteen years since Oliver died. This particular anniversary hit her harder than most.

Each year she had quietly celebrated his birthday by blowing out the requisite number of candles, indulging herself in a cry and wondering what he would have been like at five, twelve, etcetera. But, eighteen, my... he would be off to uni to study zoology or music possibly, or to the pub legally with his plumbing apprenticeship mates. Claire realised she was painting a picture of him following his grandad's footsteps and that thought punched her in the solar plexus. She had recently read anxiety could cause acute pain in the solar plexus stemming from the adrenal gland kickstarting the fight or flight response. She could write her whole life-long case study, or maybe a novel this time, based on her own "adrenals" – she would call it *Heartbeat Hotel* – hah!

She'd had a "Thinking of You" card from her mum and dad and she'd put it on her sparse mantelpiece alongside Oliver's plaster footprints. The only things she had to offer at this newly created altar were his birth name-band (which she had lifted from her jumper drawer, hitherto untouched since she had squirrelled it there on moving in) – and his poem.

Each year she added a line to her "Oliver poem", summarising the latest missed milestones and more, forcing herself to live out each stage missed. It began:

"My Oliver,

Cradle-capped head turns, crusty eyes open, perfect pools of past wisdom anoint mine,

Never to be dry-eyed again.

Sodden nappy trampolines you to standing, first uncertain steps into my astonished arms.

A shape of you, and for you, remains.

Pureed ammunition hurled from highchair battleground, victory of spoon in gurgling Cupid's bow. Laughter lost in time.

Sturdy arms banging drums, knocking down brick towers destroying my hard heart, I'm undone. And remain an unclosable wound."

... etcetera.

This year, she added:

"Hug now so strong, yet still never to be fiercer than mine. Go forth, my Oliver, I couldn't and cannot hold onto you anymore..."

Writing was becoming her main source of catharsis, however maudlin her verse; a glass of fizz and a piece of his birthday cake were a balm. But nothing really helped, and she had never felt so lonely. She thought of ringing Jenny, but Claire had never told her of her baby's birthdate or any information at all and so didn't know about this particular hole that annually gaped a bit wider.

79
Olivia

Liv wanted her eighteenth birthday party at Aunty Jan and Uncle Jeff's local village hall, as she had her previous parties there and it wasn't that far for her friends to come. She also wanted to feel "'other" somehow by not having it somewhere predictable.

Before her guests arrived, she was in the toilets reapplying her "natural look" makeup (which her Uncle Jeff had teased added inches to the circumference of her head) and she overheard her dad and Aunty Jan talking about her, so, of course, she had to tune in.

'Well, I'm sure she will see it through – the number of times she watches "Waterloo Road" she won't even need the teacher training!'

'She's done so well, bless her, despite everything. How proud are you, eh, Tony?'

'Hugely. And you. If it hadn't been for you two... well, I'd never have managed on my own. But we've got her to adulthood between us.'

'Don't set me off!'

At that point, her Uncle Jeff came over and said the DJ had arrived. It was then all hands on deck to bring in lights, speakers, etcetera, and to find a suitable place for Ella's cake which was the centrepiece of the huge buffet. Ella had excelled herself; it was made in the shape of an open book with a tennis racquet "bookmark" and a black spider's web covering it all, representing her Goth era. Liv insisted food wasn't needed but, of course, the "adults" overruled: 'As there's going to be "some" alcohol, there has to be food – no arguments!' As if a sausage roll could filter Noah's hidden half-bottle of vodka!

The party was a great success, with the adults staying mostly out of sight in the kitchen. The DJ played *Hips Don't Lie* by Shakira at least five times, and it was only when Jan recognised another song that Liv played a lot, *Bad Day* by Daniel Powter, that a cloud gathered over those same adults.

'Listen to the lyrics, Jeff, this is the one she's been playing over and over.'

'And?'

'The line "You tell me *don't lie*".'

'Jan, love, you've got to let this go.'

'What kind of Christians are we though, Jeff, to keep this from her now she's officially an adult?'

'It's her dad's decision, Jan.'

'No... Yes, you're right – it's never been mine.'

At that point, the inevitable unstable conga wove in every way possible, signalling the end of the night.

THE TWENTIETH ERA

2012

The year the UK hosted their third Olympic games.

80
Jenny

Jenny and Claire were both turning fifty that year, born a month apart yet they couldn't have been more Different. Their approach to that big milestone was obviously very different too.

Claire would only agree to a sleepover supper at Jenny and John's, saying she wanted to get hammered whilst eating vats of John's special beef bourguignon. Of course, they spoiled her with a box of fifty silly and touching individually wrapped presents, such as a monogrammed trowel. And, of course, Claire went all out for Jenny's fiftieth and uncharacteristically even sent a card, not just signed, "from Claire" but it had been positively gushing:

"To my dear Jenny,

You don't realise what an amazing woman you are. I wish I had just half of your warmth, wisdom and humanity. Please believe in yourself and live your best life now.

Happy birthday and I wish you deservedly many happy years ahead – you old soak!

Much love

Claire X"

Claire "teenage sat" for Evie, as she often offered to, this time, so John could whisk Jenny away for a mystery weekend, which wasn't a mystery in the end as Jenny had wheedled it out of Claire. Evie wanted to stay with a friend, but Jenny won as she wanted to know exactly where Evie was, as recently doubts were creeping in about certain of her daughter's "arrangements".

'Mum, you've got to trust me! Tasha's parents are going to be there and it's not "really" a party…'

Jenny knew how much Claire adored Evie and wished she'd show it so Evie would love her in return. She sometimes caught Claire suddenly looking teary-eyed at Evie and always interpreted it as Claire's empty nest feelings bludgeoning her when she least expected them. Claire hid it by being the bossy Aunt: "feet off the sofa", "wash your hands before tea" and demanding pleases and thank yous, as if she was still a child.

'Well, you and Aunty Claire have fun too, she's so looking forward to it.'

'Oh, yeah… to torture me some more!

'Drama queen!'

'I'm serious, Mum. You don't know what she's like when you're not here. She'd have been an awful mum.'

'Well, just be kind for one night. Pleeease! And if you're good, we'll bring you back a stick of rock!'

They had one special night and two days in the lakes where they had honeymooned and, this time, it didn't rain a drop. Although the weather was perfect for the Champagne picnic hamper Claire had hidden in John's car, they had it on their four-poster bed overlooking Lake Derwent water, revisiting those early married days. Claire had also booked them into a very swanky restaurant, although they didn't have the heart to tell her they overslept that very afternoon and missed their booking. Instead they ate later at a simple local pub they found themselves eight years ago.

So, apart from birthday celebrations and breast cancer clinics, the years slipped by with them cherishing more "Evie firsts": the first school uniform hung on that labelled peg and that wobbly-lipped day from all three of them as they parted at Mrs Channing's door. It all seemed an age away. Next came her first big part in a school play as the narrator, her first and last violin concert and then, all of a sudden, her first day at secondary school with not a backward glance as she boarded the school bus into town, her mandatory school hat worn at a defiantly jaunty angle.

Two further miscarriages made Evie even more precious if possible, but John and Jenny steeled themselves not to mollycoddle an only child, as they had finally accepted that was what she was destined to be. Or rather, John had. Jenny tried so hard to hem in that over-protectiveness and also hope. She knew even, say at eighty, she'd never give up hoping and that possibly it would be hunger pangs that were joyously mistaken for a miracle baby growing in her old womb. All very characteristic of Jenny: that never-ending hope.

81
Claire

Claire was lucky her employers had always been so understanding of her little "wobbles" and "life events" as they so genteelly put it. Over the years, certain triggers meant Claire retreated for a few days or so to reset before she could brave the world again. When she asked for time off for her father's funeral, she had to remember if she had used his death as an alibi already, before this very real event.

When her brother had unusually rung, she had planned to make an excuse and not go as she normally did, but he had issued an ultimatum:

'Claire?'

'Nigel! What on Earth are you phoning for?'

'Hello to you too!'

'Sorry, well?'

'It's Dad; he died in hospital this morning. His lungs finally packed up.'

'Oh... god!'

'I'm sorry... It was fairly quick and peaceful apparently and Mum was there...'

'Oh... How's Mum?'

'In denial, so in organisation mode already. She's got half-written lists all over the house about numbers of pork pies, for god's sake... She wants you at the funeral, of course.'

'Oh, I don't know—'

'If you don't show up, I promise I'll bring Mum to stay with you when it's all over.'

That sorted it and only eight days later, her brother pulled strings (with a fellow Mason, no doubt) and sorted a gap in the busy crematorium's schedule. Claire donned one of her many black outfits and drove "home" – whatever that meant.

The first shock was seeing Jenny's blue Volvo parked outside the crematorium with Jenny sitting in it, waving at her to park alongside. She not so much parallel-parked as swerved alongside, wanting to take Jenny's mirror off, but opened her window and aggressively thrust her elbow out instead.

'What the—'

'I thought you'd like some company.'

'Well, you got that wrong. It's not *Mamma Mia*, Jenny.'

(Another dig at Jenny's outing with her "cancer friend".)

'Don't get spikey. I knew you'd be like this, so I just came. You were there for me at my mum's funeral, remember.'

'But I don't understand; how did you know?'

'Don't get mad, but your mum wrote and told me.'

Claire didn't have the space to get mad, as the hearse pulled up with her dad inside and she could see the single DAD floral tribute on his coffin – and thought she was going to faint. Jenny took her arm and led her inside, where she insisted on sitting at the back despite her brother looking daggers at her for not joining them.

It was one of those soulless local authority crematoriums, where you decided if you wanted the one cross available as decoration or not. Her parents, being religious of course, had at least got the wall art to break up the cold magnolia, which Claire was now training her eyes on. As she hadn't ever spoken to either of them about death wishes or indeed anything recently, she could only wonder why her dad had chosen to go off in this way. There clearly hadn't been any services before this as the building was cold. Or was it just Claire, as she couldn't seem to get warm at all?

Her brother got to his feet, took his place by the lectern, blew his nose, and then read the eulogy. She fixated on his white and, no doubt, monogrammed handkerchief still in his hand – and the germs that would still be on it – being waved around, as punctuation to his words. Claire didn't recognise the man he was speaking about.

'*He never got any educational qualifications, so was very proud of my sister and me becoming a physiotherapist and accountant respectively. He was a man of few words as Mum said it all! The few he did say were always suffused with love.*'

Her mum leant on her son and daughter-in-law as they all stood to watch the curtain swishing possessively behind the ornate casket, presumably containing her dad, and Claire felt even more the odd one out in the family.

She kept her gaze firmly on the coffin until it receded, then on the priest; a replacement, of course, for Father Duncan from remembered Sunday school days. Out of the corner of her eye, she caught askance glances from former foster children, remnants of them as children in those grown-up faces, now with children of their own.

She breathed deeply during a period of reflection on his life. It was accompanied by *Hymn to the Fallen* sung by Katherine Jenkins and she had no idea again as to why? The dad she remembered was a big band man.

But then they were all outside under the suitably grey skies and all she had to do was stand quietly for just long enough – and people would leave her to her presumed grief. Then she was free to waltz past Tony, seeming not to see him (especially as she hadn't bargained on him being there), quickly hug her mum and get her jangling car keys demonstrably from her handbag – black and borrowed from Jenny months ago. As her mum had a melee of mourners around her, she couldn't remonstrate and thus Claire quickly kissed her cheek. She was almost gone until Jenny stayed her arm and drew her attention to a young woman dressed in a dark purple coat also retreating in an outer circle of mourners.

'She looks kinda familiar... Claire?'

Claire looked as the younger woman also locked eyes with her. Janet, at that moment, was released from the flock of black around her and witnessed the encounter. She stepped forward as Claire gripped her chest and sank to the ground.

Claire's mind felt foggy, she felt sick and couldn't get her breath but knew she needed the flight adrenaline to kick in instead of the fright version.

As she looked up, her mum was by her side, as was the young woman.

'Liv, go get some water. Now!'

All she could do was sit on the damp gravel enduring the nightmare until her legs would take her to her car.

'I'm fine, don't fuss, Mum. Please, I've got to go, I can't do this. Sorry.'

Claire struggled to her feet with Jenny's help and she hissed at Jenny to get her to her car: 'NOW!'

Her mum followed her and went to hug her.

'Come back to the house, love, please, we'll sort it.'

Claire felt cornered and inadvertently lashed out, pushing her mum away. Then, the deed done, she compounded it with:

'For Christ's sake, Mum, I don't want to "sort it"!'

'Claire!'

'Agghh! Just leave me be! Do I have to spell it out: I don't want to be part of this sham family.'

With that, she slammed the car door shut on her mum's crumpling face.

Jenny couldn't persuade Claire to calm down and wait a while. She said that "no, she certainly wouldn't *fucking rest* at the wake at her mum's or anywhere else". So all Jenny could do was agree to follow her home. From both cars' rear view mirrors a backdrop of black mourning clusters could be seen with bent heads standing awkwardly, giving space to the bereaved wife in the foreground, who was being comforted by her son. And sipping water from a glass proffered by a tall slim young woman.

In Claire's mind, this was another "unstable relationship" finished – her body belying her cold analysis as she shook at the wheel, all two and a half hours back to her own home.

Although rocked by her Uncle Jeff's death, Liv, now a self-assured twenty-four and an English teacher, had written her own eulogy and was hoping to deliver it herself. However, her Aunty Jan had persuaded her to leave it to the priest and, as she wasn't "real family", Liv hadn't pressed the point.

Liv stayed the night before the funeral, as had Ella, who at thirty-seven had a family herself and lived locally. The two young women put together a huge spread of the usual sausage rolls, tuna, egg and ham sandwiches and enormous cut pork pies displaying incongruous pink firm flesh. It was held at the village hall as there was plenty of parking. Ella, of course, had been busy baking her signature cupcakes which had become quite a lucrative business alongside her hairdressing. Janet had sat still in the kitchen, blankly watching them beavering away, her own feverish beavering suddenly dissipated, but occasionally getting up to look out the window when a car passed, still looking for Jeff coming home.

The crematorium was packed full of their fellow churchgoers, all the cul-de-sac's neighbours and Jeff's golf mates, old plumbing colleagues and former apprentices sitting shoulder to shoulder, drawn together both by lack of space and the comfort of having living beings beside them. And Liv was amazed, although shouldn't have been, at the huge number of former foster children who turned up to honour her uncle's passing. Most of whom she recognised from home, occasional visits or from the huge photo albums kept by the hearth, which Janet liked to pore over over and reminisce.

Nigel and his wife, Christine, were sealed in the black limousine with Janet. Liv drove Ella in her old Fiat Panda, as her husband was picking up their eldest, Alfie, from school and meeting them there. They all stepped out into drizzle with Liv worrying suddenly that her purple coat was too bright. With grief seeping into their best clothes, shoulders shivering and on Bambi legs, they both walked into the murmuring silence pre-ceremony. Once sitting on the unyielding pews, their hands gripped the order of service displaying a much younger Uncle Jeff's kindly face incongruously beaming at them. It was Liv's first funeral and for the first time in quite a while, she wondered if she had missed her own mother's funeral. She drifted in and out of the service, only able to register snatches due to the unexpected intensity of emotion. Uncle Jeff had been like a grandad to her.

'In the rising of the sun and in its going down. We will remember him.'

She saw Aunty Jan sitting directly in front of her sway, and went to steady her but her dad who was next to her got there first. Everyone, somehow, got through it and then they were outside, the drizzle having reduced to a token spit.

An eruption of voices, piercing and real again after the hush of the church, ricocheted around Janet, who stood inert until her foster children broke the spell. Liv stood off to the side and re-hugged all the foster children after they had been through Jan's programmed arms, many of them like long-lost siblings. She noticed a slim, dark-haired woman approach Jan and hug her briefly. Just as she was about to follow her and ask if she was Claire, Aunty Jan's daughter, her dad grabbed her arm and steered her away, asking her to help with the flowers.

The day passed fairly undramatically apart from this woman seeming to faint, but by the time she got her some water, she had vanished again, leaving a strange fall-out and at the epicentre Aunty Jan standing stock-still.

Soon, she was scooped up by Ella and all was bustle back at home: kettles boiling, corks popping, memories tumbling and laughter full-throated and cathartic and then quiet again as even the very drunk nextdoor neighbours left, somehow sensing they should.

There were no other foster children currently since Jeff had begun to go downhill last March. Ella wanted to take her home with them, but Jan firmly put her foot down saying she needed to be in her own home; she'd feel closer to Jeff there. So, Liv cleared it with her school and agreed to stay with Aunty Jan for a week after the funeral.

Janet's son, Nigel, was "terribly busy" doing important things and Claire, well, she never had been around. Thus, Liv felt she'd crossed the threshold and became the "carer" not the "cared for". As she washed up endless cups of undrunk tea, a heaviness of adulthood and an escort of mortality arrived in the familiar seventies kitchen. Liv then had her turn to cry, being careful to muffle her sobs, in what turned out to be a teatowel of stick figure families that she herself had created at playgroup – all those years ago.

The long week settled into a new routine for Janet of early morning tea by the window and watching the birds peck at the seeds, which Liv kept topping up. Liv hadn't realised how insatiable a sparrow's appetite was, unlike Janet's, who pushed Liv's food temptings around the plate in a desultory, lovesick, teenage fashion. Liv took her to see Ella's children after school each day, which was the only time she had a hint of both a smile reaching her eyes and of being present. The rest of the day was spent gazing, unseeing, at formerly unknown daytime TV, interspersed with fevered bouts of non-productive activity, such as putting washing in the machine and not turning it on. Liv picked out lighter news topics to read to her in the evenings but who knew what was landing in that far-off land of grief?

The week over, Liv couldn't wait to get back to school and be surrounded by the arrogance of innocence, however sad Aunty Jan looked waving goodbye from her gaping doorway.

83
Janet

That first night, Janet sat unmoving by the dying fire and eventually had to be taken to bed like she used to for Liv. In the morning, she had woken early and Liv found her crying, submerged under bin bags of Jeff's clothes like an abandoned puppy. When Liv remarked that it was a bit soon to be clearing his things, Janet uncharacteristically snapped at her and then collapsed in on herself, with no energy to make recompense in any way. She didn't recognise herself anymore and so had no route map to follow, and was relieved when Liv left at the end of the week as she couldn't be chivvied into life as it was before. However kind Liv was being, she needed to figure this out for herself.

Janet opened the odd-sock drawer weeks later and realised how many of Jeff's things she had dispensed with; she even missed his crusty old flannel. Thus, she couldn't bear to be parted from the motley assortment of his socks: golf socks, walking socks, work socks and smart socks, all waiting to be re-united with their pair. She saw pairings everywhere and would cry at the "twoness" of two squirrels, two chops under cellophane, even two cars parked near to each other, and also cry at the "oneness" of her solitary coffee mug, solitary toothbrush and letters addressed just to her. And then, of course, there was the complete, glaring absence of so many things now. She missed his grunt in the morning when he levered himself out of bed, the cuppa he always brought her to start her day, the way he'd always ask "shall I wipe?", even when she always washed up and he always dried. This was a dance they retained even when Ella had bought them a dishwasher and despaired at them using it as "storage". And, more recently, his laughter which lately always ended in a coughing fit, but he still loved to laugh, mainly at *Only Fools and Horses* repeats. Even with the television on all the time, it was still quiet; *how could that be?*

When Ella brought Alfie around, she could see him looking around for Jeff and that hurt so much, but he was also the only person who could make her smile. And the first time she laughed again it was because Alfie was gigglingly licking her teary, salty face. Maybe it was time to start having him on her own again.

When she mentioned this to Ella, her response was a fierce and lingering hug which awoke something in Janet. She hadn't wanted to live without Jeff but now she did. It also got her thinking that what we take to our graves is important, and she had a duty to sort out certain secrets before her own death. However, she couldn't go there yet; she had plenty of time.

84
Claire

Weeks went by like a listless queue at the jobcentre. Claire looked up the word "fugue" and found a meaning to fit: "fugue from the Latin 'fuga' meaning flight. In a fugue state, like fleeing from your own self". Spot on.

She went to work, went grocery shopping and, occasionally, actually cooked said groceries – to all intents and purposes, a pattern of "normal life". However, the swell of emotion at the funeral left a fierce undercurrent so that Claire, now permanently estranged from her mother, had no one else to vent these feelings to other than Jenny, so she paced her house with mobile in hand and vented away:

'You had no right to barge into my personal life like that.'

'I'm sorry. I realise that now, but I just didn't want you to face it alone.'

'Did you think there were some spoils to be had?'

'What?'

'A share of the estate, now you're buddying up with my mother too!'

'I'm not having this conversation, Claire. You know I'm your friend and I wanted to help. This is grief talking.'

'You're not a fucking psychiatric nurse anymore, so get off your high horse and be honest; you've groomed me!'

'What the..."

'And you've used our so-called "friendship" to feel good about yourself, feeding off my misery; you're a leech, a parasite!'

'Oh, come on, Claire – the opposite! I think we help each other.'

'How!"

'By realising we don't have to follow life's script; we've made our own literally! And you helped me like me at last – and to feel I deserve happiness and I hope—'

'Oh, Jenny! Bloody perfect Turner with your perfect life, go swivel! I hate you! I always have.'

Claire was now screaming banshee-like down the phone at Jenny.

'I'm going to hang up now, Claire, until we can talk calmly. I'm sorry you feel like this.'

Claire was left holding, or rather mishandling, a heady concoction of outrage, fear, loneliness and grief, which was magnified by the nagging sense of "other" truths than hers. So, she went immediately to the back of her wardrobe, to the "Jenny" section, and pulled out the first item she laid her hands on: a voluminous beach cover-up in gaudy blues and yellow. Claire had taken to wearing it occasionally after a bath. She yanked both floaty sleeves from their arm holes but felt worse and not better. This resulted with no option other than to reach into the bathroom cabinet. Behind the inserted mirror was her stash of razor blades, hidden only from herself. She selected a brand-new blade and sat on the edge of the bath. Slipping her jeans down, exposing her right thigh, she cut down, more firmly than usual, into the ever-yielding skin.

Claire hadn't had to self-refer to casualty for years, but even though she knew she hadn't hit the femoral artery (she usually placed her blade very carefully), the bleeding wouldn't stop. She clearly hadn't been careful enough and had nicked some vessel offering a Vesuvian flow of blood which she hadn't accounted for.

After a one-handed, hairy drive (the other hand was on several tea towels pressing her wound) to the thankfully very local hospital, running a red light and then eventually being bandaged up, she had to run the gauntlet of psychiatric assessment.

Claire was left in the casualty cubicle awaiting the dreaded consultation with just a set of flimsy sky-blue curtains to stare at. That environment was never further from nature and sky; stark fluorescent light illuminated the sharp edges of machines which beeped their own belligerent birdsong, with a background chorus of plastic apron busy-ness and urgent solos of consultants' orders. In a neighbouring cubicle was an affable drunk singing *O sole mio* who, at that very minute, Claire would gladly swap lives with, so she could be gently reprimanded, head neatly sewed, and be back on the road again.

Instead, she lay there painfully aware of her attempt on her life and wondering if she really meant it this time.

'Claire Hetherington?

'Hello, Claire, I'm Dr Fernandez from the psychiatric team. You knew I was coming?'

A tall, striking forty-ish woman took a chair from outside the curtain.

'May I?'

Claire shrugged. So far, she didn't <u>dis</u>like her. She was polite and unpatronizing, and she had a gentle way with her.

'So, tell me how you came to be in hospital?'

'You know.'

'Yes, but your version is more important to me.'

Ooh, she was good.

'My mother died recently – and I'd been having a bad time anyway… just in the moment things were overwhelming me, but I'm okay now.'

'And this "overwhelm-ment" caused you to cut deep into your leg?'

'Yes.'

'I know you are a physiotherapist, so you have anatomical knowledge and must be aware this was a serious injury… that we need to take seriously.'

'Yes, I know it sounds like an excuse, but my hand slipped as I was in such a state, I didn't mean to…'

'You didn't mean to take your own life?'

'God, no! I feel awful now, for all this trouble I'm causing you too.'

'Have you had thoughts that life isn't worth living before?'

'Haven't we all! I mean, sorry, no, I just feel so foolish now. I just want to go home.'

'We would like you to go home too, but we need to be sure you are safe.'

'Oh, I am definitely.'

'I see you have had ECT before.'

'Yes, that was years ago.'

'For post-natal depression?'

'Yes.'

Ooh, this was getting too, too deep.

'Look, I know you need to do your job and so do I. I am a senior physio and I need to be back at work on Monday, so I just need to get home and sort myself out.'

'Do you live alone?'

'No, my partner will be back tonight; he's been away on business. I'll be fine when he's back, honestly.'

'Have you been cutting regularly?'

'God, no!'

'Can you show me?'

'Look, I feel this is an imposition now. I have no intention of getting undressed again; can't you see I am ashamed enough!'

Dr Fernandez wavered and so Claire, skilful now at this manipulation of people trying to help her, pulled out all her armoury.

'You can check in with Senior Physio Dr Hoskins, she's my boss, and she will vouch for my level-headedness. Look, I've had enough now... I am going to discharge myself. I thank you for your time and care, but both you and I have more important calls on our time.'

And with that, knowing she was testing whether Dr Fernandez thought she was sectionable or not, she gathered her things as calmly as possible and strode away, saying as she went:

'I will fill in the self-discharge form at the desk, so you can get on with your next patient.'

Thus, her knowledge and VIP status helped her dodge proper treatment once again. Claire pushed to the front of the remonstrating queue to pay the car park charges, eventually found her car and then sat exhausted at the wheel.

Claire went home on auto pilot, googled seamstresses to mend the damaged cover-up, curled up in one of Jenny's nighties and slept for nearly two days.

85
Jenny

Ever understanding, Jenny put the acrimonious phone-call and Claire's subsequent cool behaviour and tetchiness down to grief and left her alone for just over a month. However, the conversation didn't fail to cause Jenny to examine her best friendship. Not for the first time did she ponder on that social model of psychiatry, and the impact on not just her friend. Not one to blame others, but she could see how events such as Claire feeling shunned by her parents (even though that wasn't true) and her own need to be perfect as an only child could shape one's approach to the world and adversity – and, consequently, mental health. No wonder they regularly re-invented themselves! Maybe Claire was right; she had used Claire's need to be a different person, to try on other selves herself, and just happened to be lucky that the "real" Jenny she had settled into had become happy. However, she was worried that Claire's own troubled ego would eventually self-combust.

Jenny wondered about contacting Claire's mother, Janet, to try and explain her daughter's frostiness towards her. But concluded that she just wanted to share their shunned feelings. This, coupled with the inevitable fallout if Claire found out, she soon buried under her own preoccupations.

Evie was sixteen and was "seeing someone". John and Jenny had, at last, got a name from her: "Jez", from which, of course, they had come up with many identikit characters, some more preferable than others. Maybe Jez was short for Jeremy and he was also sixteen, studying hard at the local boys' school, played cricket, planning to work in a caring profession and they met at a joint school social. Or maybe Jez was twenty-something, a local drug dealer and had her under his bony, tattooed thrall? All they had to go on was a glimpse of him in town, when Evie had them duck uncharacteristically into a failing fishmonger to avoid being seen with her oldies and, even worse, Jez meeting those same oldies. The fishmonger got all excited about custom and Jenny found herself buying crabsticks, the cheapest, least fishy-looking item she could see, which later was given to the neighbour's cat. The Jez they glimpsed was neither a drug dealer nor cricketer but a somewhat spotty, callow youth with slumped shoulders, which Jenny hoped was born of shyness, not shiftiness. The brief vision was better than the worst nightmare, so, both parents relaxed a bit and tried to remember when they too had doodled and dreamt about gawky unsuitable suitors, when they should have been studying hard for their O-levels (as they were called in that faraway time).

'Chill,' Evie said and so they tried to chill.

Jenny stored such exchanges to share with Claire when they were once again on speaking terms and maybe her friend could learn to "chill" too.

86
Claire

After five weeks and three days, Jenny knocked on Claire's door one Saturday morning and handed her an envelope.

'What is it?'

'Why do people say that! Open it and you'll find out!'

Claire, keeping Jenny on the doorstep, as churlishly as possible tore open the envelope. A voucher fell out.

'What the...'

'I just thought the lotus flower was a good choice as it symbolises self-regeneration, but you can just ask the tattooist for anything.'

'Oh! I need to regenerate, do I!

But, for once, Claire had no other comeback; she had so missed her smiling friend. Since her last cutting, which had terrified her, she had been trying an online mindfulness class. She was on week three of an eight-week course, which encouraged "paying attention to thoughts and feelings, reactions to difficulties and considering relationships with self and others". All this was particularly difficult for Claire and what she really needed was just a good laugh with her best friend.

She had also been wondering about tattoos for some time to cover the unsightly scars on her arms, but Jenny had known when the right moment was to nudge her forwards. She both loved and hated her for her saintly empathy.

'You better come with me then... Hey, you must get one as well.'

'I thought about that, but Evie may decide she wants one too!'

'No, you must. Hey, I know, a halo on your hairline!'

'Come again?'

'For Saint Jenny. I'll get devil's horns.'

'A clown's face more like, or I've got it, a cork-screw!'

After a successful tattooing debut, feeling more confident and as she had nothing better to do, she agreed to indulge John and Jenny in a few more blind dates. She insisted that she would only go ahead if they made up the foursome and didn't abandon her. Claire made short shift of them all. Date one was with Bob even though Claire had said she would burst out laughing every time she had to call him "Bob".

'It's just a ridiculous name.'

'Why?'

'Bobble, Bobsleigh, Bobbin, um...'

Jenny came back with:

'Bobtail!'

'Case dismissed!'

So, of course, when poor Bob did come to supper, John was very bemused when the conversation turned to winter sports, something he wasn't aware either Claire or Jenny were interested in:

'Have you ever bobsleighed, Bob?'

'Or isn't the term bobsledding?'

Poor Bob didn't last longer than Claire asking if his jumper ever bobbled before Jenny realised it was going nowhere and needed to save Bob by yanking Claire into the kitchen for a talking-to between courses and a moment to swallow her own fit of giggles.

'Sorry, I can't help it! Please don't do this to me again!'

There was a date two with Paul, which Claire had been "ill" for and it was never re-arranged, and date three with Johann. Claire had looked up the meaning of his name:

'It means "God is merciful".'

To which Jenny had replied:

'Let's hope you are this time!'

Johann, a colleague of John's, was charming. He had a good head of hair, presumably his own teeth and the evening had gone reasonably well, until Claire learned that, at age fifty-two, he was still living with his mother and had to go early as his mum would be worrying and wanting her cocoa.

Jenny and John admitted they had been scraping the barrel a bit with eligible single contacts and no one was surprised when nothing came of any of them. Claire said clearly once more that particular ship had "up-anchored" long ago – that everyone wasn't as lucky as Jenny and John who were sickeningly made for each other. She had long since realised that her feeling of being adrift from relationships wasn't to be solved by being fully lashed to one.

87
Olivia

Ever since Liv could remember at least part of Christmas had always been spent at her Aunty Jan's and Uncle Jeff's; her dad's appalling cooking being the excuse, which was trotted out annually. Apart from one year, when she was sixteen, her dad had a lucrative contract and so had spoiled her by booking a hotel deal in the Canaries, the two of them. Liv hated it. It was full of old people; tinsel in the sunshine was just plain wrong, and the waiters kept coming onto her with "Ola! Beautiful Oliv-ola...".

"It's Liv!" she'd say angrily, and her dad was rubbish at helping her fend them off, but insisted she went and danced with them to the lethargic hotel band, who clearly didn't want to be there either. In fact, she was convinced the drummer had died over his cymbals. And as for "enjoying herself", huh! That Christmas had even relegated the Canaries to second in the league of worst family Christmas's ever.

Liv had an invitation from her still fairly new boyfriend, Conor, to join him for the Christmas school holidays with his folks, who ran a bed and breakfast in the Lakes. It had been a very beguiling offer; real log fires, not the old gas-effect one Aunty Jan held onto (which she was sure was slowly emitting brain-cell-killing fumes) not to mention the traditional Christmas with "the works" which he had tempted her with. Liv would have felt very guilty absenting herself, especially as her poor old dad had agreed with his new girlfriend to sacrifice their first Christmas together for this good deed. He had, at last, got together with Samantha from work and, just when he should have been having cocktail-filled fun, he was sitting in the decoration-bare front room drinking pale ale, "entertaining" Aunty Jan, that is, watching *Dad's Army*, whilst Liv basted her very first and avowedly last turkey. Nigel, of course, was sunning himself with his new family on some Caribbean island and Claire, well, there was nothing new there; sometimes she wondered if she actually even existed.

After Christmas cracker jokes, obligatory Christmas pudding and washing up, they embarked on a game of Monopoly, during which all three forgot who had the racing car, top-hat or boot and even whose turn it was. They were all hoping that the others would get hotels on Park Lane so it would all be over. She knew if Ella came over with her family it would lift spirits, but it was her turn with the in-laws. Without her adored Alfie to pander to, Aunty Jan hadn't the heart to even put the tree up and so Liv had twined some fairy lights around ivy from the garden. They all watched them twinkle away until it was a respectable time to take much-needed antacids and retire to bed, Christmas over.

THE TWENTY-FIRST ERA

2014

The year the words "twerk" and "selfie" were added to the dictionary and Gangnam Style reached two billion views on YouTube.

88
Jenny

It was on December 23rd, the country abuzz and ablaze with tinkly, twinkly Christmas, that Jenny had an appointment with Dr Perry, who was coming up to retirement and Jenny couldn't imagine seeing anyone else. He had seen the family through her miscarriages, pregnancy, Evie's first immunisations, chickenpox, tonsillitis galore, Jenny's breast cancer diagnosis and treatment and John's prostate scare.

She sat in the waiting room with a pasted smile for the young mums cajoling their offspring out of the plastic playhouse to have their snuffles kindly dismissed by even younger GPs. And the elderly couple sat as two gnarled oak trees, leant into each other after a lifetime of sunshine and storms, patiently waiting their turn to discuss his prostate maybe, or her arthritis.

Jenny picked up a three-year-old Golf Monthly for distraction, but immediately her mind went to John – "afterwards" – maybe taking up golf to fill the empty weekends. She replaced the magazine and sat back, trying to sink into the persistent pain in the back of her head. Her handbag (whichever stuffed portmanteau she grabbed) always had an assortment of painkillers along with the usual handbag habitat, a Tardis of tissues, keys to unknown places, dried-up mascaras, melted lip salve, receipts (to check one day), pizza, Jehovah's Witness leaflets and assorted photos of Evie, which she had kept meaning to put into a handy pocket-size album. She had gone beyond sniffing lavender now and, although it seemed wrong taking drugs in the surgery, she couldn't wait and so put two dry tablets on her tongue and tried to summon enough spittle to swallow, before "Jenny Turner" was called – and she would know.

And now, here she was sitting opposite Dr Perry, wondering how his health was, whether he was going to have years of golf and cruises, or not. He seemed so timelessly robust and she sat staring at his four grandchildren smiling at her encouragingly from a large, proud, gilt frame, willing Jenny to be there for grandchildren of her own. She'd be happy for just the one.

The bargaining had begun.

She knew as soon as the headaches started but only made the appointment when the sickness began. Dr Perry was kind and upbeat as always, but there was an edge of resignation in his voice that he couldn't disguise that signalled "brace yourself" and, of course, he had said "that word" again.

She hadn't taken John, buying him a little more time until this news was too real to hide. Besides, it was soon Evie's sixteenth birthday. She was having a party at the village hall on the final day of term and, although she only wanted a mobile disco and "just a bit of booze, come on, Mum!" Jenny felt she ought to make some food to soak up the allowed and supervised shandies. Then there was actual Christmas to get through.

89
Claire

Claire knew she hadn't handled it well... once more, she had been found wanting as a friend. Jenny had come to share with her the news: she probably had secondaries in the brain, and Claire's response? She got angry with her.

'What do you mean you've only just found out?'

'Well, I actually saw Dr Perry before Christmas and I couldn't tell anyone then. I've still not told John... or Evie.'

'God, Jenny!'

'I've got to go to the hospital for a brain scan.'

Her tone brightened:

'He put me on the two-week pathway.'

'For Chrissake, Jen, it's the cancer pathway, not a route through a fucking arboretum!'

Jenny looked hard into Claire's eyes.

'I know.'

'Why didn't you do anything sooner?'

'What do you mean?'

'You're so dense sometimes.'

'Not the reaction I was expecting!'

'You said you'd had headaches. I just assumed you'd get checked and that it was okay? That's so irresponsible.'

Needless to say, Jenny left soon after and Claire went and knocked on a neighbour's door and rollicked them for leaving their bin out days after rubbish collection. Still full of anger, she donned her gardening gloves, pulled out all the rhubarb, dug over the frozen bed and, hours later, after three glasses of red and several reckless cuts to her thigh, cried, as she was about to lose her best and only true friend.

90
Jenny

John booked a night away as his Christmas present to her and so Jenny had vowed to herself to let them both enjoy that. She would tell him over breakfast the next morning in a neutral place away from Evie, so her emotions could be held in check and maybe it wouldn't all seem so real.

Claire's many characters and scripts had rubbed off on her and she was able to play healthy-Jenny, forward-looking-Jenny, well, for a short time at least. Evie was allowed to stay over at a friend's without too much interrogation, which amazed and delighted her. So, off John and Jenny went to a posh hotel in Brighton with not too many backward looks. On arrival, they meandered the cobbled streets and it was only when Jenny wanted to buy a couple of special, discounted Christmas baubles that she got a bit teary wondering how different a Christmas the next one would be.

'Are you crying? You silly mare!'

'It's just well... "Christmas". Must be getting sentimental in my old age!'

'We've only just got through last Christmas! Anyways, you've always been sentimental!'

'True! I think Evie's inherited your more practical approach, don't you?'

She desperately wanted him to say "'yes, she'll be fine, Jenny, when you go. She's made of stronger stuff than either of us". But, of course, she couldn't discuss any of that just yet, or maybe ever. They had sex amidst high-thread-count Egyptian sheets which also made Jenny cry.

'What now, love? I wasn't that bad!'

'No, I think I must be allergic to luxury! It's all too much.'

'Shall I cancel the dinner booking then?'

'Don't you dare!'

That night in the hotel's Michelin-star restaurant, they had oysters for the first time ever – well, they tried them, and Jenny tossed one back and pronounced them:

'Gobby slimy things. I just wanted the pearl!'

Chateaubriand was wolfed down. They were on safer territory there but then, for dessert, they had chocolate "air" as Jenny called it; she liked her puddings more substantial and with custard – she craved familiarity. Champagne headiness and nostalgic conversation stemmed any forays into the future, so Jenny had managed it all thus far. Breakfast was a different matter.

'You're quiet, love?'

Her eggs Benedict had been pushed around the plate one too many times to avoid comment.

'I've got something I've been wanting to tell you. I've been waiting for the right time, but there is no right time.'

'You're scaring me now. You're running off with Bob?'

Jenny wanted to stay within this familiar banter but took a deep beath as she registered John's sudden awareness and spoke the words that ended their happy weekend – their happiness full stop.

'I'm sorry, love, I saw Dr Perry and—'

"When? Why didn't you say?"

'Because it's not good news.'

John sat very still and very quiet. Jenny reached for his hands which were propping his recently greying beard (when did that happen). He looked up at her, grasped her hands tightly, released them, shook his head then beckoned the waiter and asked them to prepare the bill as they had to leave.

They silently went back to the room, packed and Jenny waited for him to talk, but he said he was unable to talk about matters of such awful reality surrounded by the "banality of generic hotel art". Jenny fixated her thoughts on the very un-John-like comment and followed his hurt, hunched shoulders to the car. It wasn't until they were nearly home that he pulled the car over into a layby and said they needed to prepare themselves to tell Evie.

'So... what are we facing?'

Jenny fixedly looked at his knuckles getting whiter as he gripped the steering wheel incrementally tighter with each piece of the awful news: headaches, dizziness and nausea that she'd ignored for too long and kept a secret, the booked MRI, the possibility of more chemotherapy and who knew what else.

Evie, at sixteen, was devastated and clingy one minute and, the next, seemingly too busy pouting in front of the mirror, trying out new looks for party after party. Jenny was worried her exams would suffer but, in reality, Evie wouldn't have studied hard anyway, even if cancer hadn't taken up residence in the Turner household for good. John, on the other hand, immersed himself in work, finding solace in drainage plans and costings, trying to dream of revamped mansion wings and not his wife's decaying body.

91
Claire

On a rare clearing out of cupboards, Claire found the pictures she'd painted years ago of her brain – the irony wasn't lost on her – and of Jenny's brain scan, full of all the wrong colours. Her grieving was happening already and in all the wrong order; typical. She desperately wanted to leave this depressed phase and re-enter the more familiar "anger phase". That, at least, had a bit of action to it, not this strange moping she had sunk into. It didn't help to read a name for it: "anticipatory grief"; it made it sound exciting, like counting the weeks before a trip to the Canaries – this was no holiday. On finding some photos of the time they went to Amsterdam, she determined to ignore the diagnosis and make a lovely album of all their old memories and put suggestions in blank pages for new places to visit and new memories to make.

She sat on her bed with a shoe box of photos, still preferring actual pictures to anything virtual and, to her, thus unseeable. By midnight, she had only sorted a small pile as she got lost in each image:

Jenny with very scarlet lipstick smudged on her grinning teeth in Fortnum and Mason for a Prosecco afternoon tea. They had bet each other the cost of the bill; the winner had to be the first to have their lipstick-stained glass replaced by a fawning waiter. Neither had won, despite numerous lipstick stains all over the flutes reminiscent of a Jackson Pollock. They were clearly judged not worthy of such attention, which, of course, had stoked Claire to become very demanding about the tea leaves:

'Are they really jasmine?'

With Jenny backing her up, saying they knew their teas:

'My dad is from Yorkshire,' said in a very bad Yorkshire accent, which caused them to laugh uproariously, as per usual, and the waiter to retreat.

And another of Jenny with hooped earrings and a turban, teetering at a very precipitous angle, carefully holding the top of Claire's table lamp, that is, her "crystal ball" in a scarf to conceal the lightbulb socket! That was the trendy party in a nearby warehouse where Claire had a client contact and they had provided some of the "entertainment".

They had repeated the successful clairvoyance routine at another warehouse party they blagged their way into whilst away in Blackpool. Claire had to drag Jenny away as she proved so popular; she had a queue of customers clamouring for her psychic abilities who wanted to arrange future sittings. After the high of their escapade, it took them hours to fall asleep and, the next morning, they overslept and missed breakfast. The cheap hotel they had booked was very strict about just one sitting. Thus, they had gone to a local greasy spoon and were converts after tasting their first fried bread. There was a picture of Jenny, eyes closed, in raptures – over a piece of soggy bread.

They weren't always "naughty". Claire found a picture of them both outside the Royal Albert Hall when they had gone to the Proms. They had gone more than once but this was taken after *Beethoven's Symphony No. 5* in 2012 and they were both still looking so obviously moved. Claire found the piece on YouTube and lay on the bed, suddenly back there again experiencing the same dark and dawn as she had alongside Jenny two years ago.

She had managed to lift a dressing gown from Jenny's on her last visit and wrapped in Jenny's recent changing smell, she fell asleep dreaming of Jenny wearing stupid heels that she never ever wore, slipping in the mud.

THE TWENTY-SECOND ERA

2015

The year that a migrant ship sank off the Libyan coast and over 400 refugees drowned.

92
Jenny

Jenny agreed to the surgery as it would slow the progress of the tumour, singular at the moment but the size of a golf ball and then, "whoop, whoop", it would pave the way for radiotherapy, chemotherapy and then maybe buy a little more life. The appointments and then admission date hurtled towards her ever more quickly – and then it was over.

Luckily, Evie had gone to the hospital canteen for more snacks and a teen magazine (as she was bored), when the consultant came to break the bad news to Jenny and John:

'How are you feeling, Jenny?'

'A bit woozy still but thank you... for everything, doctor.'

John was watching the consultant's face closely.

'As I said, the operation went according to plan; we removed most of the tumour. But I am so very sorry I have some difficult news for you... You know I told you we were going to take a biopsy of it? The biopsy showed a grade four cancer which is very aggressive. Even if we had been able to take it all away this time, it would have come back very soon.'

John found his voice first:

'How long are we talking then? We've both talked about it and we want to know.'

'Well, I am sure you realise we cannot accurately predict how long anyone can live with such a diagnosis... and some patients always do defy the odds—'

'Worst-case scenario?'

'I would say, do all you want to do in the next few months. I am so sorry, I truly am, that I have no better news. This is a lot to take in, so I'll leave you for now, but do get the nurses to bleep me when you want to talk again, and we can plan the next steps... I'm so sorry.'

They must have crossed in the corridor, as Evie burst in with:

'They only had prawn cocktail flavour, but I got some Cheddars, and I got some Lucozade for you, Mum.'

'Thanks, love.'

'Why are you looking at me like that?'

She wanted, she needed, more rows with Evie about too much foundation, mobile phone bills and its usage at the table, heart-to-hearts about being dumped by Kieran and life decisions about art and design or history, Exeter Uni or staying closer to home and trying for Canterbury. She wanted to see her throw a mortarboard in the air, cry at her wedding and soothe her crying babies. And John: she craved silent side by sides on the sofa, the silence, not from cancer taking their brains to the wrong places, literally, but the silence of satisfied commune and then only punctuated by a shared snigger at politicians on the telly, or shared sighs at Evie's remonstrances when in late again. Moaning about creaking joints and leaky bladders would be heaven. Just a bit more normal, please, nothing more.

93
Claire

Maybe John was too close or just not trained to spot symptoms but Claire had noticed every step change in Jenny's condition: when she swayed walking up the garden path and when she knocked her mug of tea over that first time. Each stage of her decline took Claire a bit further from her friend. She was disgusted at the loss of Jenny's beautiful hair again taken by a surgeon's crop this time, and angered by her fortitude and cheeriness.

This anger was becoming a problem again and, after another cut of her own that could have been "it", she ended up back in hospital and couldn't pull the wool over the doctor's eyes any longer. So, Claire, for the first time in her adult life, had a label for her whole struggles: BPD, her new diagnosis.

Wanting, of course, to take the treatment into her own hands, Claire decided to go privately. The therapist she found was equally surprised that Claire had not formerly had any support with her BPD.

Rachel was a dialectical therapist who specialised in equipping people with skills to deal with difficult emotions. As Claire had returned to long sleeves pulled down over her hacked, scarred Lotus flowers, she was hoping Rachel could equip her with the skills to stop venting her anger on the person she loved most – and on herself.

As a lover of words, Claire had obviously googled "dialectical" many times before the appointment: "describes the notion that two opposing ideas can be true at the same time... The therapy itself enables people to view issues from multiple perspectives so that they can reconcile seemingly contradictory information". *Good luck with that*, Claire thought, her whole life had been a series of contradictions; wasn't everyone's?

Rachel was, as Claire expected, wearing that look of indiscriminate taste and age, possibly between thirty and fifty, "BBC", that is, "bum back in chair" straight-backed, smooth hair scraped back in a ponytail that negated the need for any distracting fiddling of hair-strands, gentle but impassive expression and head seemingly permanently cocked to one questioning side. And surely, she needed a physio with that neck; maybe they could do a skills swap, as these sessions certainly weren't cheap! All thoughts logged to share later with Jenny but she checked herself once more – she wouldn't be sharing much more at all.

'I'm glad you've sought help at last, Claire. Living with BPD without the right strategies can hurt very much; has this been your experience?'

'I guess so. I have only me to compare myself with and sometimes I feel as if I don't exist at all.'

'May I ask at what age did you get your diagnosis?'

'I've never officially been diagnosed until, er... my recent hospital stay... but an art therapist got to know me reasonably well and thought the diagnosis fitted, and I've googled it lots, of course!'

'You've had other hospital admissions?'

'For depression and post-natal depression.'

For the first time ever, Claire was able to calmly describe her psychiatric history, confident that these divulgences were in confidence and, as she was paying, she could just walk away.

'I've been relatively okay for years now. I think it's just when a major stress comes along it knocks me for six, well, more like sixty.'

'And you've had a major stress recently?'

'Yes, a few...'

Claire wasn't ready to share, particularly Jenny, with anyone just yet and the silence grew.

'You probably know from your research that people with BPD have very intense emotions that can last a few hours to days; does this sound familiar at the moment?'

Yes, too familiar and, suddenly, all too much. Claire was finding it hard to remain in the room and Rachel, of course, saw this.

'Claire, you have taken the first enormous step by coming here today. I just want to assure you that people with BPD do get out of the mental health system, so this doesn't have to be a repeated pattern for you. I can help you regulate these difficult emotions. You just need to give yourself this chance of an "easier" life.'

Claire certainly didn't want to ever return to hospital and knew this was a pivotal moment, but her legs stood her up and walked her from the room and straight to her car, without explanation or a backward glance. Damn those opposing thoughts; she'd scuppered her chances and now it was down to her alone – physician heal thyself.

94
Olivia

Liv had just got in from her first day at her new "special measures" school. Her form had the notorious reputation of being badly behaved apparently. She had opened with a firm but fun approach and hadn't had anything thrown at her, so it had gone surprisingly well so far, she thought. She was eager to share her day, with Conor especially, and then later on the phone with her dad. Her dad had been worried about her leaving the high-achieving school and opting for this new challenge. Conor was worried about the stress on her and their new happy lifestyle. Neither man liked boats rocking, but Liv needed to rock boats to test her own balance.

She picked up the post from the doormat, put the celebratory wine in the fridge and flicked the kettle switch. The post was mostly election leaflets, but there was one letter in an unfamiliar hand.

She sat with her strong builder's tea and peeled the layers of Sellotape from the back of the envelope. Someone almost didn't want her to open it. She saw the cheque first and thought there must be a mistake, but checking the envelope, it definitely had her name on. It said clearly Olivia Thomas and it was the right address. She looked at the amount again: £50,000. No! Who!

There was a notelet with a beagle on the front, and inside the only words printed in Lucida font handwriting were:

Olivia,

To right a wrong. No questions asked please. No tracing. This is a gift to use for your bright future.

From a well-wisher.

Liv had finished writing her diary (with the accompanying fact-finding of her past) a long time ago. She had decided to accept and embrace both who she was now and those who had always been important in her life, that is, Dad, Aunty Jan and Uncle Jeff, Ella and her family, her close friends and, now, Conor. That had been enough – until now. So, her first emotion wasn't curiosity but anger at this unwanted reactivation of the old holes in her life.

Conor texted to say he was running late, so in her inability to sit on the news, she rang her dad. Her dad's reaction wasn't surprised as she had expected, which gave her cause to question if it was him which he, of course, denied. Liv didn't know what to think as this was just the sort of gesture her dad would make not wanting the accompanying fuss. But his business certainly wasn't that flush and he and Samantha were about to get a place together at last too, so she doubted he would have this amount of money spare.

Conor's reaction was uncomplicated: 'Who cares who sent it! Holiday first, then, woohoo!'

His excitement was infectious and thus calmed Liv's thoughts, but ever respectful, she felt she couldn't be frivolous with the money. Instead, she realised that this could really enable them to get on the property ladder at last and would satisfy the "bright future" element of the behest.

Thus, within twelve weeks, they not only had their very own mortgage broker, Jon, but had exchanged contracts on a tiny but perfectly formed first-floor flat, aptly converted from an old Victorian school, which was midway between both their schools, complete with a village pub and the owner had warned, possibly, a resident cat. Thank you, well-wisher.

95
Jenny

Evie took it upon herself to be the cancer stylist. She shaved Jenny's once wayward curls when they first began to appear as springy moss in the shower again, and she tie-dyed funky head scarves, winding them in heightened turbans that suited Jenny's more steroidal, swollen face.

Jenny was aghast that Evie might curtail her ambitions and talents to stay near her mum, wasting her young life "waiting".

'You need to concentrate on <u>your</u> image now, Evie.'

'What do you mean?'

'For uni. You'll need to go shopping for some new clothes. Dad and I thought two hundred might do it?'

'Mum, wow, yes! When can we go!'

'You won't want me suggesting all the wrong things; go with Lauren.'

'I'd rather go with you. We can have lots of coffee stops.'

'Bless you, love, but you'd be better with Lauren.'

'Is it you don't want to use the wheelchair?'

'No, it's just I haven't a clue about surfer looks.'

'You what?'

'Well, Exeter'll be all surfer-ish, won't it?'

'I haven't decided, anyways, I might take a year out first.'

'And do what?'

'I'm still thinking what. And I can be around more for you.'

'Well, while you're thinking, you could have done a year already; imagine being right on the coast. You've got to seize these opportunities, love.'

'But...'

Jenny uncharacteristically tried to toughen her stance saying that she didn't need the continual grooming and fussing, much as she cherished every careful touch from Evie.

Jenny had taken to encouraging Evie to see Claire on her own, ostensibly to check she was okay as a distance had crept in again, but she knew Evie realised she was grooming their relationship to be a surrogate mother/daughter one, for when the time came.

She had Claire accompany John when Evie visited Exeter and made Evie promise to take up the place when of course she fell in love with it: the coast, the lecturers and the boys too were apparently all "soo hot". But, inside, she was hurting more from this readying for her premature removal from Evie's life than the excruciating headaches themselves. John would often come home and find her curled up in Evie's bed, hugging some tattered old blanky of her daughter's or hands clasped around some misshapen playgroup clay offering. Jenny kept everything Evie had ever made. Whenever she unearthed an ashtray Evie had made, it had made them all laugh afresh, as neither parent had ever smoked! John would lift his wife (now easily liftable) still sleeping and tenderly put her back in their bed, to spare Evie from finding her mum so laid bare.

96
Claire

Sitting beside John in his steady Volvo estate (Evie in the back with her headphones on, listening to some cacophony or other) with Radio Four playing *Woman's Hour* (courteously, for her benefit, Claire thought), she felt "at home". Being shown around the accommodation blocks, she felt it was her duty to inspect the shower power, mattress quality and kitchen cleanliness or lack of. This was despite Evie's obvious mortification and Claire found herself enjoying conspiratorial looks with other "mothers" whilst their offspring were raising abashed eyebrows at each other – and, yes, it felt good.

Although Evie did her best "truculent traipse" around the campus, she could tell she wanted to flee permanently to this place of future promise – and felt she understood this young woman. She was her "sort of" godmother after all and both of them were coping by gripping onto their new selves for now.

Claire suggested she treated them to tea on the way back, but they wanted to get home to Jenny so she had packed a picnic tea instead for the four-and-a-half-hour journey back from Exeter.

'Ham sandwich anyone?'

'I'm vegan now.'

'Yes, but you have bacon, Evie; ham's the same.'

'I know what ham is, Dad!'

'Well, I've got cheese, hummus, you name it, and your favourite brownies, Evie!'

'I'm not eating chocolate anymore.'

'Evie!'

'But thanks, Aunty Claire.'

Claire could turn on a sixpence with her emotions so she should have been able to understand Evie's nought to sixty, from fury through to fun, but wasn't practised at defusing Evie's moods. Thus, she was grateful to John for making the journey back as prickle-free as possible, under the circumstances.

She thought a firmer hand was needed. Jenny and John seemed to forgive her all sorts of cheek, attributing her behaviour to her fear of the future, both uni and her mum's demise. If she had been Claire's daughter, well – *but let's not go there*. For starters, she wouldn't have let her wear so much black eyeliner, today of all days. And she thought she was certainly old enough to help around the house. And to have a Saturday job.

At her age, Claire remembered working at Clark's Bakery. When people came in asking for a bloomer or a cob, she would just reach for any bread until, at last, she got the right one, as she was far too shy and proud to ask the staff to give her the loaf "low down". This obviously slowed the queue's progress somewhat and so she had been transferred to the kitchens, where orders for the attached café were prepared. She had to make teas and coffees and also put Welsh rarebits under the grill, and then when an order was complete, had to shout "Welsh rarebit" very loudly until it was collected by a customer. Many a cheese topping went cold awaiting ownership, as despite her elocution teacher's efforts, she was still not projecting her shy voice. But this had been good for her, or so her dad said every Saturday evening when Claire said she didn't want to go back the following week. Thus, she also felt she knew best about cultivating Evie's work ethic.

She did concede that maybe everything adults felt was good for their teenage daughters wasn't always, and secreted her own can of gin and tonic in a napkin with a can of diet coke over the seat into Evie's surprised and delighted hands.

'Thirsty?'

'Thanks, Aunty Claire.'

97
Evie

Her mum had fallen asleep while Evie was trying to talk to her about her prom – she kept doing that. Evie could see her battling to keep her eyes open, so had once again retreated to her room. Then the home phone rang; she sprinted to get it, so it didn't wake her because as easily as she drifted off, so she awoke, usually in pain. It was Claire, again.

Evie couldn't keep the annoyance out of her voice. Only earlier she had said to her mum that, every time she wanted time alone with her, Claire phoned. Or worse, popped in uninvited, with embarrassing photos of stupid girly weekends away they'd had, and she'd been excluded from the conversation as usual. Her mum tried to mollify her, but Evie wasn't having any of it:

'I can't work her out, Mum! When she comes round and you drop off, one minute she'll sit like a statue and stare at you for hours. Then, if I come in it's as if the statue sprang to life, cos she'll turn on me! Like my hair needs brushing or "have you washed up for your mum and dad?" treating me like a kid. The next minute, she'll be nice as pie and talking grown-up stuff like careers. She's like some seriously weird chameleon.'

'She's not got children, love. She doesn't know how to be around you. She really loves you and just wants to be there for all of us, honestly. She said she wants to take you prom shopping.'

'That's your job'.

Her mum pulled Evie to her.

'Oh, love.'

Evie bore her weight on her arms, conscious of crushing her mum's always longed-for and now painfully skinny torso.

Thus, Evie later rang Claire, who delightedly arranged to pick her up at the weekend for prom shopping, a movie and a meal. As her mum seemed pleased, Evie really tried to be "nice" for her sake.

'Ooh, Aunty Claire, look at this black one.'

'Black's too old and, anyway, it'll be too draining for your colouring. How about this turquoise; your mum's colour?'

'I'll be wearing lots of foundation or maybe a spray tan.'

'You don't want to look cheap.'

'I don't intend to, Aunty Claire!'

Evie couldn't stand the joy-killer taking over anymore and so they came back with nothing and short-circuited the movie and meal, saying she had a headache, conveniently. There was only so much duty a daughter could bear, thus she escaped to order her dress online, stalking the postman and squirrelling it away from prying eyes until the prom reveal.

When Evie appeared dressed in the short black and plunging number showcasing her ample cleavage, it was to her parents' utter shock – and her prom partner, Luke's, very apparent pleasure.

Her mum beckoned this vision of confidence and sass to her and could only whisper: 'Be careful' and Evie was made to hear, more loudly from her dad:

'Have a great evening' and meaningfully: 'See you at eleven!'

Evie's mum had asked her dad to wake her when he brought Evie home. However, her mum looked so peaceful neither liked to disturb her. So, she didn't get to hear how Luke had gotten too "fresh", she had ended up slapping him and had hidden crying in the loos with her best friend, Lauren, for most of the night.

The next morning, Evie was awoken by her mum bringing her a cup of tea which had obviously taken every ounce of her remaining energy. She sank onto Evie's bed, eager to hear all.

'Thanks, Mum, you needn't have.'

'Well, how was it?'

'Oh, great, you know!'

'No! That's why I'm asking!'

'The bands were really good, even Tom Johnson's band, you know, from sixth form?'

'Oh, yes! Have you got pics on your phone of everyone?'

'I was too busy dancing.'

'Oh... Luke looked nice.'

'Yeah, but I've decided I just want to be a free agent.'

'Good for you, love. As long as you enjoyed yourself.'

'Yeah.'

Her mum gave her one of those "you can tell me anything looks" and Evie would have loved to... normally.

'You sure?'

'Yeah, just tired. Do you mind if I go back to sleep for a bit?'

'Of course, love. You looked beautiful, you know, even if your dad wanted to cover you up with one of my oversized cardis!'

Last night's events all seemed so much less important in the grand scheme of things, even to an eighteen-year-old.

THE TWENTY-THIRD ERA

2016

The year the United Kingdom voted to leave the European Union
and the year that five Brits were among the Mars One applicants
shortlisted for a one-way trip to Mars.

98
Claire

Jenny's world had shrunk to John, Evie and a series of pale blue uniforms that came to inspect her flesh for sores, leave her a cup of tea to go cold and write up the story of her demise in a "handover" book.

At first, Claire had tried to read these entries out to Jenny in funny voices until Jenny no longer laughed and Claire had no purpose to stay. She called out 'bye' each time as she closed their front door, noisily with a slam, but knowing there would be no answer. They were all in the upstairs hinterland of Jenny's departure lounge, oblivious to anyone other than an occasional doctor, who may, just may, extend her stay.

Claire took to writing again, darker and darker short stories, which to her surprise won her another prize, again with a presentation. She dressed in Jenny's "going away" lilac linen trouser suit that she had altered to wear in private, little knowing that she was to wear it for quite a few such public occasions. *Who'd have thought it, me a published writer!*

She felt safe in the knowledge that Jenny wouldn't be reading her latest short story now: "*floating face-down in the pretentious spa bath with requisite scented candles shifting the light, the chiffon bat-winged sleeves looked like gossamer wings ready to transport her to her next incarnation. Adult monarch butterflies live the longest at one hundred and eighty days, this woman was definitely a Painted Lady, who lived a mere fourteen days. She had to go."*

99
Evie

It was 4 a.m. and Evie's head was inevitably banging from the alphabetical alcohol challenge. She remembered getting to "F" for "Fuzzy Navel" (a peach schnapps) had them giggling uncontrollably, but the rest of the night out was lost. However, this added awful screeching sound was actually outside her head.

Disorientated in her tiny box room of only five days, she eased her head off the pillow and trod carefully to the window for clues. Other students were already gathering. Her heavy brain deduced that someone had set the fire alarm off; just one of the "multifarious taboos" they had been lectured about by some draconian fascist ruler. Still in last night's crop top and jeans, she grabbed her freshers' sweatshirt, more paracetamol with her water bottle and headed outside, as if a reluctant conscript to battle.

'Evie! Thought you'd be crispy bacon by now.'

'Can you not mention food.'

'Lightweight!'

'So, who was it?'

'Alex. Dom dared him.'

Evie's spinning head spun anew. She had scoped both boys out as potential allies on her corridor and now, although she was up for fun in her uni escape, there was a limit to the high drama she could cope with; she had enough of that at home. And now the fire engines' sirens split her head both with their insistent sound and the usual subtext of danger they semaphored.

'Evie, you okay? You look kinda green?'

The bilious taste in her mouth wasn't just a hangover but a visceral reminder of her life elsewhere. Only days before she left for uni, her dad was at work and she had called the ambulance when her mum became unresponsive. As the very same "nee naw" sound approached then, her knee-jerk response had been that it would delay her leaving for Exeter, thus all that she'd miss out on – and she'd hated herself.

However, her mum had rallied once more and came home stoically insistent that Evie didn't miss a moment of her new life. Anyway, Claire had muscled in (as usual), assuming she knew best and whisked her off to uni, alongside secret teddy, spider plants and kitchen paraphernalia destined to remain mostly unused. And where it should have been her mum and dad on that momentous journey, she had left her mum behind, who was forcing gaiety.

'And ring us and share all you dare! Then we can live it too.'

And Evie hadn't looked back – at that point; she had already been to three different nightclubs, eaten packet upon packet of Oreos, discovered she liked fish after all, cooked a first full meal for more than three, skinny dipped in the sea after dark, blown her allowance on a new surfer look and had a gym induction for some reason. She signed up for shitloads of societies, some of which she would actually attend, for example, acapella, martial arts, yoga, fencing (chosen for the advantageous boy: girl ratio) and the obligatory Marxist Society.

Whatever ensued, she had acquired a great supply of pens.

A select few of the thousands of selfies taken made it back to her parents on their nightly FaceTime calls. Evie felt she had just been on the steepest helter-skelter and on her very coarse mat, was sliding to an ungainly stop, trying to orientate herself again back to the start. And there was her brave mum holding up a mat for her to get back on the ride of her life.

'Dom looks nice!'

'Mum! I'm not going to get "entangled" with anyone. I'm here to have fun – and work obviously!'

'Obviously!' her dad interjected. Evie knew it was to save her mum's breath, as formerly he always used to let her take the lead in any conversation, particularly around boys.

'No lectures then yet!'

'It's still freshers, Dad! But I have met a girl, Ava, on my corridor who's doing the same psychology course. She's Polish and a bit homesick too.'

'You know you can come home anytime, love.'

Her mum, again hampered by emotion and weakness, struggled to speak:

'But you'd miss... out... You're missing nothing... here, love – I promise... You know Dad'd call you if '

Her dad, rescuing both of them:

'What your mum means is we haven't got nearly enough biscuits in for you. And anyway, we've rented your room out already... to a Hungarian circus duo.'

'Haha.'

'No, really. Gabor and, er... well, I forget her name! So, you'll have to wait a while to come home. You can always get us... anytime.'

Evie wanted to ring them right now to share this bizarre but somehow meaningful moment, as she was shivering outside her student block in the dawn of her new life – but realised she was being selfish. She knew her dad would be awake though; she pictured him right now, lying rigid next to her mum (in the new hospital bed which had to replace the one he had lovingly made for them) drinking her mum in. Just last week she'd come in late from a few farewell nights out, crept upstairs and caught him... waiting; she knew. *That was the start*, Evie thought, *of her own leaving – she'd always had to go first... whether it be Monopoly, a bath or... this.*

'Evie!'

'What?'

'I said, there's no point going to sleep now. We're going to Leah's, coming?'

'Oh... yeah, sure.'

100
Jenny

Jenny was increasingly tired now and was thus grateful that she'd already made her time capsule for her possible grandchildren. She had enlisted Claire's help to bury it in the garden and instructed her to tell John where it was when the first grandchild was born, or if he was to move. She had used a metal container Claire sourced for her and Claire had wound duct tape around it to seal it tight. Claire had left Jenny to fill the box herself and didn't ask what was in it; Jenny could see such "future" thoughts weren't Claire's cup of tea. Inside, Jenny put pictures of her own parents' wedding (an inexpensive town hall quickie and local pub reception with the rest of their police colleagues) in borrowed clothes, but they looked, as they were, blissfully happy. Other items included more photos, school reports and press cuttings over the years, her watch – an eighteenth present from her mum, always "kept safe" and was too ornamental for Evie to wear. Jenny felt it was an apt token from the past and she believed in energies passed on through such items. She didn't expect Evie's clay thumb pot to convey any such energy, but it told a tale, as did wrappers from an assortment of their favourite chocolate bars, and John's only poem he wrote for their first anniversary. It was difficult to prune these memory items to fit into such a small space, but Jenny filled every corner with charms – Evie's scan picture and a lock of all their hair – and love, so much love.

The days and nights became a blur of visiting Macmillan nurses. The list of things she'd wanted to do "before..." hadn't been touched and the Christmas angel and snowflake (she'd bought in Brighton) lay somewhere in their weekend bag, now lying unneeded in the loft. She hadn't even had the energy to get John to unearth them, even though the tree looked somewhat lacklustre – it was probably their perspective and not the decoration.

She was glad her mum had died last year suddenly of a heart attack whilst out at bowls; how perfect an end. This was no life and soon it would indeed be exactly that. So, Jenny had enlisted her regular and favourite nurse, Evelyn, to scribe those important last letters she had been meaning to steel herself to do a few months ago when the treatment fatefully shifted to just palliative. John and Evie, however, were investigating treatment trials for some months more, angrily refusing to accept her very acceptance.

John had a very old-fashioned attitude to her privacy and Jenny's bedside cabinet was to him a strange "woman-only domain" of "goodness knows what", so she knew he wouldn't look in there until he was ready to clear out her belongings. Little did he know that there was nothing more exciting in there than old evaporated lavender oil bottles, "must reads" that weren't ever read, a crystal she had been given to help with Evie's birth that she had thrown across the room (swearing with one particular climactic contraction), a travel iron that had never been used (who irons on holiday?), a silk sleep mask with a broken band and a tiny wooden Buddha that hadn't lived up to its promise.

Thus, she safely deposited the letters to Evie and John in there. She had struggled with Claire's and, in the end, had decided to get Evelyn to send it to her on her way home to see if it provoked a better farewell than was currently happening and, well, she would just have to read it prematurely.

101
Claire

The postman rarely came to Claire's door as Tony's letters, which remained resolutely unopened, gradually slowed to just one update at Christmas and she'd put a stop to all other junk mail. So, she was surprised to hear her letterbox hinge creak and even more to see Jenny's blue stationery. She took a strong coffee and the letter to her cherry blossom seat, as she knew it wasn't to be an easy read.

"Dear Claire,

I couldn't rely on John or Evie to remember to give this to you when I die..."

Claire had refused to discuss the "d" word with Jenny, so was already irate.

"... so, I am afraid you are going to have this early and maybe are reading this before I've gone. Don't worry, this isn't going to be one of those end-of-life letters telling you how to live your own life, 'make the most of every day', etcetera – except DO!

"I just wanted to tell you how much you have meant to me in the last twenty-five of my fifty-two years. You will find this soppy, I know, but I often thought we were two sides of a coin meant to find each other to balance and help each other through this strange life. You are definitely the spikier 'tail'! And now one side of that coin is wiped out, I'm sorry not to be there for you but do so hope that the family you have become to Evie and John will sustain you through any future emotional blips

you may have (sorry, 'blips' seems wrong, but my addled brain cannot find the right words). I know you may well have screwed this letter up by now, but I am going to plough on.

"As you know, I felt as if I let you down badly all those years ago and have wanted to make recompense, but it became more than that. We were two people plagued, then bonded, by our own insecurities and I was lucky to find people, including you, to bolster me through what turned into such a happy and fulfilling life. I have few regrets (don't worry, I am not breaking into song!), just that I didn't speak out for you all those years ago and didn't enable you to get your possible BPD diagnosis sooner..."

'What!'

Claire felt sick. How did Jenny know, how? After much pacing and a tumbler of port, as that's all she had left in the cupboard, she read on:

"... but then we might never have met again, and I am too selfish to think of not having had you as part of my life's fabric. You are sooo bloody-minded, have awful dress sense, are resistant to any attempts of mine to hug you for longer than a nano-second, fiercely independent to your own detriment, but are an amazing physio, artist, writer, comic and the best confidante (you'd say 'who else would you tell!'). You are my gardening and Prosecco pal and the driest, wittiest person I know, who can test my pelvic floor to its absolute limits! I so want you to be as good a friend to someone else; they are missing out at present, and so are you.

In my experience, there are all sorts of friends one can have: the casual Christmas card contacts either from nostalgia or pure nosiness; the school friend whom you have nothing in common with anymore, and you hate their FaceBook politics but with whom you shared awful school dinners and they knew your parents when all were young; the first flatmates who flung themselves into adulthood alongside you, kept your basest secrets and you kept theirs, so you're bonded and on social media and keen to see them happy; work colleagues whom you share coffee break confidences, moans about superiors and so many hours of your life that they 'get you' or part of you; the school gate friends, who through shared lack of sleep have seen you at your worst - and you, them. And (I'm sorry, Claire) they know that primal fear now of possibly losing the most precious being in our lives, our own child. And then there is you who lost your precious Oliver and was so misunderstood, but you gave all of yourself to our friendship, even endangering yourself by visiting Tom that time. You became the friend that became the 'best'..."

At this "best", Claire laid face down on her bed and howled years of tears into her pillows, then took the rest of the port out to her seat again.

"... but you became the friend that became the 'best' because I know of those dark places, we visited many of them together, as well as the 'real' places we visited, albeit as very 'unreal' people. How I loved that pretence! You allowed me to escape from everyday life and myself, and push a few (who am I kidding, LOADS of) boundaries! I think all that roleplay helped me to be happier with the me I discovered and returned to at last. Thus, we are bonded forever.

"And, also, no one else has cleared up my sick-stained, best top after a girls' weekend away, to a spa of all places, where, do you remember, we only had one treatment: a sadistic body massage. So, we said we were ill and spent the rest of the weekend calling room service for the cheapest but turned out to be the most throat-stripping and extortionate house wine! Remember, you laundered it and popped it round when I was out, telling John you'd borrowed it – as if you'd wear anything of my, quote, 'clown outfits'!

You keep the best secrets (including the unmentionable one) and have never judged my worst traits, some shared only with you. I love you, my friend, and wish you real happiness wherever you may find it. Please, as you are doing already, keep an eye on my John and Evie, but also on yourself.

Your forever mate, Jenny xxxxxx"

Claire did make it to the end of the letter and decided she wouldn't tear it up just yet, but she wouldn't visit Jenny again, she was gone to her.

102
Jenny

Jenny was surprised to hear Claire's voice on the stairs as John had said he'd phoned and phoned and asked her to come, but she had declined in that very blunt Claire way, saying: "there was no point". But he had kept ringing and here she was. Jenny was so relieved. She could only be totally herself with Claire and she was so tired of pretending to be brave and embracing her dying when she was still greedy for more time. John ushered Claire in and left them to it.

Claire sat as far away from Jenny as she could in the overstuffed bedroom, which was now full of hospital detritus and chairs for hushed visitors. Jenny struggled to prop herself up a little more so her blurry eye line was level with Claire's, but she slid back down again trying to disguise her pain-wincing with a smile. Clearly, Claire wasn't going to play nurse.

'I told John not to get Evie back from uni yet; she's so enjoying it, but I'm so glad you came.'

Claire just fixed her with a resentful look.

'I know you're angry with me for going. I'm angry with me too.'

Jenny now found talking exhausting, but she was compelled to discharge her fears.

'I haven't had... that dream yet.'

'What fucking dream?'

If Jenny had it in her to laugh, she would have.

'The dream you're... meant to have at the end... the one with light... and the tunnel... and my mum and... my dad waiting for me.'

'That's crap!'

'Don't say that... I need to know it's not the end—'

'Now who's the deluded one!'

Jenny did manage a smile, but it was extinguished by an excruciating wave of pain and she saw the pain-wincing had been registered by Claire this time (she had refused her medicine earlier as she wanted to be more awake, just a little while longer). However, these efforts and exchanges exhausted her and she drifted off once more. She remembered John coming in saying he was just popping out to get some milk, if Claire was okay to stay – and then sleeping again until she thought: "this is it".

She couldn't breathe. And it was all dark. Where was the goddamn light that was meant to appear? She struggled against the dark and gulped for air, and as she did, it went light again and she saw Claire's face, the unrecognisable look in her eyes and the pillow she was holding. She managed to find a sound from deep inside her – and Claire ran out of the room.

She tried to call out John's name when she heard him come back, but they were talking downstairs. She fell back against the pillows, wondering if it was the morphine as she couldn't... and yet so could, believe what had just almost happened. She reached for the pen and paper with which Evelyn had written the farewell letters and managed to write:

"John–– Don't trus Claire anymor... tried smother me... she's mad... so, so sorry"

She put it in an envelope and put it in her bedside table, and exhausted with these exhortations, fell asleep.

103
Claire

Claire had seen Jenny struggling to breathe, had seen the tiniest of tattoos, the butterfly she had talked her into getting as a symbol of the transformational change she had enabled in Claire. It just settled near her collarbone and that had done it for her. She had snapped. And then ran home and holed up, yet again.

104

John

In Jenny's final winter, her chest gently rose and fell. John, his exhausted head propped in his big hands, waited... and realised he was holding his own breath as the time between her breaths lengthened. She and so he too, had been like this for days now. Even as the newly-inserted syringe driver whirred its persistent doses (hooked onto her borrowed hospital bed), the catheter bag drained the last of Jenny's life's juices. The digital clock by her bed clicked to 2:07 a.m.

He held her loose wedding-ringed hand on the crisp white bedlinen; he had remade it only that morning – a lifetime away. The detail of death. At 2:09 a.m. the air changed; she was really gone.

Nothing had altered in the room and, yet, everything had. At last, stirred by a brazen chink of light which seared through the straining blousy curtains (Jenny never did master sewing), he tucked her in tenderly and laid the picture of Evie, gap-toothed at seven, face down on his wife's quiet heart, bringing the sheet up under her chin, not able to cover her face, not yet, and switched off the clock at the wall. Wrong that time was still moving on.

Amidst the detritus of final days – the wet wipes, valiant room deodorisers and drug timetables – John found Jenny's lists of things to do and people to ring – now death was an official visitor.

Amongst the bottles of morphine and rescue remedies, he found a bottle of sherry. This and vodka jellies had become her new five-a-day. He poured himself a large tumbler and went into the garden, shrouded by the long unpruned leylandii, standing like white sentinel, still in his shirtsleeves, oblivious to the chill air.

'Claire?'

'Oh, John... has... Oh, god!'

'At 2:09 this morning. She just didn't wake up. Sorry, I didn't know if it was too early to phone you?'

'I couldn't sleep. I had a feeling. Do you want me to come over?'

'No!'

This was said too forcefully. He didn't know why, but he knew Jenny wouldn't want Claire there, or anyone just yet, and neither did he. He had just needed to say the words to someone. He softened his voice.

'Thank you, but Doctor Perry's on his way. I ought to phone the funeral directors. I just don't want to set all that in motion somehow, not yet. I want to sit with her awhile. That's okay, isn't it?'

With the saying of these words, it was all becoming more real and John, a previously unfaltering man, began the "falterings".

'Of course. There's no right or wrong way. Take your time... Does Evie know?'

'No, I should tell her now, I just...'

'I'll call her right away.'

'It should be me.'

'No "shoulds". I'm family really too, remember? And I'm here for you.'

'Thank you.'

'I'll come over this afternoon to be with you. No arguments.'

When the doctor had left, John bolstered himself with another sherry and coke. It felt wrong to open a red just yet. He filled the plastic washing-up bowl with warm water in their newly replaced country kitchen and carried it carefully up to her bedside. Then, dipping her flannel, he soaped it up with some lavender soap he found at the back of the bathroom cabinet. The cloying smell hit the back of his throat and he knew Jenny would say it smelt of old ladies, so he emptied the bowl and started again with her everyday soap.

'No fuss, Jen, I know, but got to get it right, eh?'

He spoke, wanting to believe she was still listening, still there. The washing was easy compared to the hugely difficult dressing of her unhelpful body.

'Sorry, love, never was much good at bras, was I? But this is a first, doing one up!'

Yes, this had to be right, this last act of love. And he had all the time in the world. He was glad of the time – seven, then eight o'clock – so that rush hour was over and the road outside was rightfully quiet. And he hadn't wanted strangers turning her flesh, although he knew soon they would have to handle her. But at least he had done this, prepared her in the chosen dress. A mauve silk that she had selected online, knowing that it would suit this new pallor and would shroud her – gossamer clouds enveloping her (she had joked) "once in a lifetime svelte figure". John had mostly mourned cancer stealing her once fulsome body, her supine splayed belly that used to shake with their Sunday morning lay-in laughter – she had always loved a lie-in.

He arranged the silk folds around her legs – fanning the fabric out – and stood back like a window dresser appraising a mannequin.

He tried a wolf whistle, but it petered out, and every ounce of John's six-foot-two and sixteen-stone frame folded in on him:

'Oh, Jen.'

Feeling this weight of his fifty-four years corpulent past and empty present, he traipsed downstairs to the notepad of IMPORTANT

NUMBERS. He slumped onto their well-worn leather sofa. Their Labrador, Lewis (after the detective), found his lap and weighted him still with his big heavy head. He fondled Lewis's velvety ears, stalling just a little longer. Then, when Lewis finally sunk by his feet, he set the whole funeral fiasco in motion. He made his way through all the unsurprised relatives and friends – calling them, ticking their names off Jenny's list, crossing through her feeble handwriting.

'Hello, Jan, I didn't know what time it was out there, but you'd said to ring whenever...'

'Margery? It's John... Yes, early this morning.'

'Laura... yes, I'm so sorry.'

Stopping after every batch to climb the stairs and check in again on Jenny.

'Daft.'

The saxophone doorbell rang. Jenny had chosen it ironically for their unmusical family and he welcomed the sound as the noiseless funeral directors hushed in. Each item of furniture these men slunk past screamed Jenny at them. John couldn't understand why they didn't see that. Her console table in the hall piled high with hats and scarves nobody wore but Jenny kept in case visitors needed one. The desk on the landing with drawers stuffed with Evie's playgroup paintings and displaying her wonky clay pots and netball trophies. Their marital bed where she had revelled in her Sunday lie-ins, until life was all lie-in. They lifted her, *tenderly*, John thought, and then they hushed out again.

He hoped they had Bob Marley, or Led Zeppelin even, playing at full volume, when safely alone in the hearse with Jenny. From Beethoven to The Backstreet Boys, she'd had an eclectic musical taste, or "tragic" as Evie had described it – but her mother had just liked human family noise around her best.

He was sure they had to keep the hearse free from crumbs too and obviously couldn't be seen to eat when on view at traffic lights, say, but, maybe on the open road, they could go about their normal lives; perhaps stop for a Big Mac. Maybe they had special compartments under the coffin bit where they could store their rubbish. She would feel more at ease if it wasn't too tidy though. She had always prioritised living rather than tidying the house.

"Lived in, that's what it is, and the cobwebs? They're performance art!"

He went back upstairs, pulled back the curtains just a little and sat on their empty bed. Then he opened the "D-Day note" Jenny had penned for him:

"Now you're reading this, I am presuming the cheery coffin collectors have carried me off and you are left on your tod, or with Evie if she's back. Sooo, first make yourself a milky coffee and a cheese and pickle sandwich to soak up the booze. See, I know you so well! Then, why don't you put the football on, or an episode of Only Fools and Horses, *and then face another day? Live your life to the max for me and encourage Evie to never look back... Always yours, loveliest man, Jenny xx"*

And overleaf he saw:

"P.S. longer epistle to come!"

The funeral day arrived. Sitting in the pew, Evie on one side and Claire on the other, John turned to see moving up the aisle the ridiculous bright turquoise box she had insisted on and riding inside his Jenny. Then, somehow, his legs took him to the lectern.

'She always said she left nursing to spare humanity but was never happier than—'

He caught Evie's eye and coughed away the lump of emotion wedged in his throat.

'And the Christmas Jenny got us all to volunteer at the soup kitchen. She was put on the cooking team but had misread the quantities. Maths, never her strong point, she had made the treacle for the sponge pudding into brittle, that could have kept dentists in business forevermore.'

'Evermore', another cough and he was nearly at the end.

'Jenny had the largest capacity to laugh and to love that I have known or will ever know… it was just a shame she couldn't cook.'

He had wanted levity at this point and a few friends tried to support him with a faded chortle, but the swallowed cry in his voice soon smothered any further laughter.

'… otherwise, she was the perfect person and my perfect life companion.'

"So brave" and "did her proud", all the usual platitudes followed, then back to theirs for a spread that materialised on actual tablecloths he'd forgotten they possessed. Claire had pulled this off, not him – what would he have done without her – he had no other family now and Evie was only eighteen and snatched back from freshers' week into premature adulthood. But what next? Evie was adamant she would go right back to Exeter, not able to stay on in the house without her mum just yet. Claire insisted she'd take her. John just acquiesced; he couldn't deal with his own emotions let alone those of their beloved Evie.

The kitchen radiators were draped with drying baby clothes and the fridge magnets still held the first precious purple daubings of Alfies. It was Janet's own version of *Homes and Gardens*; she loved this feeling of new life in her house. Ella had Ailsa, the bonniest of babies, six months ago and so she was now back at work. Thus, Nanna Jan was called on more and more. Janet was in her element but was increasingly tired lately. Ella had collected Ailsa and left Janet with a lasagne for tea which Janet just moved around her plate; she had no appetite lately. She'd just picked up the paper to see whether *Antiques Roadshow* was on to while away some of the evening when the phone rang.

'Is that Janet?'

'Sorry to trouble you, but I know you knew my wife, Jenny?'

Janet clocked the "knew" and held her breath. Jeff had been dead for almost three years, but each successive news of a death plummeted her into others' grief.

'Yes?'

'Well, I am just going through her address book to tell everyone.'

Janet heard this deep voice catch and wanted to hold him.

'I am sorry to have to tell you she died two days ago, and I wanted to let you know when the funeral is – in case...'

Antiques Roadshow was a repeat and Janet couldn't settle for knitting or anything. She couldn't decide if she wanted to go to the funeral for Jenny's sake – she hardly knew her, but she felt they had formed a special bond – or whether she hoped to see Claire there and maybe have a chance to talk. *Death prods you to have these conversations before it's too late*, she thought, like the one she needed to have with Tony about telling Liv about her mum.

Janet wrangled with these thoughts in bed for hours. She got up once to find some antacid, as she had that pain in her chest again. It must have been the little lasagne that she ate resting heavily on her.

106
Claire

'Claire?'

Bloody Nigel again.

'Everything okay?'

'Well, you must know as we never do social calls, that it's Mum.'

'Go on.'

'Apparently, she had a massive heart attack last night and died. The doctor said she wouldn't have known anything about it.'

'Oh... Was anyone with her?'

'Ella found her this morning.'

'Ella?'

'Her adopted daughter. Our "sister"!'

'Oh... yes.'

'Well... I'll call you back with all the funeral arrangements. As I imagine, you'll want to leave that to me and Ella?'

'Don't bother.'

'Oh, Claire! Don't be like this. She was your mother too, for god's sake!'

'I'm not "being like" anything. We're all entitled to deal with loss our own way. You do the dutiful son bit and leave me be.'

'Oh, typical! Why did I bother? Well, fuck you, Claire.'

Claire had taken a week's compassionate leave and the hibernation spooled into months, with only necessary outings to work as all food and wine were delivered now. Evie had exams and said she didn't want visits as they were distracting and John was lost in his grief, so she had no human contact and could think of no reason to live.

Conor was at swimming training and so Liv had been sitting with a cup of tea ploughing through her year seven's marking of *Sherlock Holmes* so they could enjoy their evening when he got in.

She was kept on her toes by the students at her school, but she was never bored and had a few gems stored up to share with Conor on his return, such as: "Benedict Cumberpatch has got squinty eyes which help him find clues, but then he smokes weed and he forgets so the Doctor has to help." Priceless!

Then Ella telephoned. Her reverie was interrupted; Aunty Jan had died. Conor came home to find Olivia sitting in the dark, rocking.

Ella, on hand and practical, had taken on the organisation of the funeral and Liv helped shoulder some of the phone calls. This time, only ten days from that phone call, they were back in the same crematorium (Janet wanted the same low-key send-off as her beloved Jeff), but Liv did get to deliver a eulogy this time:

'My Aunty Jan had the biggest heart of anyone I know or will ever know. That is why it seems understandable this extremely hardworking heart should wear out too soon. What a lot of use it had. As well as her own biological children, Nigel and Claire, that heart loved thirty-seven other children unconditionally. These also lived with her – and they had many more who visited for various lengths of time. She joked she was like the nursery rhyme: The "old woman who lived in a shoe, she had so many children she didn't know what to do". But she knew just what to do. And we all fitted happily into the tiny kitchen for after-school cookies and in the garden, kitted out with every swing and slide combination possible, and there were always random mounds of earth where buried treasure excavations were ongoing. She carried child-like enthusiasm and wonder throughout life and gave them as gifts to all of us. This is shown by Aunty Jan's favourite poem which she had up on the sitting room wall: *My Heart Leaps Up* by William Wordsworth:

> *"My heart leaps up when I behold*
> *A rainbow in the sky:*
> *So was it when my life began;*
> *So is it now I am a man;*
> *So be it when I shall grow old,*
> *Or let me die!*
> *The Child is father of the Man;*
> *And I could wish my days to be*
> *Bound each to each by natural piety."*

'Aunty Jan's heart leapt at the sight of rainbows too. Yes, always recognising every happy omen but mostly when she saw happy children. And our own hearts leapt when we had her attention; her oft-given hugs on her accommodating lap, her reading *The Hungry Caterpillar* and *Harry Potter* – for the trillionth time – her famous suet puddings and her encouragement to be exactly... who we are.'

Liv was very touched to be left a surprisingly large legacy in Jan's will and, because she was now twenty-five, in a relatively secure job and a homeowner (even if it was only the airing cupboard she officially owned), she felt she needed to honour Jan's life in some way. After talking it over with Conor, she decided to set up a local charity for those children without an Aunty Jan to have a mentor in their lives. These mentors, "aunties/uncles", would, say, once a week, take their mentee skating, to the cinema or an art gallery to encourage them to develop interests and discover who they were. Aunty Jan had taken her to umpteen tennis tournaments before Liv discovered she really wasn't going to be the next Serena Williams, but Aunty Jan had backed her all the way. She equally understood and allowed her to stop when she had fallen out of love with tennis and in love with the band *London After Midnight*.

This action helped with her grief which she hadn't ever anticipated being so huge. Mostly it arrived when she was cooking. She could hear Aunty Jan's gentle instructions: "Maybe turn down the gas a fraction and it won't catch as much" – meant she was burning something; "Try a bit more salt maybe" – when something was particularly tasteless. Ella and Liv had divided up her dogeared, chocolate-stained, well-loved cookbooks between them. She then discovered cooking wasn't just a necessity for survival but could be enjoyable and, most importantly, it was a bridge across the divide she was feeling. Conor complained he would have to train harder as he'd sink in the pool, but he appreciated the spoils of her efforts, as well as the therapy for Liv.

108
Claire

Claire lacked the will to carry out any of her suicidal thoughts. Work kept her tied to life and, amazingly, she still had a diary full of patients in her own private practice. She had decided to go fully out on her own, partly because she told colleagues she wanted time for her writing, but also following a sticky supervision in a hot office with her old boss, which resulted in Claire, unfortunately, telling her that body odour wasn't an asset for management!

After the first few months, John began occasionally dropping in on Claire for what she imagined were duty visits, but she found herself almost as dependent on their chats as she had been on Jenny's former appearances out of nowhere. She still felt Jenny's presence and expected her to rock up alongside John. There was a space next to him somehow.

They spoke a lot about Evie and her way of coping which was clearly "out and out" denial. She still found it painful to come "home" and Christmas had been excruciating, with neither one knowing if family rituals were to be upheld, reinvented or just plain buried. Thus, Claire had a mission: Mission Spoil Evie and Create New Rituals. She turned up as a surprise with what she felt was a grown-up hamper of Champagne and seafood straight from Exeter's shores. Evie didn't seem overjoyed to see her, but that was teenagers she felt. (Evie, in fact, had hidden her current beau under her bed when Claire called "Surprise!" over the intercom. A surprise indeed it was.)

It was very apparent, after said picnic, that Evie would rather get on with her life without Claire's input. Evie had cited very important one-to-one tutorials, which Claire saw through and so came home, calling in on John to update him on his daughter, omitting the rumpled sheets and neck foundation disguises.

John had just gotten in from the shops with what he admitted was a rather large bag of ingredients for one. He still wasn't used to a meagre shop, even though Evie had been away again seven months now and Jenny longer still.

Evie and he cancelled Christmas and even her birthday celebrations in the end and had stockpiled takeaways in the freezer, but his New Year's resolution had been to take better care of his daughter – and himself. He kindly invited Claire to stay and eat with him and, while he was cooking, they fell into easy inconsequential chatter about Claire's broad bean crop and John's forsaken vegetable patch. Then, he admitted to not getting on top of the garden jobs – Jenny's garden – and it spooled into not even sorting Jenny's clothes yet. Whereupon Claire said with her usual directness that there was "no time like the present" and, while John cooked, she could make a start on Jenny's clothes.

Jenny had an affliction for keeping old clothes that she may well slim into one day, or that Evie would (never) wear. So, a feverish hour of fixedly remembering so many of Jenny's clothes – particular character costumes she'd kept for particular outings – and eventual bagging meant she had still only made a small dent in Jenny's stash (and, of course, selected those she might gradually also bring into her own wardrobe) before supper was ready. But it had stilled her mind somewhat.

Claire felt she could get used to this; John at her side pouring the Malbec solicitously and drawing conversation from her tricky depths, even when he was still obviously grieving. They had this in common even more so now, and she felt also so much more.

Several Friday evenings were thus spent with Claire sorting and bagging Jenny's clothes for the various "charity shops", having been told curtly by Evie that she didn't need clothes to remember her mum by. John had exhausted his culinary repertoire and had been trawling the internet for different countries' cuisines to try out on Claire on these "sorting" evenings, with appropriate wine pairings.

One night, they had both "paired too many" and Claire had to sleep in the guest room, thus sorting could happen on the Saturday morning too. John joined her and sat by Jenny's bedside cabinet, confiding that he felt he was rooting in Jenny's deepest secrets.

'Not that we had any.'

'Surely you did?'

'No, we spoke about everything or at least I think so unless you're going to tell me otherwise?'

And, of course, at that moment he reached in and found the envelopes addressed to him and Evie. He asked Claire if she minded leaving then, as he was suddenly overwhelmed. Claire left and went home via the off-licence and had wine for lunch.

THE TWENTY-FOURTH ERA

2017

The year that Manchester Arena was attacked by a suicide bomber
at an Ariana Grande concert.

109
John

He knew he would wait until Evie came home at Easter to hand over her mum's letter so he could be with her, but he had no such delay tactic for his. His wonderful wife, selfless to the end, had charted all their best memories, excerpts from their wild, themed parties, the birth of their beloved daughter to their quieter sofa side-by-side times...

"... and the first time we took Evie abroad. We had obviously got food poisoning from the unwashed salad in a snatched street food burger on the way to the airport, and the whole of the flight home we were trying not to be ill. Remember, we even allowed Evie to be passed around and cooed over by complete strangers, almost forgetting to take her back, as we rushed for the plane's exit and the nearest loos! We vowed never to go back to Turkey but, of course, we did. How wonderful were all those holidays, from the early, always rainy, camping ones, when every other family seemed to remember the washing-up bowl for the dirty crockery, and the tea towels. We only ever remembered the cork screw – we weren't natural campers, were we! On the other extreme was the more ambitious sailing one in Greece, when poor Evie had her first unrequited crush on that awful prig of a boat hand, 'summering' on the seas!"

Although Jenny's tumour was stealing her memory, she had forgotten nothing from their shared past and then said that it was time for more...

"... *sooo, I hope that very soon you will start making more memories with just Evie and then maybe with someone else. And you know what an integral part Claire has been to my life, our lives; she always 'had my back' and now I know she will have yours.*"

She went on to urge John to be kind to her and so generously suggested Claire should become more a part of their lives, and now that he realised that was precisely what was happening already, he felt suddenly sick.

There were more envelopes for Jan and Tom in Australia, for other friends, his sister and colleagues. She had thought of everyone, of course she had, and momentarily he had forgotten her.

One last unlabelled envelope was left, not in the nurse's hand, but Jenny's own shaky one and so he opened it and the sickness returned. He rushed to the bathroom and remembered the time when he had gone down on one knee to Jenny by such a toilet basin. And here he was retching about his betrayal, but more sickeningly Claire's final betrayal. But what to do?

IIO
Claire

It was early on Sunday morning and she was sitting in the garden with a first cup of Earl Grey, having just prepped one of her, hopefully, last roast beef meals for one – a memory of her mother's Sunday roasts pinched her consciousness, but she denied it entry. She was mentally deadheading but also wondering how much she'd miss every plant if, or indeed when, she moved in with John and Evie. She would definitely dig up the Ceanothus. After all, Jenny had given her that, blue again, of course. She'd ask John to help her take the pergola apart, which would work in the corner of "her new garden" with honeysuckle to sit beneath maybe, or a white climbing rose.

And there, as if she'd conjured him up, was John striding through the garden gate, unusually for him letting it clatter shut behind him.

She rose eagerly to greet him, hoping he wouldn't notice (or maybe that he subconsciously would) the Jenny top she'd altered and was using as a gardening smock. An easy smile on her face ready to mirror his, she held up her teacup questioningly to offer him one. As he strode purposefully towards her, he was unrecognisable.

His usually open, calm face was twisted and red with rage. His arms were flailing, and he paced around the garden spitting venom at her, just "like the murderous snake in the grass" he said she was. He trampled her flower beds, upended her bird table, snapped her broad bean canes and wielded them in her face.

This formerly mild-mannered man didn't know how to vent this unfamiliar, apoplectic rage, and only when he frightened himself with "you don't deserve to live!" did he calm down. He suddenly started sobbing, uncontrollably. Then, as quickly as he arrived, he turned on his heel and ran out of the garden.

She couldn't, wouldn't, recall all the words he'd flung at her. She sat unmoving with her cold cup of tea in her lap throughout his barrage – and until the sun went down, then somehow went inside.

III
John

John and Evie found a lovely Airbnb that Jenny would have chosen too, right on the coast in Budleigh Salterton, fifteen miles from Exeter. John wanted to be regularly on hand just in case she needed a good meal out or a supermarket shop. Therefore, that particular weekend, John left Claire's house and went home to make some calls and then drove straight there and walked along the coast, only messaging Evie his whereabouts when he felt in control enough of his emotions.

Once sat at their favourite cream tea shop with an obligatory cake stand crammed with calories, John had to talk. He didn't tell Evie the full story, of course. He'd had to do some digging into Claire's past to piece it all together. He had spoken to her brother, not an only child after all then, and found out about her suspected borderline personality and the double life that Jenny had been duped into believing and, so, had carried her for years at her own expense. And had only found out at her own terrifying end.

Claire had tried to kill her and, to John's mind, she had done just that. He couldn't bear to share with Evie that this python had been entwining herself for years into their lives, he just said that he'd discovered that Claire had been deceiving them after all.

'She just wasn't the person we thought she was, and your dear mum had been propping her up for years; I've told her we don't need her in our lives anymore.'

'I could have told you that, Dad!'

There it was – an era and friendship ended. So, it wasn't until John got home late on Sunday evening and saw the police car outside his house that he allowed himself a thought of Claire again.

112
Claire

The method always worked before, for her "attempts" anyway, so Claire saw no reason not to think third time lucky. She always knew this day would come, had been deluded to think otherwise. Having written the note and locked up the house (she didn't want burglars after all), she took the bottle of wine and her only remaining crystal glass into the garden, sat under the cherry tree and drank quickly. There was nothing to savour, even though it was a good Rioja bought for next Friday's meal with John. The sobs came at this point. Once the bottle was empty, she hit the glass against it and the dying light entered the crystal, just as she had written it would. She placed the shard's tip against her jugular vein this time and lay down on Oliver's cold bones.

113
Olivia

Six months after Aunty Jan's death, Liv was once again marking piles of schoolwork whilst Conor was at swimming training – and bad news came in a different form.

The doorbell rang and her dad was standing sheepishly on the doorstep with flowers, which took her aback as her dad had never bought her flowers. He favoured vouchers or money, always apologising for his lack of imagination but Liv was always touched, as she knew he worried he'd get it so wrong otherwise.

'What a lovely surprise. I thought you and Samantha were on holiday still?'

'Got back last night. I'm not interrupting, am I? Looks as if you're marking?'

'I'm always marking, Dad. Don't be daft, this is a treat.'

'Well, not so much a treat, I'm afraid.'

'What do you mean? Are you okay?'

Liv almost dropped the coffee percolator she was about to fill – suddenly terrified that her last remaining family member, now that Aunty Jan had gone, might also forsake her.

'Yes, I'm fine, love. There's no easy way to say this other than this – I've just heard that your mother has died.'

Liv's "oh" held a million meanings and questions.

'How do you know, I mean, I didn't know you were in contact, or I had presumed, you never...'

'This is huge, I know, love. But she, your mother, wouldn't let anyone tell you. But now she's dead, well...'

'Go on.'

Liv managed to pour them both strong black coffee, stir much-needed sugar into hers, pace, sip despite scalding, anything to keep "doing" and not be still, which would let this all sink in. Not yet.

114
Evie

Evie was home from uni for the summer break and steeled herself to find a job locally that would peg her down to stay for some of the holiday with her dad. Last Christmas had been shite, of course. It was their first as just the two of them (except for the unmentionable Claire sticking her unwanted oar in until Evie had given her short shift), but anyway, after two weeks, Evie had escaped back to uni to breathe and live again. Then at Easter, she got a job in a bar in Exeter, but this time knew she had to find a way of being at home again, for a month at least.

When she heaved her bags up to her old bedroom, she couldn't believe how dated it seemed and so, at last, she had a project to distract herself with. So, with the bank of Dad, Evie bought a new bed, a double instead of the impossibly narrow bed of her childhood, and set to painting over the past with ombre effect walls. All this helped somewhat and they fell into a safe easy rhythm of preparing tea together. On the evenings that she wasn't out with friends or on shift at the local Italian, he indulged her with the TV remote. He became an expert on all the reality dating shows and knew who really shouldn't stay with whom, but neither of them talked of him ever dating again; an impossible thought for either of them.

They didn't begin conversations about the past much either as when Jenny came up, emotions stalled them and it was easier to just live in the present for now. So, it made Evie even more angry when a letter came from the Coroner's Office for her dad and she was forced to talk about those times – and Claire.

'But why do you have to go, Dad?'

'I've got to, to give evidence.'

'Of what?'

'They need to get a better understanding of why she took her own life.'

'What's the point, she's gone now?'

'They need to understand the circumstances that made her want to do that.'

'Well, whatever it was, good riddance, I say.'

'You don't mean that.'

'I do and so do you!'

'It's complicated, Evie, but I can't bear that you are so angry.'

'She tried to be Mum. Even you said that, and she couldn't, nobody could!'

This was the crux of it all, the attempt to steal her mum's place in the world, and she knew it compounded her hurt and loss. Her dad was powerless to help her grieve, as he still didn't know how to either.

THE TWENTY-FIFTH ERA

2018

The year that Professor Stephen Hawking died.

115
John

John had been hanging on, but then it was as if the bungee cord he fell with, and was dangling on since Jenny's death, had been cut. Now he was in freefall. Colleagues clearly thought he should be "moving on" by now, and as John hadn't shared this latest twist in Jenny's story, he felt on different wavelengths to them all.

Like so many, particularly men, he realised he was holding his pain deep within and that cold stone twisted its jagged edges at the most unlikely times. On an inspection of a new estate, he found he couldn't breathe and had to stagger to his car. He had gone to have a closer look at the proposed foundations of the last house to be finished (as there was a tree preservation order on it), and a piece of blue plastic had been whipped up by the wind and flew at him, catching him in the eye. It was the combination of staring into the frozen, clay earth below and the elements conspiring to bring him up sharp that had him fleeing home. There he sat with Jenny's urn in his lap sobbing. He still couldn't bring himself to scatter her ashes in such cold inhospitable ground.

John's formerly pragmatic and positive approach to life had been shaken; the only person left to believe in and live for was Evie. The way she coped was to look forward, just as Jenny wished, and he so longed to reminisce with her about Jenny but dared not reactivate her grief, especially by discussing his latest conundrum.

John was the reluctant executor of Claire's will. Indeed, he had said yes after two bottles of Rioja on an empty stomach a full two years ago when they decided to have these conversations to be "sensible" about the future, never knowing these would be the circumstances. He had been physically sick at seeing his name as a beneficiary. He couldn't accept any money from her estate; he had to sort out this other unknown beneficiary but what to do about Evie? Almost half of a decent house sale was a tidy sum of money that would set her up for life. John was still mulling how to broach the subject with her as he began the clearance of Claire's documents explicitly left for him to deal with.

He had been unusually terse and tight-lipped when Claire's brother called regarding the funeral arrangements and had evasively said he'd be "out of the country", as would Evie, which sadly the brother seemed to accept as part of people's lives moving on. How wrong they were. His own life still seemed unable to shift from the overwhelming angry stage of grief for his beloved Jenny.

EPILOGUE

2019

The year Greta Thunberg made a historic speech at the UN Climate Change Summit.

Evie and her fiancé had come for Christmas; now a slightly easier time with new traditions in the making. Over many meaningful mealtime conversations, Evie had enabled John to reach the decision he had been grappling with ever since Evie and Harry had bought their first house. He had enjoyed being entrusted with rubber stamping their choice of home and enabling them both to gather DIY skills, but this also made him redundant in many ways. Dad was no longer needed to fix the leak or build a shed; they were doing it themselves.

He had rattled around in the family home for too long, and realised it just wasn't needed anymore and it was time to move on. So, as soon as January began and his new year's resolve was still strong, he had rung a colleague at the local estate agents. When the For Sale sign went up, he realised he needed to prune his belongings if he was to achieve the downsizing Evie had told him he needed.

'Just three bedrooms, Dad; one for you, of course, then one for Harry and I and one for the grandkids. Oh, and a small garden so that you can put my swing in a tree; you must still have the swing.'

John was happy with that spec and added an outbuilding to his wish list; he soon planned to retire there and potter with his beloved tools. Maybe he'd make a cot for "Alfie or Eloise"; Evie had proclaimed the names to Harry and her dad a while ago, very keen to recreate a whole happy family.

He had surprisingly quickly (maybe with Jenny's help) found a three-bed cottage the right distance from Evie and also in need of the right level of TLC to keep him busy – and ease the transition away from their special home.

Evie and Harry took a few items of furniture (to upcycle of course) and, after several trips to charity shops, the skeleton of his old life was laid bare, except for the dreaded paperwork. Thus, he was ready for project SORT. Jenny had been a hoarder, and while Evie said it was now fine to throw her playgroup paintings away, he knew he would be doing it with Jenny's retrieving hand over his.

He set aside two hours each evening to be brutal with the paper shredder and was getting into a confident rhythm, with the "keep pile" being more sparingly added to every time. Then, he discovered Claire's letter. He moved to put it in the shredder immediately, but curiosity stayed his hand, and once more with chaotic emotions, he read a missive from the dead, written for him:

"I never felt I was meant to have a happy life. Jenny's open acceptance of all the sharp edges and dark parts of me and the generosity of her friendship made me feel truly known and whole for the first time ever. I loved her totally. In her absence, I just wanted to be close to you, as she had been. I never wanted to replace her. I couldn't bear her abandoning us, but could bear her suffering even less and, yes, in an impulsive..."

He dropped the letter on his desk as if scorched by her somehow and there it stayed until one evening, when the doorbell rang its unchanged tinny saxophone sound.

A young woman stood uncertainly on the doorstep, hugging her very bright purple coat taut over what looked like a very pregnant bump. As John opened the door, he was sure he knew her, but from where? Big brown beagle eyes looked up at him beseechingly.

'Sorry to trouble you, but I think you knew Claire Thomas, nee Hetherington, and I just wanted to ask you a few questions?'

'Sorry, but who are you?'

'I'm Claire's daughter. Olivia, Liv.'

John felt the portentous penny drop; of course, the other beneficiary! He didn't know how his legs carried him into the kitchen or how his hands made them coffee, but they sat at the breakfast bar (which John had made so all three of them could eat their cereal while looking out at Jenny's garden) now patinaed with their past morning lives. When the courtesies of coffee couldn't delay the conversation anymore, John realised it was incumbent on him as the senior and host, to initiate the many questions.

'May I ask, what made you seek her out now?'

Liv glanced at her seven-month bump and said it was time for family truths.

'You said when you arrived "knew" Claire, so you realise she's -'

'Dead, yes. She didn't want to know me when she was alive. I grew up living with either Dad or at my Aunty Jan's and Uncle Jeff's, foster carers, who I now know were my grandparents. Your wife apparently met my gran, Janet, at Uncle Jeff's, her husband's funeral but you probably don't remember.'

'Oh, yes, yes, I do...'

'Dad was a bit useless, bless him, especially when I was a teenager, so I had two homes and used to make up all these fantasies about who my mum was – and why she left.'

'So, you didn't have any contact at all?'

'Never and when I was old enough to find her, I s'pose I was too scared the truth wouldn't live up to my fantasies, till now.'

'I'm sorry. I'm still trying to take it all in. We never knew. Jenny, my wife, who I presume you know was her friend—

393

'Yes, Grandma told me.'

'Well, Jenny found out about a baby boy who died at birth, but not a girl.'

'Oliver was my brother, my twin. I was what's called a hidden twin, so she never knew I existed in pregnancy, and then, when I was born a few minutes after Oliver, well, later she refused to believe I existed, so I remained the "hidden twin".'

'Oliv-ia, wow... I don't know what to say. Gosh... So, she never saw you?'

'Not even just after I was born. Then, I gather, she tried to avoid me at all costs. I was "persona non grata"! I feel worse that my actual grandparents and my dad were forbidden by her to tell me, or anyone. That power she wielded from afar.'

'My word...'

'I just want to know more about her, for the next generation, you see? My dad apparently sent her pictures of me every year, but she never replied, so they weren't in contact and their marriage was brief. He said he never really knew her. I know how she was can be inherited and I need to know. I don't want any more secrets.'

'No. God, that was quite a secret.'

'You're telling me!'

'Well, I'll do my best with what little I know.'

'Anything.'

'But, Claire, your mother was a very private person.'

'I know she was difficult, but you were friends?'

'Well, my wife more. I think Jenny "managed" her well and Claire could be great fun and very...'

John was finding all this reminiscent of a therapy session; traumatically dredging up buried memories and re-ordering them. He knew he couldn't rearrange lives like an extension that didn't have building permission, pull it down and rebuild it, but all this was making him look at the actual "original plans" anew.

'... generous and warm at times. She was a bit like strong sunshine coming out on a cloudy day, and then from nowhere, the clouds would obscure her again. And she was always very honest, yes, fiercely loyal, very fierce! And real, I suppose, in a very raw way. I think that's what Jenny, my wife, appreciated, your— Claire's uncompromising take on life. She always knew where she was with her – or thought she did.'

'I've read her short stories, which are incredibly dark. I can't believe she was just that one dimension.'

'Nobody ever is, I suppose, but, no, Claire didn't allow the light in much. I think Jenny brought that in; she did for all of us. They had quite outrageously fun times together. I don't think I even know the half of it. They had a close bond like that.'

John was saying more than he thought possible.

'I can only admit it now; I think I was a bit jealous of their closeness, their shared jokes. She could be a compelling presence, a great raconteur. I s'pose that's why she became such a good writer – and actually, well maybe it was a quest to be understood... in an arms-length kind of way.'

'Have you got any letters from her or anything like that?'

'Er... No, sorry, but I have got some old photos spanning the years.'

John, from his piles of "keep" photos, found some with both Jenny and Claire in, that had thus far, escaped his pruning of her presence. So, he tried his best for this vulnerable young woman to paint a fuller picture of her mother's life. But who, indeed, was she?

'Grandma said she was very shy. She doesn't look shy here.'

She was holding a photo of Jenny and Claire who were dancing on the garden table at a party for Jenny's fortieth.

'I think she felt safe with us, to let go a bit.'

Yes, she had.

'Take it, and these.'

'Are you sure?'

'Yes, of course.'

'Did she ever talk about wanting children?'

'No. She tried very hard with my daughter, Evie, but I'd say she wasn't very maternal... Sorry. I don't know why she shut that part of her away. She baulked at getting involved with anyone actually – apart from us. I don't know why that was... I'm sorry.'

Liv got up to go.

'Well, I mustn't take up any more of your time.'

In that moment, she was so like Claire, needing to take control when Claire had wanted an escape from so many awkward social events at his and Jenny's.

John had dug up one of the younger Ceanothus, planted not long before Jenny's death and had put it in a pot to take to his new house and was now glad he had.

'Hang on a minute; I've got something for you.'

'Oh, it's beautiful; I love blue flowers.'

'So did your mother and my wife. They gardened a lot together.'

"I can't possibly—'

'Please, I'd dug it up to take with me, but it feels right that...'

And now he was blathering emotionally, unusually for him, wanting to connect with this newfound child of Claire's.

'In fact, I had nearly given up as my spade had hit something hard and immovable and it can't have been a pipe as well... but here it is.'

And, before he got any more emotional, he took it to her car and popped it in the boot.

'Well… good luck with your baby. Take care. Will you let me know what you have?'

'Babies!'

'Sorry?'

'I'm having twins.'

When this remarkable young woman had driven off, John had taken the remaining photos back to his study and saw Claire's letter once more. He went to put it in the shredder but needed a certain symbolism that honoured Jenny and all the parts of her life – and also Olivia now. It was now time to move on. He poured himself a generous glass of Merlot (his new tipple) and walked out into the garden.

He stood by his fading bonfire of winter leaves raked from Jenny's favourite oak tree, and took Claire's letter from his pocket and piece by tiny piece fed it to the renewed flames.

Then he went inside, and before he changed his mind, had a quick milky coffee and cheese and pickle sandwich to mop up his Merlot, grabbed Lewis's lead and the old Lab heaved himself to his feet and John lifted him into the boot of the car. He went back inside and took Jenny's ashes from the mantelpiece. He strapped them carefully into the front seat of the car, with a tartan picnic blanket cushioning them, not sure how long a journey it would be, or of his destination – but her final journey at last. He was peering out of the car window through the rain, and just as he switched the wipers off, he realised he had reached a favourite walk of theirs. Without letting himself think too much, he leapt out of the car and found a fold in the green, velvety hills just for her. Yes. Some ashes nestled in the fold of the hill, others caught the breeze. He heard walkers' voices puffing as they approached, so he put the urn under his coat and, nodding to them, walked back to the car, with Lewis plodding behind him.

On his way home, he went to Jenny's favourite garden centre and bought two new Ceanothuses, one for each of them. He thought he would plant them in his next garden.

AFTERWORD
by Matt Williams

The experiences of individuals living with a personality disorder, whether this has been formally diagnosed by a clinician or not, are varied. As *Edges of Me* so vividly details, the impact and implications of a personality disorder are myriad and wide-ranging.

Personality disorder, like so many mental health related diagnoses, remains a controversial and contested label. In our world of increased awareness of identity and attendant identity politics, the term is often embraced or roundly rejected by clinicians and individuals with the condition alike.

Personally, the very term "personality disorder" has always struck me as a particularly cruel and unhelpful label. Suggesting, as it does, that our very essence – our personality itself – is faulty, defective, and well, quite simply, disordered.

Borderline Personality Disorder describes a discreet group of personality disorders. Also known as Emotionally Unstable Personality Disorder, or more snappily EUPD, this represents another potentially prejudicial label. For women, it smacks unhelpfully of the misogynist trope of the "hysterical woman" and potentially emasculates the man who has this unenviable and unhappy title bestowed upon him.

Since the turn of the century, it has been increasingly recognised that those with personality disorder require greater understanding and support from those working within healthcare and, we can only hope, that in time this will extend to our wider society and communities. Such steps and attitudinal shifts are to be applauded.

I am fortunate to work with inspirational clinicians and to meet the patients whose lives have, in some cases, been transformed by the care and support they have received within the NHS. One such clinician, Dr Rob Schaffer, alongside colleagues within Oxford Health NHS Foundation Trust, has created training called the Personality Disorder Positive Outcome Programme (PDPOP), which can be delivered to all staff within a GP surgery.

Training programmes, such as PDPOP, show what engaged and inspiring clinicians can – and do – achieve, as they help those providing support with concepts and a common language around this diagnosis, such as considering where one sits on the "Rescue-Blame seesaw" throughout a consultation, and encourage professionals to take the time to really consider what the meaning of a patient's unmet need may be.

I hope *Edges of Me* will provide readers with the time, space, and raw ingredients to stop and think. To consider personality disorder in all its messy, difficult angles and shapes. To see the person behind the diagnosis, and to promote compassion.

Matt Williams is the Senior Programme Manager for Mental Health, Health Innovation Oxford & Thames Valley; Co-Founder and Chair of the Oxfordshire Men's Health Partnership, and Chair of the Thames Valley Suicide Prevention and Intervention Network (SPIN)

SUPPORT AND INFORMATION

Increasing numbers of GP surgeries have local support groups and networks which welcome participants – and those who care for them – to connect and learn from each other. To feel less isolated and alone.

The charity **MIND** provides information and services (including helpline support) nationally and regionally for all mental health and related issues, including personality disorder. **www.mind.org.uk**

Rethink provide helpful information and factsheets around personality disorder and other mental health conditions via their website. **www.rethink.org**

The **Royal College of Psychiatrists** website also provides information about personality disorder and other conditions for clinicians and the public alike. **www.rcpsych.ac.uk**

Helplines, like that provided by Samaritans, can offer a non-judgemental, anonymous, listening ear for those times when everything feels like too much to cope with. Or just when things feel as though they are about to unravel or become difficult. In the UK and ROI, **Samaritans** can be reached at any time on **116 123**.

ACKNOWLEDGEMENTS

At the risk of this reading like an Oscar speech, I have a list of people to thank. Firstly, thanks to my lovely sons, Jack and Barney, who read a first draft and still encouraged me to continue. To my midwife-daughter-in-law Adele, who guided me through the birth scene (in a literary way). Special thanks to my writing mentor, author Stephanie Butland, who somehow saw inside my muddled brain, helped me sieve the contents and pick through what a reader would like to know. And to Cranthorpe Millner, for kickstarting my longed-for career – proving our sixties is definitely the new forties. Finally, thanks to my lovely artist friend Mary Jane Ansell for the beautiful book cover, and to my legion of inspirational female friends.

ABOUT THE AUTHOR

Gaye originally trained as a general nurse, and then as a psychiatric nurse, but felt she 'saved more lives' by leaving! However, she has used all those human stories in the rest of her life: firstly, as an actor, then a playwright and now, in her first novel. Gaye lives in Wales with her husband and labradoodle.